'DAN COOPER'

Based on the real story of
the relentless pursuit of
the Northwest Orient
Flight 305 hijacker...

Contents

Part One

"Up, up the long, delirious burning blue
I've topped the wind-swept heights with easy grace
Where never lark, or ever eagle flew —
And, while with silent, lifting mind I've trod
The high untrespassed sanctity of space,
Put out my hand, and touched the face of God."

John Gillespie Magee Jr.

Chapter 1

SeaTac

Clifford Harding, November 24, 1971

Many of us know where we were at certain historical moments; some of us were involved directly in them. Those of a certain age tend to know where they were when Kennedy was shot or, for those younger, where they were on 9/11. These seismic events shook the world for many people, but lesser-known people and events can have a huge impact on us as well. I am now seventy-one years old and retired from the Seattle Field Office of the Federal Bureau of Investigations (FBI). I retired in May 2002, a week after my sixty-second birthday, to enjoy more time with my two daughters and three granddaughters.

I wanted to become a full-time grandparent. I love picking my grandkids up from school, watching them grow, and watching them smile. With my girls, I didn't see them smile much as children. Not because they weren't happy, but because I was seldom there. I was on a wild goose chase across the United States and eventually Canada to look for someone who has now become wrongly engraved into folklore.

I may have shrunk slightly below my peak height of six feet. I have more wrinkles on my face, and my hair is as white as it gets, but when I become Grandpa Cliff in the park with the girls, I feel like I am twenty-five again. My youngest granddaughter, Maria, is a real rascal with a sassy little smile. She loves when I chase her around, catch her, and fling her over my shoulder. She isn't afraid to get covered in mud and ice cream and often ruins the nice clothes my daughter Celine gets for her. When I chased people before, their clothes tended to be left in worse condition.

Everyone is always on their phones these days, buried in this alternate reality where the truth becomes skewed and monsters can become figments of fantasy and speculation. There are adoration pages for serial killers, for Christ's sake! Sure, I like reconnecting with old friends and colleagues on Facebook, but the man who ruined my life and destroyed most of my happiness is hailed as a god by some people online. In some spaces, there are huge gatherings in his honor to celebrate his "achievement." You can buy t-shirts and beer mugs with his face on them, and I have had to look at him on television several times in documentaries.

His name was "Dan Cooper." You might know him as "D.B. Cooper," the unidentified hijacker of Northwest Orient Flight 305 on November 24, 1971. I have been inundated with emails and messages asking me to speak about him, and I've always declined. I thought, *I don't want to give this slimeball any airtime because he doesn't deserve it.* However, one evening I finally caved after agreeing to have coffee with someone keen to talk about the case with me, and he said something to me that stuck:

"This is your opportunity to tell your story and tell it only once. If you don't tell it, it will die with you. Who knows? What if there are technological advancements in decades to come that will finally show the world who Dan Cooper was? In 1971, I bet you couldn't have imagined the advancement of DNA analysis. What if this is the same?"

I remember asking how I should start, and it started with a simple question asked to me:

"What was your journey up to and beyond the 24th of November, 1971?"

***

My parents welcomed me into the world on the first day of May, 1940. I was an only child, and my mother gave birth to me when she was forty-eight years old after years of believing she couldn't have children. My childhood was a happy one, and I grew up in North Capitol Hill, an affluent area in Seattle. My father was Dr. Marcus Harding, a specialist pediatric surgeon, and my mother was Susan Harding, who ran a private preschool daycare from our home. My father died when I was nine years old, and my dear, adoring mother died when I was twenty. My mother home-schooled me during the war, and I used to play with the other children in her care. We lived in a beautiful art-deco home that had a huge garden at the rear and seven bedrooms, despite only three of us living there. The only room that was off-limits was my father's study, where he hosted medical students and gave lectures and demonstrations.

I can't recall where my interest in criminal justice came from, but one topic that fascinated me as a teen was the Whitechapel murders carried out by the unidentified killer known as Jack the Ripper. The idea that in the late 1880s someone could just get away with butchering five women in the streets filled me with wonder and a naïve attitude that I would want to catch a Ripper if one were to resurface. I hate unresolved stories as much as I love them. Closed cases give a feeling of satisfaction, but open and unresolved ones provide some sort of psychic tension that draws people in, including me.

Garfield High School was where I was educated, then I

went on to Washington State University to study sociology, which had elements of criminal justice. I wanted to join the cops upon graduation, and that was the goal I set for myself.

College life was fun. I had the odd fling, drank the beer, smoked the pot, and lived the life of every other college kid before I graduated in the summer of 1961. I have always awakened at 6 a.m. because I believe an extra hour in bed is an hour wasted. When I joined the cops, my ambition was to become chief, but after seeing and hearing too many things I didn't want to see and hear, I jumped ship relatively quickly. I had no plans for a wife or kids into the sixties because there was a ladder to climb, and I wanted to quickly get up as many rungs as I could.

I joined the FBI in 1963 after a miserable two years as a beat cop upon finishing college, and it was tough to get in. The age range was twenty-three to thirty-seven years old. Being an American citizen was a must, of course, as was a bachelor's degree. I had experience in the local police force, which wasn't essential but helped me get in. They also required a good level of physical fitness signed off by a doctor, a background check to make sure I wasn't a crook, and a willingness to relocate. The willingness to relocate was always going to be okay for an unmarried twenty-three-year-old with no kids, which I was when I joined.

The training was tough. We had grueling physical drills like running and assault courses, legal training to know the laws of the land, firearms training, investigative techniques, counterintelligence, and counterterrorism, plus the one I struggled with most: ethics and professionalism.

But as far as love goes, I've found that it often comes at you when you either least expect it or don't even want it. Upon meeting my wife Charlotte in 1966, my steely eyes turned to wide-eyed ones, and I was smitten from the get-go. Charlotte was so fun and full of laughter, bringing out a side of me that was always there. She had that Marilyn Monroe look, so effortlessly beautiful in every way, and she also had the inner beauty to match it. Time vanished when we were together; we never ran out of things to talk about, and she called me out when I said or did something that didn't meet her standards or expectations.

I just adored her, and as far as the saying goes, when you know, you know. I knew I would never have a connection with anyone else like her, and I didn't. We married only twelve weeks after we met.

Our first bundle of joy, Celine, came on September 1, 1968, and our second, Helen, on Christmas Day of 1970. Celine is a modern-day version of Charlotte, and Helen looks more like me. Helen also inherited my temperament, and I asked her to make her Daddy one promise: to never join the cops. She is an assistant chief now.

By November 24, 1971, I was a fit and enthusiastic thirty-one-year-old, with all my black hair intact and a suave suit collection to make up for my biggest insecurity that I had to wear glasses. It was the day before Thanksgiving, and it was a horrible day. The rain was coming down hard, and I remember hearing it batter the office windows. In those days, our offices were on the second floor at 1015 Second Avenue in Seattle.

The FBI office in Seattle was quite large in those days, with around 250 agents. I knew every last one by name, rank, desk, susceptibility to bribery, and even what cigarette brand they smoked. We were a dynamic force, and I was promoted to supervisory special agent and worked on some high-profile cases still classified today.

There are two Clifford Hardings: the one pre-November 24, 1971, and the one post-November 24, 1971. This day was the end of the Cliff that most knew and loved, and it was the beginning of me evolving into the Clifford Harding I became. It all started with a telephone call that reached me at 3:30 p.m. that day. Everyone was getting ready to shut up shop early, and I was happy to let everyone get home to their families. When the phone rang, I picked up the receiver and inadvertently left down the man I was.

"Cliff, is that you?" a rushed and familiar voice said to me.

"Yes, Margaret. This better not be too terrible because I got a turkey to pick up before 4:30."

"We have a hijacking in progress," she blurted out to me.

My first instinct upon hearing this was to not take it too seriously. "A hijacking?! Probably some hoodlum taking his grandpa's truck for a joyride. This isn't for us, dear; call the cops!"

"Northwest Flight 305 from Portland to Seattle. A gentleman in the back row of their aircraft handed a stewardess a note stating that he has a bomb in his briefcase and wants two hundred thousand dollars in a knapsack by 5 p.m. and four parachutes—two chest packs and two backpacks."

I gripped the telephone receiver so tightly that I thought it would shatter in my hand.

"Hold on, Margaret…an aircraft!?" As I shouted this out, some agents filing out of the office turned around and crept toward my desk, curious to know what was happening.

"Yes, Cliff. The flight deck is in comms with the radio tower at SeaTac Airport."

"Are there four hijackers?" I inquired because the demand for four parachutes was perplexing me.

"Not to my knowledge, sir, just one from the SITREP given from the flight deck. One of the stewardesses is sitting beside the man, and passengers are seemingly unaware, but I can't be sure how a hijacker with a bomb can go unnoticed."

"Do we know who the hijacker is? Did the motherfucker give his name?" I snarled at Margaret.

"No, and please mind your language, young man."

"Sorry! Margaret, contact the ticket booth and get me a list of passengers, please, and relay it on to the Portland Field Office too. We can run the names by everyone here and see if we can make a positive ID."

"Okay, sir. I will do that right after this call."

On the notepad beside me, I scribbled, "$200,000, FOUR PARACHUTES, TWO FRONT AND TWO BACK BY 5 P.M., HAS BOMB IN BRIEFCASE." Six or seven agents huddled around my desk to hear more of what was unfolding. I ripped the page from my notepad and held it up so they could see it. All their eyes opened wide, and one even mouthed the word "shit." I nodded to agree.

"Margaret, has anybody spoken to the chairman of the airline?" The festive Thanksgiving Eve atmosphere evaporated from the room and was replaced by all our cigarette smoke.

"Yes, sir. Mr. Donald Nyrop has authorized meeting the hijacker's demands and the payment of the ransom money to the hijacker. You will need to source the cash from different banks, most likely the Seattle Federal Reserve Bank, but you will also have to source the four parachutes. The aircraft will circle overhead until the money and the parachutes are delivered to SeaTac runway."

"Okay, noted. Thank you. One more thing, Margaret: please instruct air traffic control to radio the plane and tell them to circle over the Pacific. If this guy detonates the bomb, we don't want it to rain wreckage and body parts all over the suburbs."

"Understood," said Margaret, and then the line went dead. There was a stunned silence among us all. This wasn't the first skyjacking we'd heard of in recent years. It was becoming a growing issue, but it was one of those things we thought would never come to our door on the eve of Thanksgiving. The men looked at me, and I think they knew from my face that I had no clue what to do. They all leaned in, hanging on to every ounce of silence from my mouth. In times of extreme difficulty, what comes to one's mind is very peculiar. I had my wide-eyed stare on. They had their wide-eyed stares on, too.

I thought, *I'm going to be late picking up this turkey. What if the butcher shop is closed? How am I thinking about a turkey while there's a bomb on an aircraft circling above our heads? I need to eliminate this thought; why can't I get rid of it? Do other people think like this in a crisis? Is my brain protecting me?*

The deafening silence in the room was broken when the phone rang only once, and I leapt onto my desk chair, grabbed the receiver, and had my pen and notebook ready. "Okay, Margaret. I'm ready."

"Okay, sir. I have the list."

"Go ahead!" I half-shouted, with the intention of repeating each name after they were read to me so everyone could hear and hopefully recognize a name.

"William Mitchell, Dan Cooper, Roy Clouse, William J. Murphy, Floyd Kloepfer, Dennis Mickelson, Jack Almstad, Adrian E. Menendez, Daniel Rice, George Labissoniere, Lester Pollart, Wesley Jensen, Larry Finegold, George Kurata—"

At this name, a few agents nodded heavily, given some anti-Japanese sentiment.

"—James Wornstaff, Robert Gregory, Lavonne Conley, Cord Harms Spreckel, Helen Connors, William Keats, Michael Cooper, Nancy House, Scott MacPherson, William MacPherson, Paul Weitzel, Clifford MacDonald, Patrick Minsch, Richard Simmons, Barbara Simmons, Raymond Donahoe, Charles Street, Albert Truitt, Arnold Andvik,

Lynn Cummings, Adele Cummings, Robert Cummings."

None of the names were familiar to me. We knew and would have recognized any names of those wanted by the feds or high-profile police cases involving fugitives. Everyone was quite dumbfounded because we were relatively close-knit and knew one another's cases and who our wanted men were. However, we realized quickly enough that our guy was using a false name. It is important to state that getting on a flight in 1971 was the same as getting on a bus today. There were no airport security checks, no ID checks, no body frisking, and nobody's belongings were searched. Hand over the cash, and you get a plane ticket. That was it.

"Thank you, Margaret—anyone from the Portland Field Office give an ID to any wanted fugitives?"

"No, Cliff. None of the names were immediately recognizable to that office."

"Thank you, dear," I said before putting the telephone back down.

My partner, one of the first Black men recruited and respected by the feds, Steve Johnson, was lurching over my desk when I looked back up through the cigarette smoke cloud. He must have come in as the passenger list was read out. He used to do this stylish trick with his hat, where he would flick the underside of the brim, so it spun a couple of times before landing brim-side down on our adjoining desks.

"Cliff, we can rule out the broads for sure, right?" he quipped at me.

"Yes, Johnson. They said it was a lone man."

The other band of agents was heckling us, saying that there were a lot of Russian and German names on the list and that there was no doubt one of those would be our guy. I didn't know what to do, so I called for patrol vehicles in the area to make their way to SeaTac Airport. One team member also informed me that the ransom money was obtained from the Seattle Federal Reserve Bank in twenty-dollar bills. The serial numbers were microfilmed before being placed in the cotton money bag and in a car destined for the airport.

We needed to get parachutes by this stage, and nobody knew where to begin. The obvious answer was to take some from McChord Air Force Base, which is only a twenty-minute drive from SeaTac Airport. One of the guys had a contact at McChord, an old army buddy, and rushed off to give him a call. I needed clarification on the parachutes, as I didn't know the difference between front parachutes and back parachutes. It was explained to me that the backpacks are the main parachute, and the front parachutes are reserve parachutes that are chest-mounted and clipped to the shoulder straps of the backpack.

Time seemed to fly at this stage when I glanced at the wall clock and noticed it was 3:50 p.m. We were all eager for telephone updates. The frantic rumbles ceased when my phone rang; a gunshot wouldn't have been nearly as effective as that phone in quieting everyone down. Margaret had called again.

"Yes, dear?" I said sarcastically. Margaret and I went way back. She was like my "work mom" and fluctuated between calling me sir, Cliff, Clifford, Mr. Harding, or other names that would make most ladies of a particular vintage blush. She has been a radio and telephone operator since the war. It didn't matter that I was of decent rank then; I was thirty-one, and Margaret was probably in her early fifties.

"The gentleman has more requests."

"Who does?"

"Our friend, of course."

"Requests? Do we have a choice?" I sighed at her, gesturing for everyone to gather around the table.

"Air traffic control has contacted us to tell us he wants a fuel truck on landing and that the parachutes must be civilian parachutes with manual ripcords on them. No flashing lights, no cops or FBI, and only one representative from the airline is allowed to approach the aircraft with the money and the parachutes. No funny stuff, or he will do the job."

"Shouldn't he be telling this to the control tower so Flight Ops can be notified?"

"Indeed, but I am keeping you up to speed. Flight Ops are in communication with the aircraft, and they are in touch with us, hence my call to you."

I felt so helpless and over a barrel that I slammed the phone down and looked at everyone around me as I walked out from behind the desk.

"I understand wanting two hundred thousand dollars, gentlemen, but four parachutes for one man? Why?" We were able to figure out at this point that the parachutes were going to be used to escape after a second takeoff.

Roger Williams, another senior agent, suggested that we get four fake or non-functional parachutes to the airport and return the cash from the hole in the ground left by the hijacker afterwards.

One of the junior agents whispered to me, "Maybe he is going to take an airborne hostage, sir?"

I suddenly felt sick to the pit of my stomach. I roared out, "Fuck! Is he going to make someone jump with him? The parachutes have to be good ones—no duds!" At this stage, the atmosphere in the office was becoming frantic, and I ran after him and ordered him to contact local skydiving facilities and airfields to get functional civilian parachutes.

After much to-ing and fro-ing, we eventually got two civilian-owned NB6 backpacks with manual ripcords and two front chest reserves. I sent them to the airport without delay to meet with the people handling the money. The next step was to call Margaret, and the phone rang forever. I repeatedly shouted "pick up!" and looked at the clock to see 4:45 p.m. It was only minutes away from our deadline of 5 p.m., and I put the phone down. I buried my head in my hands and was sweating profusely. Any time I've experienced a hot day since, it reminds me of that moment. Eventually, I got Margaret and was almost out of breath updating her on the latest developments, and she said she would tell the radio tower.

At the last minute, I received another call from one of the field agents informing me that they had provided three functional chutes and one dud. This wasn't intentional, and in the rush, a dummy front parachute was included. It was a student rig that was sewn shut. It was so close to 5 p.m., and my permission was sought to try and source another or to send it to the airport. We were so close to our deadline that they had to proceed. Then again, my initial thoughts were that if the fucker was silly enough to jump with the dud, I would still be able to sleep at night. Plus, it would help us develop a better profile of the hijacker after the fact and determine if he was an expert parachutist or military jumper.

I decided we should go to SeaTac, so Johnson and I scurried out of the office to the parking lot, and I decided we would travel in my car. It had reached 5 p.m., and I looked up at the darkening sky to see if we could see or hear an explosion. A few minutes later, we got into the car after hearing nothing. It was a nice, new Chevrolet Nova that I got after my promotion in August 1971. We had thirteen miles ahead of us to the airport as we raced toward SeaTac.

Chapter 2
Fort Smith

Dan Cooper, February 27, 1921

I was born on February 27, 1921, in Fort Smith, Territoires du Nord-Ouest. My father, Hugo, was a sailor. Just before I was born, he began working for the Alberta and Arctic Transportation Company aboard the steamship Distributor, transporting cargo along the Slave River and overland. My mother, Amelie, was a nurse and midwife at the local St. Anne's Hospital. We certainly were not stricken with poverty, and we were all very happy for the most part. My parents had seven children, with five of us surviving past the age of four.

Of the seven children, the two siblings to perish in childhood from typhoid were my older brother Mathieu, who was one year older than I, and my younger sister Lucille, who was one year younger. I managed to escape it, as did my younger brother Eric, who had his own challenges. Mother worked long hours, and we had a nanny at home, Madame Laroche, who adored us, particularly Eric.

We lived in a large farmhouse in idyllic, rural Canada. We ate, prayed, went to the local church, played around our land and nearby woodland, and led a quiet and peaceful existence. We had five large bedrooms at home, and I shared a room with Eric and Mathieu. Our room had three beds: my bed, Eric's, and Mathieu's. One of my earliest memories is of my mother insisting on making Mathieu's bed for years after we buried him, but she didn't do that for Lucille. We were never allowed to touch it, nor were we allowed to mention his name to Mother. Mon père being my father, he didn't show how he felt after both Mathieu and Lucille's passing.

Eric and I were very close. He was full of fun and mischief, and so was I. When we were little, we used to run around the woodland together, and we laughed a lot. Despite our closeness, I noticed that there were some things about Eric that were different. I remember asking my parents why Eric wouldn't talk much, why he didn't understand certain games, or why he became upset so quickly at things I thought were trivial, like it being too hot or too cold, or if Madame Laroche wasn't nearby. Eric stayed the same as I grew older, at least in his mannerisms and mind.

Eric was slow. He was very childlike for a twelve-year-old and didn't attend the local school. Occasionally, Eskimo Elders came to the house to chant or pray with him. I don't think he knew what it all meant, and it was more for Mother's peace of mind than his. Most of Madame Laroche's time was spent with Eric. If Eric did not have access to his toys or blankets, our house would look like a tornado zone by the time he was finished. Mother kept her jewellery and glassware hidden away, as Eric would have destroyed them in his fits of rage. We ate and drank out of tin military ration trays and goblets, so if Eric didn't like what was for dinner, we wouldn't have shattered crockery or glasses strewn around.

When I looked at Eric, he had this look in his eye—a lost and bewildered look that I will always remember about him. He liked my company and loved feeding our chickens and watering Mother's plant bushes. In the few family portraits I still have, Eric isn't in them. He got his picture taken as an infant, but he seemed to remember the flash hurting his eyes and never posed for a portrait again. He was overweight, and Madame Laroche had to ensure that Eric didn't choke on his food when we had meals together.

I took Eric fishing a couple of times, and he used to clap his hands when I pulled some trout out of the lake. I think he liked the peaceful surroundings because our home was loud. People came and went with mail, our floorboards creaked, the horses neighed, the chickens clucked, and the wind whistled through the slats of the wooden frame house when the gales and gusts hit us.

Beyond our house were stables, and my sisters Annette, Angelique, and Simone used to tend to them and ride them around. We didn't have a post office in the village, so my father volunteered himself and me to take local people's mail to Fort Fitzgerald on horseback. Perhaps this is where my preference for speed comes from. My father would taunt me to race him on the open roads and roar, "Allez! Allez!" but he never liked it if I whipped the horses too frequently. When I reached twelve or thirteen, he would send me alone, and I pushed the horses to their limit.

Fort Fitzgerald was around twenty miles away, and Mother took issue with a twelve-year-old travelling twenty miles away alone on horseback with potentially sensitive mail. Father's argument was that sixteen-year-olds had gone over the top at Le Somme only a handful of years earlier and that I would be fine. When he started questioning how I had returned so quickly on my mail trips, I started milling around town and waiting an additional hour before gingerly returning home so Father would never know I pushed the horses too hard.

School was okay for me; I didn't love or hate it. What I did love was the outdoors. I demanded that my father give me money for some of the mail runs I was doing, and he would give me one dollar for every run I did. I asked for a raise on a few occasions and instead got a raised hand each time. In the summer evenings, when daylight was longer, I would do two runs a day and get two dollars.

We spoke French at home, which my father enforced, but we spoke English everywhere else and away from our father's earshot. We lived in a multicultural community with Inuit families, and we were olive-skinned ourselves. Luckily, the racial bigotry that plagued Europe and the United States was not commonplace here. During the harsh winters, we needed one another to survive, and the fur trade was what kept food on our tables and some money in our pockets. I'm not quite sure of my ancestry, although both of my parents had Cree blood in them, that's for sure.

We all took turns taking Eric for his evening promenade with Madame Laroche. She had been our family nanny since my oldest sister, Simone, was born in 1907. By 1934, she had greying hair and was slightly slower on her feet. She was large and in charge, but she could no longer restrain Eric if he decided he was deviating from our path. When the girls were growing up, Madame Laroche taught them to cook, clean, and be perfect wives, despite not having children of her own. We were her children, yet our mother was always our mother.

Crooks like me always have mommy issues, but I had the privilege of having two mothers who loved me very much. The three older girls became closer when Lucille died, and Eric and I became closer when Mathieu died. Even though we were from a generally nice community, we found storeowners and innkeepers would close their doors and slats when they saw us coming. Eric had no concept of handing over money for items—he would have lifted apples, potatoes, and meat and eaten them if given the opportunity. People would whisper under their breath, pointing at us, and the reason the Inuit Elders came to pray was that our local church, St. Joseph's Catholic Church, would not allow Eric to enter.

Eric wouldn't run too far when I was with him. Despite being quite skinny, I was strong and could wrestle him to the ground if needed. I could take Eric out without Madame Laroche, and one day some kids started shouting at us. This was not the first or last time, but Madame Laroche and my parents were the ones to turn the other cheek. I was not. The kids and young men would shout things like "imbecile" or "idiot."

One kid in particular, Philippe, was particularly nasty. His family was the old money in the area and owned acres of farmland in the surrounding towns. They were vegetable farmers, and because they stopped us from starving to death, they could treat people however they wanted without consequence. Eric certainly wasn't feebleminded in some areas and understood when people weren't being nice to him or when I beat the stuffing out of Philippe for abusing us.

It became routine; the same kid called Eric the same names and got the same level of beatings from me, yet it never stopped. I was glad to learn early on that violence wasn't overly effective in getting my point across. Like every good bully story, Philippe got his comeuppance when he drowned while fishing the Coppermine River. I didn't shed a single tear.

***

During Christmas of 1935, Eric developed a nasty cough. Mother's nursing background caused her to become concerned, especially after losing two children, but the doctor always insisted that it was because he had eaten too quickly and was overweight. Yes, Eric wheezed when he exerted himself, but this hacking cough was serious. So much so that Father moved Eric downstairs into our reception room and quarantined us from him. Of course, this upset Eric, which exacerbated his cough to the point that it produced blood.

When the bloody cough got worse, the doctor returned and told us that because Eric was screaming from downstairs, he had damaged his throat and lungs. But he assured us that Eric would settle down soon. He was right— Eric did settle down once he was too weak to move and confined to the chaise longue in the room. He didn't know what was happening, but we knew it was tuberculosis. My heavy, playful brother became my sad, withered brother. He only spoke a few words, even at his best, but at this time he kept saying, "Paradis avec Mathieu. Paradis avec Lucille." Children have a very innocent view of death and dying; he was thinking about angels, Mathieu, and Lucille.

The girls were constantly coming and going to tend to Eric, bringing him water and wiping the sweat from his brow. Simone had a beautiful singing voice and would sing "Un Canadien errant" to him. This was a very fitting song choice, given that it is about exile. The girls still had their chores to do, and despite Eric's illness, they still had to tend to the horses and help around the house. Madame Laroche couldn't bear to watch Eric deteriorate, so she mostly stayed away from him. She had her own limits; despite everything, it was her job, not her family.

I sat with Eric often; he liked me being with him. As we slept in the same room, I set up camp on the floor beside him, although I had to wear a handkerchief over my mouth and fasten it around my head with string to avoid catching the disease. I sat on a chair beside him, and he tried to smile, but the pain was just too much for him to smile authentically. He seemed to like people tending to him individually, but he never permitted us to be in the room simultaneously—too many people, conversations, and hushed tones. Before long, the doctor just advised us to keep him comfortable, and for the most part, he was—it was the rest of the family who felt the least comfort. Mother and Father were praying, and the Eskimo Elders would burn lavender tea in a lamp, bringing a calming aroma and atmosphere to the house. It removed the smell of disease, dying, and sadness, if only for a short time.

It was difficult for Mother and Father when Mathieu and Lucille passed, but it killed them when Eric finally joined them on May 4, 1936. He was thirteen and a week short of his fourteenth birthday. Although they both lived for a few decades afterwards, Eric's passing removed a part of my parents that never returned. I couldn't adjust to Eric being gone, and I often awakened at night to look at the empty bed. I was alone in our bedroom, and the place wasn't the same without him. When Eric was happy, he was infectiously happy, and when he was upset, the surrounding towns would know about it. I missed his laugh and would have done anything to hear him cry again.

Eric didn't really have a chance in life, and I felt a certain sense of guilt after he was gone. What could I have done to improve his life and make him happier for the short time he was here? I cannot say what the answer is, but it was something that I often pondered. My father was the same, and we grew somewhat closer, having to be the stoic faces of our household. The ladies could cry and grieve, but we were not afforded that luxury. What used to prevent me from crying was the genuine belief that Eric was a tortured soul and was probably better off wherever he was.

My parents' relationship became volatile in the months and years after Eric passed. My father would drink and quarrel frequently. My father always enjoyed a drink and was a keen singer after having a few, but when he drank his

bottles of Old Tub Sour Mash Bourbon, his temper came
out. The first and only time he struck my mother happened
to be in front of me, and I remember feeling frozen to the
spot. The girls and my mother left, leaving my father and
me in the house. Madame Laroche remained to clean up the
house and ensure that Father was lying on his side when he
passed out in our sitting room.

They moved to be with my Aunt Cherie, about twenty
miles north of where we lived. Father would go to work, and
I would deliver the mail and tend to the horses. I was doing
all the mailing work, as my father was in no condition to do
so. I spent my sixteenth birthday alone up until three o'clock
that day. I was throwing pails of water over the horses when
I turned around and saw a girl looking me straight in the eye.

"I like your horses!" she said.

Jumping back, I exclaimed, "My God! You frightened
me—how did you get in here?"

"I'm responding to the notice seeking someone to tend
the horses here. I knocked on the front door but didn't get
an answer, so I let myself in."

Strangely, in a rural town of less than five hundred
people, I thought that I knew everyone, and it turned out I
didn't. Her name was Yvonne, and she was an odd girl the
same age as me. She was nearly as tall as I was at five feet ten
and wore these giant glasses that took up almost all of her
face. My father had advertised for someone to tend to the
horses given that the girls were gone and Madame Laroche
had allergies. I could only do so much on my own between
delivering mail and going to school, and my father was still
too busy drinking. From that point on, Yvonne was at our
stables every evening. She loved the horses, and her love
for them was very endearing. She used to stroke under their
chins, and the horses really responded to her. We grew closer
every day, and she became prettier and prettier to me as the

days and weeks went by.

Yvonne and I would ride the horses around the country, and she would come with me to deliver the mail. She loved being outdoors as much as I did, and I suppose this was our form of dating. A happy coincidence was that our birthdays were on the same day, and we took the horses and went out for dinner on our seventeenth birthday. Even though we had grown close over the past year, she blew me away when I went to pick her up. She wore her hair in pin curls and removed her glasses, and she was the prettiest girl I had ever seen. We were officially in a courtship then, and we were both very happy. We didn't have a bustling town or amenities to entertain us, so we had to depend on getting to know one another by spending time together meaningfully rather than being mutually occupied by a movie or theatre performance.

Thankfully, my parents reconciled after nearly eight months apart. After many months of my father attempting to stop drinking, he finally succeeded. However, what we found odd was that Annette and Angelique moved away without telling us. They moved to Toronto and later ended up marrying two brothers. We were never close, and I seldom heard from them again after they moved away to the modern world and left us out in the countryside. Simone and I became closer, and she adored Yvonne, as did my parents. Simone and Yvonne were great company for one another, as Yvonne was an only child and never had much company growing up, although neither did I, especially after Eric's passing.

Even though I was a teenager fast approaching adulthood, Madame Laroche stayed with the family until I was of age before deciding to retire. My parents gave her a thick brown envelope, and I remember Madame Laroche almost fainting when she saw the sum of money inside. I am guessing it was around fifteen hundred Canadian dollars because she called me aside as she left and insisted on giving Yvonne and me two hundred dollars. We could start a life somewhere where there were more opportunities for both of us. We were shocked, and she insisted we take it. I think it was my father's way of thanking her for caring for him without actually having to say the words to her.

***

I had turned eighteen in 1939, and the world was on the brink of war. Yvonne and I discussed getting married, but she protested because she didn't want to be a young widow. I never thought about the Army or the Navy because my father deterred me from military life. Although I feared that conscription would become the norm in Canada as it had been in the past, I seemed to lack a sense of purpose and didn't know what to do with my life. I didn't want to stay in our small town, run a farm, or continue delivering mail across the landscape for the rest of my life. Yvonne and I couldn't decide where to go or what to do.

On the usual mail run, I stopped by the post office in Fort Fitzgerald. It looked the same as a post office would in a John Wayne picture—antiquated, with the clerks separated from the public by large metal bars. There was a notice board of sorts, and a poster caught my eye. On it was a man on horseback with a fancy red uniform and a broad-brimmed hat.

The slogan read, "YOU ARE INVITED TO HELP MAINTAIN THE RIGHT." The poster was for the Royal Canadian Mounted Police (RCMP), and given that it involved horses and action, I thought I would apply. I knew the paycheck would probably be better than the one or two dollars a day I was getting from my father to deliver mail. There was no fancy application package or anything; it was just a cable with my name and address. The RCMP, known affectionately as the Mounties, were seldom seen in our town. The only crimes I ever remember were assault and reckless horsemanship, both of which I committed and referred to above.

I got a letter and nearly destroyed the contents by ripping the envelope open. I was invited to an interview in Regina, Saskatchewan at the RCMP training academy, three weeks from the date of the letter. So Yvonne and I decided to relocate—this was our chance. My mother was slightly tearful, but my father shook my hand and nodded. They must have been confident in my abilities because they never once said that I was welcome back if I didn't get in. I was the last to fly the nest from home, and my parents wished both of us well.

So in October 1939, we set off to start our new life. The journey is eight hundred miles over dirt roads and rail. It was awful, yet Yvonne and I never bickered. We had four or five different train journeys, and Yvonne spent much of the time sleeping with her head on my shoulder. We were able to find lodging in a boarding house on Victoria Avenue, not far from the First Baptist Church of Regina. The rent was very reasonable, and the house was very well kept for its size, but we noticed we were the only tenants. We found this odd, but we soon learned that the gold organ pipes from the First Baptist were almost deafening, and sleeping was a challenge for those of us who grew up rurally. We didn't have a choice and had to remain there for the time being.

***

When I arrived at Depot, the training academy for the Mounties, for my interview, I was greeted by a stern officer who asked me some peculiar questions. They had done their background checks and found out that I wasn't a criminal—at least, not yet. I recall the interview going something like this:

"Why do you want to join the Royal Canadian Mounted Police?"

I wanted to say that I wished to join because I didn't want to die in Europe at the behest of a British monarchy that had no value or significance in my life, but instead I told them that I wanted to serve and protect Canadians at home while Canadian troops joined the effort in Europe.

"Do you have any health issues or concerns?"

"No."

"Are you married with children?"

"No."

"Are you afraid of heights or air travel?"

"I don't think so." This was an odd question, as I had never flown before, not even in a hot air balloon.

"Are you willing to relocate to meet the demands of the force or assist in the war effort, both imminently and in the future?"

This was a difficult question because Yvonne and I had set up camp nearby, and the thought of moving again would impact our chances of finally marrying and starting a family. However, I knew I had to say yes. I don't recall a handshake—there may have been one, but regardless, I walked out of the room as a recruit of the Royal Canadian Mounted Police. I was to report back the following morning.

Chapter 3

Between Portland and Seattle

Dan Cooper, November 24, 1971

After we began taxiing toward the runway, a dark-haired stewardess sat in the jump seat behind me. I had the envelope in my hand and removed my sunglasses to look at her directly. I reached around my seat and put out my right hand to give her the envelope with the note inside. This was it. The rush of adrenaline I got as I felt the wisp of paper leave my hand and glide into hers was the biggest rush, positive or negative, that I had ever felt in my life. It was somewhat quashed, however, when she put the note straight into her purse without reading it. I looked at her, and she smiled politely back at me before looking away. I didn't ask anyone for their name at the time, but later learned them over the years from television shows and books, and this stewardess was Miss Florence Schaffner.

"Miss?" I uttered softly, trying to avoid attracting too much attention.

This is where the media and details become somewhat skewed. I never said aloud that I had a bomb; it was in the note. Airplane seats are close together, and there was a kid in the row to my left in the middle seat, and there's no doubt he would have heard me. In any case, it didn't matter; nobody with any sense would rush me from any direction while armed with a bomb. I don't recall telling her to read the note; I just said, "Excuse me," and pointed to her purse. She gave me a smile and took out the note to humour me.

The look on her face wasn't immediate dread or fear when she read the note—it was a look of slight amusement.

"Is this a joke?"

"No, miss. This is for real," I told her.

The other stewardess in the coach section, a young lady with blonde hair, Miss Tina Mucklow, came to the aircraft's rear just as Miss Schaffner read the note, which said I had a bomb in my briefcase and wanted her to sit beside me. When Miss Schaffner was looking at the aisle seat beside me, I removed my paper shopping bag and just sat it on the ground between my feet. Before taking the seat, she handed the note to Miss Mucklow. She asked me once again if I was serious, and I told her I was. Miss Mucklow went to the interphone attached to the bulkhead behind us to contact the flight deck to tell the captain what was happening.

I didn't seem to persuade Miss Schaffner initially, although her demeanour changed when I opened the briefcase and showed her the bomb. To avoid an accidental detonation caused by the command wire touching the battery cell, I secured the wire to the side of the briefcase with tape before departure.

I noticed a slight twitch or shake in my fingers when I removed the tape. Annoyingly, I dropped it—it was the only piece of tape I had—and I watched as it wafted below me, landing under the seat in front of me. I took hold of the command wire to hold it up and out of the briefcase.

"All I need to do is place this wire into this gadget here, and the circuit is complete."

She looked around her in a panic, and I closed the lid of the briefcase over the four fingers of my right hand. We were all gone if the aircraft took a turn or there was any turbulence and the wire touched the battery. So, for now, I was down to one hand. I would have to keep hold of the command wire with my right hand for the remainder of the flight to prevent an accidental detonation.

I asked Miss Schaffner if she had a pen and paper, and she said she did. She had a notepad in her purse and a pen clipped to the breast pocket of her uniform. That was when I requested the $200,000 in negotiable American currency in a knapsack by 5 p.m. English not being my first language, I thought that I had given away a hint of my identity. In my mind, asking for $200,000 in negotiable currency wasn't an American thing to do, as I always knew that in their minds, there was only one type of dollar in the world, and it was theirs.

I reminded her again that I wanted a knapsack and two sets of parachutes—two front parachutes and two back parachutes. She seemed to take a deep breath when I said that I also wanted a fuel truck waiting for us on the runway.

I told her, "No funny stuff, or I will do the job." Miss Schaffner wrote down four parachutes, and again, I said it would have to be two backpacks and two chest reserves.

She became slightly confused or unsure, and I just wanted to hurry her down to the cockpit because what should have been a ten- to fifteen-second interaction was turning into a minute or more on a flight that was only scheduled to last thirty to forty minutes. I told her, "Smile and walk; don't rush!" but whether this registered with her or not, I cannot say.

She took another deep breath, said, "Okay," and composed herself.

"After this, we are going to take a little trip," and I smiled at her. My strategy was to remain calm and make them feel unsettled and anxious instead of excited or desperate. When people get desperate, they become compelled to take action and often make mistakes, and when mistakes happen, lives are lost. As my mother used to say, "Attract people with honey, not vinegar." Regardless of what anybody on the flight or on the ground would do, I would never let anybody take me alive.

As she left, she asked me, "Sir, is this all you want?"

I just said, "Yes," and then she went to the cockpit. Miss Mucklow approached me and stood in the aisle while I still had my hand inside the briefcase. She had the note in her hand that Miss Schaffner had given her, and I gestured for her to sit beside me. She didn't flinch and was the epitome of calm, which rattled me somewhat. I repeated to her, "No funny stuff!" and she told me that the flight crew were going to cooperate, that Miss Schaffner would remain in the cockpit, and that she would remain with me and provide me with anything I needed. She asked me if there was anything that I wanted to eat or drink, but I said, "No." In truth, I wasn't expecting the flight crew to be completely cooperative, and I thought that I would at least have to shout or threaten. However, when she offered me refreshments, I was suspicious that their strategy was to remain calm and drug me if given the opportunity.

Again, I opened the case, and she stared into it. She seemed transfixed by it, although I suppose seeing a bomb isn't a daily occurrence for most people. I closed the case, put a cigarette in my mouth, and looked toward her; instinctively, she lit the cigarette. I never expected a lady to light my cigarettes for me, but given the circumstances of not wanting to let the wire go, neither of us had a choice.

The cabin interphone was behind the aisle seat, and Miss Mucklow could reach around and telephone the flight deck from a seated position beside me. I didn't quite understand what she was saying, but she held the receiver with her left hand and had her right hand over her mouth. I looked across the aisle at the kid looking out the window, and he didn't look around to face me. I thought he was a threat to me then, and I needed to get rid of him and the passengers in the rows in front.

"I certainly hope that none of the radio equipment interferes with this," I whispered into Miss Mucklow's ear as I tapped the top of the briefcase with my available left hand. I don't think she replied, but she moved rather quickly out of the seat and offered people to move further up the aircraft alongside another seemingly senior stewardess, whom I assume was their supervisor. I learned in later literature about me that her name was Mrs. Alice Hancock. Again, I didn't catch exactly what they said to the passengers, but gradually the passengers moved further up the aircraft, leaving me alone in my seat.

After the passengers were moved and given refreshments, Miss Mucklow sat beside me again. Mrs. Hancock had asked Miss Mucklow for playing cards for first class, but I told her to return to her station at the front of the aircraft. By this stage, the puddle jump of a flight should have been completed. Thirty minutes had passed, which was the scheduled flight duration, and we were still in the air with no indication of the aircraft beginning its descent or landing pattern.

My watch read 3:32 p.m., and I asked Miss Mucklow what was happening.

"We are doing all we can for you and getting all the items that you requested."

"Remember now, you told me you would all cooperate. I sincerely hope none of you will go against me," I reminded her, but she didn't break her composure in the slightest. She paused, closed her eyes briefly, and interlocked her fingers on her lap in the seated position. She didn't seem to be restraining herself from crying, but rather praying. Eric came into my head at that moment, and I could almost smell the burning lavender tea. It was quite bizarre, and I forgot myself for a moment.

Eventually, she broke the silence and whispered to me, "Sir, why did you choose us? Do you have any issues with our airline?"

"It isn't that I have a grudge against your airline, Miss. I just have a grudge. This flight was short and suited my needs." At this point, I had to restrain myself from giving too much information. I wasn't going to tell her that I was familiar with the terrain, that a short flight would promote urgency in the FBI or police response, and that Harding told me in Saigon that the Federal Reserve Bank in Seattle kept large sums in the event of robberies or extortion.

As time ticked by, I became more and more convinced that the FBI or the cops would storm the aircraft upon landing and that obtaining the cash and rigs should not take as long as it was taking. Planning an assault in an armed robbery situation requires careful planning when civilian lives are at stake, and the elapsed time made me believe that this is what was happening on the ground. I fell silent for a few minutes to consider how I could avoid an assault or at least evacuate the passengers in the event of a shootout or having to detonate the bomb. I was smoking a steady stream of cigarettes while planning my next move. At one point, I realized that I should offer the young lady a cigarette, and when I did, she told me she quit but, a moment later, took the cigarette anyway.

I turned to Miss Mucklow while she was still facing forward. "Everything needs to be in place before the aircraft can land. Have the pickup rig with the exit stairs ready immediately upon landing. Only one unmarked vehicle can approach with the money and the parachutes, with only one intermediary. You and only you are allowed off the aircraft, and I want you to bring on the money first. I want to see the car all the way, and I want it to park beside the exit door so I can always see it. One fuel truck, one employee—that's it! All passengers are to remain in their seats, and when the money is back here, I will release the passengers."

"Okay, sir," she whispered back. Sharpshooters weren't going to fire upon a stewardess deplaning alone. If she were to bring on the parachutes while the passengers were being taken into the terminal building, I would have everything in my hand before an arrest op was mounted against me. Like the American currency comment, I feared I gave away my law enforcement background by asking for an unmarked vehicle. Putting two and two together would have been relatively easy from these two comments alone, pegging me as a Canadian cop of some description.

Miss Mucklow used the interphone to relay these requests to the cockpit, and I rechecked the time at 3:50 p.m. Strangely, none of the passengers seemed discontented or unsettled. What I did notice that I hadn't noticed before was a gentleman wearing a Stetson. My immediate fear was that he was an undercover sheriff or an air marshal. I kept an eye on him for a bit, but he didn't seem to be talking to anybody or doing anything that indicated that he was gathering information or waiting to move against me.

I looked out the window and saw Tacoma, and after a while, I saw it again. This is when I knew we were circling above SeaTac Airport, and all the memories just came flooding back. I was surprised at the little details I could recall from the air. An announcement came over the intercom from the captain or first officer informing the passengers that they had encountered a mechanical difficulty and had to burn excess fuel before landing and to keep seatbelts fastened. I found this incredibly bizarre and immediately thought pandemonium would ensue. I braced myself for passenger panic because I was unsure that telling people in a flying tin can that there was a mechanical difficulty was a good idea. There was no panic, though, and nobody made a fuss, which was good.

"It is approaching 5 p.m.," I reminded Miss Mucklow, and she reassured me that the airline was assembling everything. All the bizarre happenings on the flight were indicative that there was a sinister plot on the ground. I was a dead man flying, and nothing would convince me otherwise. I suppose I became resigned to the fact that the operation had failed, and the calm passengers and crew were of great alarm to me. I suspected everyone had been quietly told to remain calm because I would be toast when we landed. However, I was thinking at this stage that some of the passengers and crew would also be toast, depending on how audacious law enforcement at the airport would be.

Inside the paper bag at my feet, I had wire cutters, medical supplies, a pocket knife, goggles, a first aid kit, a flashlight, and a revolver with two rounds: one to fire a warning shot and the other for the roof of my mouth, if necessary. The revolver was brought as a backup if the bomb didn't detonate. Before putting it in the case, there wasn't a way to test the dynamite to see if it was tainted or damaged.

The tension was unbearable, and I told Miss Mucklow, "Looks like Tacoma down there."

"Yes, it is."

"Ah, McChord—that is only a twenty-minute drive from the airport. We must be nearby, although you should tell the flight deck I don't want the parachutes from there. I want four civilian parachutes with manual ripcords on them. The Air Force base will likely provide static line chutes, which will be useless to me when we are airborne again." At this, she lifted the phone to inform the cockpit.

I was constantly smoking at this point. Nothing would settle me down. I was looking out the window and didn't turn my head to look at my young hostage next to me. She seemed keen to talk to me at times and told me, "If we are going to Cuba, U.S. Customs will take any cigars or rum you buy and not return them to you. We have been told to advise the passengers of this."

I couldn't help but laugh; I was disarmed, at least emotionally, and it took my mind away from what I thought would be my violent death on the runway of SeaTac airport in the next forty-five minutes to an hour. "We are not going to Cuba," I told her, "but you will like where we are going— somewhere nice. So, where are you from?" I inquired.

"I am from Pennsylvania originally, but I am living in Minneapolis now," she told me.

"Ah, very nice country." Just as I said that, I felt I had made another fatal error. In my head, I was thinking "Bonne Provence," which translates in English as "nice country" or "a lovely part of the world."

"So, where are you from?" she asked me.

"It doesn't matter," I told her, returning to looking out the window. I didn't want to face her—*I've already given too much away,* I thought—and I considered telling her because, as far as I was concerned, I was a dead man anyway. However, I held on to that toxic thing called hope and kept my lips sealed. She lit another cigarette, using the last match in the Sky Chef matchbook. She went to discard the matchbook, but I asked her for it back, and I put it in my left pants pocket. I also got the notes back, as well as the messages being ferried to the cockpit. I wanted to keep as much evidence as possible on my person, whether it came with me for the jump or was obliterated if the bomb were to detonate.

My nerves only worsened as I watched passengers

start to get out of their seats to use the lavatory behind us. I remember someone quipping to us while he waited that if we remained in the air much longer, we would have to have an airborne Thanksgiving dinner. I somewhat agreed and laughed nervously with the other passengers to save face and not arouse suspicion. The suspicious-looking man wearing the Stetson approached us and asked Miss Mucklow for a magazine because he was bored. I thought he was a little bit brash; perhaps this was part of his act. He started questioning the mechanical difficulty, and then she got him a magazine before he returned to his seat. I didn't say anything directly to him, but he stared at me before leaving.

When he was a safe distance away, I remarked, "If that is a sky marshal, I don't want to see any more of that." In the couple of years prior, the Federal Aviation Administration had piloted the practice of having air marshals on short flights, given the number of bad apples like me who were commandeering passenger airplanes.

It was getting dark outside, and I finally received the update from Miss Mucklow that everything was in place on the ground and that we would be coming into SeaTac to land. I could feel the landing gear being deployed below where I was sitting, and the time I noted was 5:35 p.m. I could feel my hand shaking on the command wire, and what was peculiar was how smooth the runway approach was from the air.

There was no turbulence or twitching, or perhaps my turbulent twitching cancelled out the movements of the aircraft. I looked out as we came in and saw the mobile airstair truck from the window and what looked like a minivan or car—I can't recall exactly which. There wasn't a chorus of flashing lights, at least not that I could see at the time, and it looked like I was in with a chance.

Chapter 4

ATC Tower

Clifford Harding, November 24, 1971

We came out of the office, jumped in the car, and raced south down 5th Avenue. It wasn't unusual to blue light or drive at a high speed from our office toward the airport if we heard that someone we wanted was touching down there, although on that evening, I seemed to become confused in the stress and missed the turnoff for Seneca Street, which leads to the entrance of Interstate 5 (I-5).

Now and again, Johnson was saying things like "Wow— wow, easy!" and he even lifted his hand as if to take the wheel from me. Eventually, we got onto I-5 South and continued. There were some other unmarked vehicles that I recognized, but I remember a Dodge Dart driving up alongside me and giving me some sort of thumbs-up or signal before racing past me. We had some marked vehicles for an emergency response like this, but we honored the hijacker's request for no flashing lights. No doubt a flashing convoy would have been visible from the air, so I felt somewhat relieved that nobody did it.

It was very difficult to keep my eyes on the road; I was constantly looking upward to see any flashes of light and seemed to be convinced that this hijacking was more than a political statement or protest of some kind. My car didn't have any flashing lights on it, but we could still drive at speed in our unmarked vehicles.

"Tell you what, Cliffy boy, I wouldn't wanna be jumping on a night like that."

"Why not?"

"Shit, even airborne paratroopers would struggle on a night like this. Cloudy, starting to rain, and the sun's going down, man." Johnson was a Green Beret and knew about parachutes and jumping conditions, which was quite handy later. "Plus, why didn't the motherfucker ask for a helmet, boots, an altitude meter, or bring his own rigs?"

"Well, maybe he brought his own boots and gear. Who keeps parachutes, Johnson?"

"Jumpers do! This dude wasn't no jumper. Let me tell you, if I was doing this job, I ain't trusting nobody else to give me no damn rig. I'd have packed it myself, knowing nobody stuck a knife through it."

This was a great observation; I would never have thought of that. While deep in the conversation and with my mind racing, I nearly missed the turn-off for 154B to merge onto WA-518 West toward Burien/Sea-Tac Airport.

We pulled up to the airport and drove up to the gate to show our badges to the guy on security, who let us through. It was just before 5:30 p.m., and all we could do was wait. The security guy told us Flight 305 was on its way to the ground, and luckily I had binoculars in the glove box. Johnson grabbed them, and we watched all the way as the seized bird screeched down onto the tarmac to greet us standing a few hundred yards away at the runway perimeter fence. Snipers had been posted all the way around the perimeter area, but even if an affirmative was given, a clear shot would have been extremely problematic.

There were other agents and cops at the perimeter fence, but all the lights were off, and nobody had weapons cocked and drawn. The atmosphere was remarkably similar, if not identical, to a situation where one of our servicemen was being flown back from Vietnam for burial. It was quite surreal, and the airstair truck was edging toward the central runway like a hearse approaching to meet the body.

A school bus approached the aircraft, and a car pulled up alongside the stairs. Johnson put the binoculars up to his face and sighed right away.

"What is it?" I whispered to him.

"I can't really see anything!"

"Fuck!" and I got to a stage where I couldn't bear looking. "No visual?"

"Not a thing, Clifford."

The fact that this man was armed with explosives was alarming. Due to our Second Amendment, the general populace tended not to fear guns or firearms because Washington State was and still is an open carry state. Ignoring his request and mounting an arrest op would have been incredibly foolish, even if this man was bluffing and the bomb was a ruse or a fake. To storm the aircraft to call this bluff would have been dangerous and foolhardy and would have been met with discipline even if we successfully apprehended the hijacker. Even if it was a ten million-to-one chance that the explosive device was real, it was a chance I was unwilling to take with American lives.

I remembered the Oath of Allegiance when I came into the Bureau: "Defend the Constitution of the United States against all enemies, foreign and domestic." *So, which was this guy?* It was very difficult to say; we knew nothing, at least not at this point.

I got a smack on the right shoulder from Johnson. "Visual, it looks like a stewardess is coming off the plane and going down to the car. She's getting the money bag. Damn, that is what two hundred thousand dollars looks like. She's hauling it up the metal staircase. If this guy lets the passengers off the plane, we should count 'em."

I took the binoculars from him to look. The same Dodge Dart that greeted me on the interstate was there beside the aircraft. There seemed to be an agonizing few minutes of staring at the front exit door on the aircraft's left side. While the passengers slowly got off the plane, I noted the aircraft registration number, N467US. It was dark, and the fuel truck was starting to refuel.

We considered getting closer to the aircraft, but seeing as the guy was armed with explosives, we decided not to snatch defeat from the jaws of victory. There were thirty-seven on the flight; we counted thirty-six getting off. Our guy was still on the plane.

The same stewardess appeared to be coming up and down the staircase to bring the parachutes onto the aircraft. The big Navy backpack parachutes looked huge, and she clasped them tightly on her way back to the aircraft. Just after the parachutes were taken onto the aircraft, the shades were put down on all the windows, completely killing any possible visual we could get of the hijacker.

"Jesus, this guy is good," I whispered to Johnson. I still maintain that; it was almost as if this guy was more than two steps ahead. Immediately, I thought, *How can anyone without a decent level of investigative or emergency response experience be able to control this situation entirely?* Anything I thought of or considered playing as a move was immediately poo-pooed, and the only strategy left for us was to hope that he wouldn't detonate the bomb.

"Do you reckon he's gonna make the bird fly again, Johnson?"

"Course he is; he's got parachutes. All he's gotta do is open the door somewhere, and that's it." It was just so simple, and I respected the guy somewhat for how audacious his plan was. It was ballsy; we were eating out of his hand

and standing there looking like a couple of lost lambs.

"Seems too easy, doesn't it?" I muttered dejectedly back to Johnson. I think at this stage, we were resigned to the fact that there was little to nothing we could do.

"No, sir. Dark and without the right stuff? That's a death jump." Johnson was insistent that this guy wouldn't survive the night.

"Well, with two hundred thousand of Uncle Sam's dollars, I would risk jumping anywhere, although one of those chutes is a dud—we should try and give 'em some sort of warning."

I wasn't sure how long it would take to refuel the bird, and we knew the guy was still aboard. After learning that it would take half an hour, we resolved to stall him as much as we could. A half-baked plan was hatched to invent a "fueling issue" to try and buy ourselves more time and to see how much this guy knew about airplanes. The passengers were ferried away to safety, greatly reducing the risk factor.

In time, a second fuel truck joined, then a third, and possibly a fourth, although I was becoming concerned that we would piss this guy off so much that he would do something stupid.

After around an hour, I decided to go to air traffic control and marched straight past the airport security guards. Airport security then wasn't nearly as sophisticated as it is now. As we marched past another security guard on our way to the radio tower, one of them stopped me and said, "Hey! Nice gun!"

Like in our beige and boring field office, staff had gathered around the air traffic controller talking to the flight deck on Flight 305. At this stage, I showed my badge. "Clifford Harding, FBI. What's the situation?" And the guy just held the palm of his hand up to my face.

Johnson also introduced himself and received the same

hand from the air traffic controller. There seemed to be quite an exchange happening via the radio to the cockpit. Then the guy said, "Roger," or whatever their radio code was to end the conversation. Air Traffic Control has its own language that I didn't really know. With all of these systems and acronyms like SAGE, NORAD, Flight Ops, and all the air traffic speak, we as FBI agents couldn't really follow any conversations or know what anything meant. I barely let him turn his head when I asked him again what was happening.

He told us, "The hijacker wants the aircraft to take off with the aft stairs down. We immediately said no, as the sparks caused by the stairs on the runway could ignite the fuel vapor, but our friend on the flight said it's possible. We got someone from Boeing who told us that the aircraft could take off with the aft stairs deployed, but that it's not recommended. They have a course set for Reno."

"Reno? Why the fuck are they going to Reno?" I yelled at him.

"Fuel stop before Mexico, sir?"

"Johnson, grab a phone and call the Reno office. Will you have them greet 305 when they land?"

Johnson gave me a thumbs-up and grabbed a nearby telephone to pre-warn the welcome party.

The air traffic controller made a sobering point to me: "By the way, Agent Harding, the passengers are fine and unharmed. I will ensure they know you were concerned for their safety."

I didn't even argue back with him, even though the comment was dripping with sarcasm. I excused myself to make a quick telephone call to Charlotte to request that she grab the Thanksgiving turkey I was now late for.

"How many are on the flight crew?"

"Six, sir, but it appears he has released two stewardesses and kept one aboard, then the captain, the co-pilot, and the flight engineer. The guy also asked for meals to be brought on board for the crew. In addition to the stairs being lowered for takeoff, he wants the aircraft to fly at ten thousand altitude, with flaps down to fifteen degrees, and at minimum airspeed."

I had absolutely no idea at the time as to why this configuration was suggested, but obviously it was to make the jump conditions as favorable as he could.

"The guy has four parachutes, five people still aboard, and one bomb. Fuck. Fuck. Fuck. Fuck. He's provided a last meal for them." I felt I had to do something and do it pretty quickly; I couldn't live without making an attempt to personally intervene.

I ordered, "Radio the cockpit to ask the hijacker if an official from the FAA can board the plane to tell him the severity of air piracy and the penalty it carries."

"Okie dokie. Can you ask our friend if he will allow an agent on board to inform the hijacker of the severity of air piracy, please?" After a few seconds, he added, "Okay, standing by." The operator tried to hide his amusement when he turned to me, saying, "He said, 'Tell him to forget it.'"

We learned that two F-106 fighter jets from McChord Air Force Base were scrambled in order to follow the plane at a distance. Additionally, a Lockheed T-33 trainer would also shadow the airliner for a portion of the flight but would eventually have to break off due to fuel limitations. This would serve two purposes: first, to track the flight from a distance, and second, to shoot down the aircraft if three were to jump with the parachutes while leaving two behind on board. This was shaping up to be quite the disaster, and the fact that one of the chutes was a dud didn't help my thinking in the moment. *Christ almighty, what if he gives the girl the dud?*

It was nearly pitch dark as the airplane slowly rumbled

toward the runway to prepare for takeoff. I could hear some of the air traffic control staff praying, and certainly at least one crying. From the ground, all we could do was wait—wait for the flight crew to die or wait for them to live. The fear among the airline staff was that the aircraft would stall or burn all its fuel before reaching Reno.

The 727 had a distinctive roar as the pilots drove the throttle forward for takeoff. Johnson asked God to have mercy on their souls as her nose went to forty-five degrees and she thrust upward, away from Seattle towards Reno.

Chapter 5
Depot

Dan Cooper, May 15, 1940

After I got home, Yvonne and I were in high spirits. I would become a Mountie, ride horses, put bad people in jail, and generally protect everyone while the world was at war. The war frightened Yvonne immensely, and she was glad that I wasn't overseas and would be near home, at least for the time being. I neglected to tell her that I agreed I could be redeployed pretty much anywhere and that if I had said no, then I would have been refused entry and we would have to make the arduous journey back to Fort Smith to live our isolated existence and raise our family in it. Neither of us wanted that. Even though the deafening bells of the First Baptist were a nuisance, I slept soundly that night and awoke bright and early to head to the RCMP training.

***

The Mounties at that time had a strength of around three thousand men that maintained the law superbly well in Canada. As the war was beginning to worsen and domestic policing demands grew, there were more recruits in my training camp than usual. The serving Mounties that left to join the armed forces had to be replaced, and the other demands that war brings needed new boots on the ground or, in our case, in stirrups.

I knew that the course would be a challenge, but I wasn't quite prepared for what was without a doubt the most challenging policing course in the world, on par with the highest order of military discipline. When I arrived at Depot, it was more like how one would imagine a military facility. There was a mix of modern and antiquated red brick buildings surrounding the Canadian flag aloft on a pole in the centre. Immediately, I was asked where my belongings were when I was registering, and I said I didn't bring any as I lived nearby. Sternly, I was told that I would stay on campus and would only be granted leave after noon on Saturday until Sunday evening.

Canadian men had travelled from around the country to be there, even though there were other training facilities in Ottawa. On day one, we got our kit, which was a blue forage cap for patrol, a brown Stetson for summer wear, riding boots, spurs, slacks, and a tunic of RCMP brown. There was something about the uniform that gave me a sense of pride, but I was also scared because I knew the training wasn't going to be easy. The first few days were spent getting to know the place, and the training would take six months. The commissioner at the time was Stuart Wood, and he came to greet us and give a recruits briefing in the Chapel, which was the oldest building on site and where meetings and occasionally some religious activities took place.

"Any lack of effort, nerve, or coordination will wash you out," Commissioner Wood told us. He stood up there with all his medals, and his voice thundered around the whole building as if God himself were addressing us.

We were all assigned a bed in the barracks, and this started the never-ending cycle of polishing and shining our boots and equipment. It was done every evening and inspected every morning. If there was a hair or a tiny scuff on my boot during the inspection, I would have to redo them.

I can't say that I mixed with anybody or put forth the effort to make friends. I had a job to do, and I was determined to see it through. Some other men would get personal with one another, but I chose not to do that. So much so that I cannot remember the gentleman who slept in the next bed. The only one I remember was a tall, bespectacled recruit called Legrand—the French name stood out, and I think we were the only French speakers. I imagine that if one were to ask any of the other men if they remembered me, I would guess that they wouldn't. Being memorable was not something I had in my arsenal, and I was happy for that to be the case.

We were told to say "sir" and to "stand up straight" around a thousand times a day, and our daily routine involved going to classes and physical training outdoors and indoors. We covered a range of different subjects: the history of the force, care and handling of prisoners, first aid, typing, report writing, the criminal code, regulations, current affairs, public affairs, and so on. If a policeman is to teach others to obey the law, then he himself must obey it best of all and set an example. This was ground into us every hour of every day.

One of the first crime laboratories was installed just before I arrived, and we were among the first cops anywhere to learn about photography in policing, using pictures as evidence, collecting blood samples, and taking fingerprints. I found this aspect fascinating, and I remember dipping my fingers into the black ink-soaked sponges to put my own prints on the paper in front of us. I looked at the ridges, lines, and patterns of my own fingerprints, and I cannot describe how innovative and cutting-edge this was to us. Some of the older and more experienced Mounties were unsure of its efficacy, but I knew it would be the future, catching the crooks red-handed even after the fact.

We were marched from class to the stables, to the drill field, to the gym, to the mess, and back to the drill field again. We were screamed at by the drill sergeant, and no matter what we all seemed to do, he was never happy. We marched every day until we had blisters on our feet and were about to collapse. Even though Canada is known for cold winters, we were marching in our brown tunic and forage cap uniforms, and the heat was sometimes unbearable. In the gym, we were taught throws and how to defend ourselves and others. The camaraderie was high even though we spent hours punching and throwing one another and using choke and sleeper holds until we fainted.

I was going home on the weekends to Yvonne, and I wasn't much company. I suffered the small talk for a few minutes before going straight to bed and remaining there until I needed to return the following evening. Yvonne had secured a part-time job behind the desk of the Hotel Norman on 11th Avenue in the city. Even though I got a small allowance of twelve dollars a week from the Mounties, she was the breadwinner for the time being, and my time would come to care for her when I graduated and had a decent salary.

What we all waited for was horsemanship training. I thought I knew my way around a horse, but I was thrown from the training horses more times than I could count. Lying on the ground, hurt and embarrassed, wasn't permitted, and if we didn't immediately remount, we were screamed at until we did. The horses were not like my previous domestic horses at home; these ones were agile and very hard to tame. We rode around and had to hold on for dear life when jumping over obstacles. It was frantic— so many horses, so many obstacles and riders, and the drill sergeants and the veterinarian screaming at us constantly added to the adrenaline.

After a few weeks, we were ready for Suicide Lane, a long, straight dirt track with obstacles. This infamous patch got its name because we were instructed to go at full speed down the quarter-mile lane with our arms folded and holding on only with our knees. Everyone dreaded this, but I got through it on the first attempt. Most of the other men tumbled off the horses or were dragged to the end of the lane.

Overconfidence on horseback is a common issue among recruits to the Mounties. One evening, a fellow in front of me was unseated, causing him to tumble forward over the reins, breaking his spine. Another man was trampled after coming off his horse, and it was all very intense. After receiving medical care on site, anyone who had accidents was told to retake the horsemanship classes. The only times we weren't screamed at were when we were grooming and caring for the horses at the end of each day. Scaring us was fine, but spooking the horses was off-limits in every circumstance. Anyone caught shouting at a horse was disciplined.

Marksmanship was taught, but there was a shortage of weapons due to the war effort. Any available arms that could be spared for the military were spared, and we went in small groups to learn about our rifles and our Smith and Wesson .38 revolvers that we were going to carry with us at all times on patrol and official duty. Ammunition was becoming more scarce, and on the firing range, we were only getting three to five rounds each. I wouldn't say I was the best shot in the world, but none of us were because there weren't enough weapons to go around for everyone to practice regularly.

We were nearly at the end of our recruit training when one of the senior drill instructors asked what my aspirations were for the force. I said that I wanted to remain local and get married soon. This was when I was told that I needed to have the RCMP's blessing if I wanted to get married, and I was so upset that I wanted to leave. I was breaking out in cold sweats, thinking that Yvonne could possibly leave me if I didn't commit to marrying her pretty soon. We were both nineteen at this point, and marriage was something that was common at our age. I was on leave that weekend and told Yvonne all about it, but she said our time would come and they would give their blessing eventually. She stuck by me, and her grace and dignity made me want to marry her even more.

***

At the beginning of May 1940, we were preparing for our graduation ceremony. Everyone who didn't become permanently incapacitated during the training made it. In truth, the force couldn't be picky as to who it accepted and refused due to the war and the shortage of national resources and police officers. We had to ride on some parts of the ceremony and stand at attention for the famous RCMP Musical Ride, which has remained a long-standing tradition and vision of Canadian national pride.

Our ceremony was on May 15, 1940, and it was a beautiful sunny day. A sunny day was great for the spectators, but not so much for us after we were issued with our RCMP scarlet tunics. Yvonne and all of our other family members were allowed to attend, and everyone looked very presentable and neat. None of us were thrown from our horses, and we all went in front of the bandstand to where our commanding officers would place our badges and insignia on our tunics. After this, we took our oath of office:

"I do solemnly swear that I will faithfully, diligently and impartially execute and perform the duties required of me as a member of the Royal Canadian Mounted Police, and will well and truly obey and perform all lawful orders and instructions that I receive as such, without fear, favour or affection of or toward any person. So help me God."

Yvonne was so proud of me, and we were all given a short term of leave, perhaps one or two days, to socialize and to celebrate coming into the force. There was a dance at a dance hall near where we lived, and Yvonne and I went. Yvonne worked the room much better than I did. I was a ghost, blended in with the wallpaper, and just enjoyed the surroundings without really talking to anybody or having anybody approach me to talk to me. I sat idly, smoking my cigarettes, and observing. Observers go far in life, I've found.

***

When I reported back to Depot as a fully-fledged member of the Royal Canadian Mounted Police, there was a sense of disarray. The war in Europe was worsening rapidly, with Hitler and the Nazis invading Europe at an alarming rate, causing more men from Canada to go to the United Kingdom to join the preparations for the liberation of Europe. The Force was losing more men than it was able to recruit, and our postings became very difficult. I learned that I would be posted to the Air Division, which was headquartered at Depot. This wasn't a posting that I wanted, because I wanted to be a regular beat cop out catching bad guys and chasing people on a horse. I felt crestfallen and had no real interest in aviation or wanting to fly to the northern territories or other areas that were difficult to access by rail or automobile.

After finishing one training camp, I was sent straight into another one. The Air Division was set up only a few years prior in 1937 at the behest of the previous commissioner, J.H. MacBrien, who died in office just before I joined. The division started with four de Havilland Dragonfly aircraft, one Noorduyn Norseman, and nine men. At the outbreak of the war, three of the aircraft and most of the men were donated to the war effort, leaving only the Norseman for police use. The Norseman was notable for its rugged construction and ability to take off and land on both wheels and floats, making it highly adaptable for operations in Canada's vast and diverse terrain.

An airfield was situated in Regina, and that was where the aircraft were kept. It was around seven or eight miles away from Depot, and ten of us travelled there in a canvas-covered truck. Our aircraft was red in colour, and it was all we had—if it became wrecked somewhere in the frozen north, then we would have nothing. We walked around the aircraft and were told of all its features and how to change the landing gear from wheels, floats, or skis. The tail could be fitted with either a wheel or a tail skid. She was a workhorse of an aircraft, and we all admired her greatly. The first time I flew, I was hooked. It was terribly frightening to accelerate at such speed before taking to the air, but being able to travel north and see the frozen wastelands for as far as the eye could see from above was staggering. One of our roles was to take aerial pictures for reconnaissance and to map out shorelines for future rescue purposes.

I was so enthusiastic about flying from the first day that it made the training a walk in the park for me. I was jumping up and down with excitement when I was telling Yvonne about it, and she hadn't seen me so happy before. What was supposed to be unpleasant—training to survive in the wilderness in the event of an accident—was no problem at all.

We learned to light a fire, use signal flares, find water sources, make rabbit snares, hunt for food, do first aid, and even use some of our equipment to make a shelter alongside things we foraged from the wild. We completed survival training in several different terrain types, including heavily wooded areas and even in the Arctic Circle. When above the treeline, survival techniques are entirely different and dependent upon fishing and making a shelter out of snow and ice. Although it wasn't what I had signed up for, I couldn't have been placed in a better posting. It had adventure, airplanes, and the great outdoors. Back at Depot, some other recruits I graduated with were complaining of the mundanity of daily patrols around the city or neighbouring towns.

Restructuring was happening all around me, and the usual uniformed clerks were replaced with women, pensioners, and anybody willing to assist the force. We were all briefed that no more of us would be released to the war effort and that our vital home duties would remain. Now and again, I had my red tunic and summer Stetson on and found myself patrolling the highways on horseback.

Resources were challenging; we had more horses than men, more men than weapons, and in the Air Division, we had more airplanes than functioning radios, of which we had one. There were tons of arrests of known Nazi sympathizers, and I played my part in that. Anyone we were suspicious of, we took in. When Italy joined the war effort and allied with Hitler's Germany, we went after the Italians too, registering them as enemy aliens. I split my time between registering potential aliens on the streets and monitoring the tobacco-growing provinces of Quebec and Ontario. A new excise tax was imposed on raw tobacco, and we had to make these new regulations known and enforce the tax payments. Even though we were registering aliens at a rapid rate, there were no sabotage efforts that I ever knew of at the time or learned about since.

***

Even though our training within the Air Division was long completed by the fall of 1940, there was another aspect of the training that none of us had covered and that we would have to learn. We didn't know what this was when told about this one "thing," but we would find out when we got to the airfield in Regina. When we got there, the aircraft was being fueled, and men were putting up a wind sock on the airfield. For about ten minutes, our sergeant, Frederick White, stared at it before ordering the aircraft to take off with none of us on board. He was Sergeant White when he was in our company, but he was called "Whitey" when he wasn't. He didn't like me much because he didn't like the "Frenchies," as he called a couple of us. There were two Royal Canadian Air Force (RCAF) personnel with him. We didn't know what was going on, but the aircraft came down again shortly after that.

We were gathered into the hangar, where a bunch of backpacks were lined up on the floor. I didn't know what they were at first sight, and my instinct told me we were going on a wilderness survival trip somewhere far away. We were asked to pick up these olive-green backpacks with leg straps and a chest strap. There were smaller, knapsack-looking bags beside them that looked as if they were meant to be clipped to our waists or worn across our chests. We stood to attention when Whitey came in to brief us.

"Gentlemen, we are at war! The Krauts could attack us at any point on land, sea, or air. Their arsenal has been able to bring planes out of the sky. If this were ever to happen, we would need to survive. We are the Mounties, and we are prepared!"

"Yes, sir!" we all roared back at him.

"In the event there is engine failure in the air or we fall prey to artillery, we need to save our own lives. The backpacks before you will be the saviours of your lives—your silky, twenty-eight-foot saviours. Leg straps on first, then the shoulder straps, before clipping the chest strap on like so."

Whitey was talking while the two RCAF men were putting on the chutes, and we were all following along with them. Canadian air personnel used the Irvin Air Chute as their primary parachute. The Irvin parachute, developed in the United Kingdom, was widely adopted by the Royal Air Force (RAF) and other Allied air forces, including the RCAF. The Irvin parachute was a round canopy parachute made of silk fabric with a diameter of about twenty-eight feet.

"You will all be given an altimeter, and you are to pull the ripcord at three thousand feet from an exit of five thousand feet. Exit the aircraft into a stable arch position, check your altitude, and pull at three and a half on the meter. After deployment, your round silk saviour should be completely opened up, and just before getting to the ground, bend your knees and lift your legs slightly to absorb impact. Got it, gentlemen?"

"Yes, sir!" was our reply, although it was a croaky and anxious one.

"Gentlemen!?"

"Yes, sir!" Our second try was louder and only slightly less anxious, but it was acceptable to Whitey.

"Very good. Now, gentlemen, let me introduce you to 'The Guardian.'" At this point, he held up the little bags that contained the reserves. The front parachute was a chest-mounted emergency bailout parachute used by aircrews. This parachute had a smaller canopy compared to the round parachutes. "This is your reserve parachute. If something goes wrong when attempting to deploy your main parachute, pull on this one. Your main parachute should take two or three seconds to inflate; if you look upward and see nothing, pull this cord on the left of the front chute bag."

"Yes, sir!" and that completed our forty-minute ground school training before we were told to grab a pair of goggles from a bucket and pile into the aircraft. We didn't really know where we were supposed to land, but it being an emergency, we were only concerned with the preservation of our own lives. On the way up to altitude, we were told to look out for the airstrip and aim for that, even though we couldn't steer or manoeuvre our parachutes very much. They weren't the steerable canopies that would become popular later on.

Since I got on the aircraft first, I was last out. When we got to altitude, my heart was in my throat, and the other men went out the exit door with no issue. I was looking at the needle on my bulky wrist-mounted barometric altimeter, and it was jiggling a little bit. I didn't really examine it on the ground, but it looked as if it was a box altimeter that had a leather strap crudely bolted onto it.

One by one, they took to the skies until it was my turn. I made the mistake of looking down as I approached the exit door, and I could see the vast expanse of woodland, trees, and lakes. I initially feared that I would be blown into a lake somewhere and that Yvonne would be left a widow. The wind was piercing, and I'd never experienced wind and noise like it. I couldn't hear a thing, and I had to crouch at the door to get out, given that I was taller at five feet ten. I didn't know I was doing this when I woke up that morning—the gravity of the situation hit me, and I found it hard to control my breathing.

When my knees started to lock, I reached the door. The Air Force man shouted, "Go!" and I hesitated. He went to lift his hand, and with a deep breath, I jumped out into the sky. I instantly wondered why my stomach didn't jump up into my throat and dislodge my heart. I felt weightless, and I remember roaring with delight on the way down. I had my eye fixed on the curved horizon ahead of me, so much so that I completely neglected to check my altitude. I even lifted my right arm to turn to look around me while maintaining my arch position. Seeing the world from above was incredible; there is nothing quite like it, but at the same time, I hoped there would never be an emergency situation where I would have to actually do it.

As the ground rushed to me, I looked at my altitude to see twenty-five hundred feet and started frantically searching for the ripcord handle on the front of my harness to pull open. I was fumbling around with the harness while still falling at 120 miles per hour and eventually found it. When I pulled, I expected the thing to open immediately, but I fell for another few seconds until I felt the opening shock, which jarred me. I looked down, and I was right above the airfield. I took hold of the risers to control my descent. The big silk dome above my head almost drowned out the light from the sun, and I was looking up at the canopy when I should have been looking at the ground. I looked down, and the ground leapt up to meet me. I immediately lifted my knees to land firmly on the soles of my boots while the silk shroud came down from the heavens and enveloped me.

I got the nod from Whitey on the ground. I suppose he created two things that day: a group of jump-trained Air Division Mounties and the man that would one day become "Dan Cooper."

Chapter 6
Reno, Nevada

Clifford Harding, November 24, 1971

We could only stare as Northwest Flight 305 disappeared into the cloudy night sky. What on Earth was this man going to do? A gentleman was standing near the window with binoculars, but given the cloud cover, they were useless as the bird ascended to over two thousand feet with all the cabin lights off; after that, we were blind. Even though the aircraft didn't take off with the aft airstairs down, it was the least of ATC's worries. When one of them said that the aircraft was "flying dirty," I wanted to know what that meant. It meant that the aircraft was still climbing to altitude with the landing gear down.

There seemed to be some initial confusion about whether we were looking at the correct blip on the radar. It certainly wasn't my skillset to read radar or understand everything everyone was saying, and we could only observe and hope the blip didn't disappear from the small, circular radar dial we were looking at. It was between six and seven thousand feet and 160 knots of airspeed when we were informed that the hijacker was attempting to get the door open at the rear of the aircraft. He wanted out very quickly, and I thought the longer he could stay on the aircraft, the higher the likelihood that his plan would fail. *Must be familiar terrain to this guy,* I thought.

The messages coming to the ground were extremely worrying, and the control tower became so tense that I think we all wanted to scream—I know I certainly did. We understood that the hijacker was frantically relaying to the cockpit that he couldn't get the stairs down. I was completely churning with fear and imagined this screaming girl with a parachute on her back or a dud parachute across her chest being dragged out the open door and thrown or forced to jump from the aircraft.

Luckily, the fear was short-lived, and I breathed a sigh of relief when we were told, "The hijacker has expelled the stewardess; she is now in the cockpit, and the airstairs light is illuminated on the flight engineer's panel." By this stage, he had the stairs down.

"Oh, thank God! Thank fucking God!" a few of us said to each other, as we knew she was at least safe and that we were avoiding an airborne hostage situation. However, with the stairs down, Northwest Flight Operations in Minneapolis was unsure if the aircraft could ascend any higher and thought that eventually somebody would have to go back and check if the hijacker was still aboard or had jumped. They recommended their airspeed be adjusted to 170 knots, and if any onboard malfunction were to occur, Portland, Red Bluff, and Medford would be able to land the aircraft if need be.

Even though the flight was airborne for around twenty minutes, the fuel flow was running at forty-five hundred gallons per hour, and getting to Reno before the fuel depleted was going to be a huge challenge. The captain radioed down and informed us that flaps were set to fifteen degrees. They were climbing up to ten thousand feet, with a further instruction relayed back that as soon as they were confident that the hijacker had left, they should land as quickly as possible. While the stewardess was in the cockpit, we got a few snippets of information, the first being that the bomb appeared to be several sticks of dynamite with wires attached to a battery.

I was reassured that he was at least making an effort to jump and that we would hunt him down like a dog when he got back down to the ground, or, in the best-case scenario, that he, the money, and the bomb would become a crater. In the meantime, Johnson was going between the tower and the first-class lounge to give updates to the passengers, but I don't recall anything he said at that time because I was looking at the hypnotic radar screen, completely lost in my thoughts.

Before climbing, the message seemed to be that, due to the cabin being depressurized at the hijacker's request, oxygen masks would have to be worn by the flight crew. I wondered if going to altitude would suffocate the hijacker so we could bag him up when they got to Reno, although with the door open and the stairs down, he had all the air he wanted up there.

By 8 p.m., the aircraft was holding at ten thousand feet, and we got a message: "Miss Mucklow saw the hijacker tie the money to himself before leaving the cabin and joining the flight crew." A decision was made that Reno would be extremely tight if the hijacker didn't leave soon. *What the fuck is this guy waiting for? He has the door open, a bag of cash, and the stairs down. It is all set for him.*

The aircraft was almost ordered by Northwest Flight Operations in Minneapolis, and I believe Kansas City, to make a secondary plan for landing in Medford, Oregon, if Reno became too difficult or an outright impossibility. All of the conversations between all the different parties by radio were very difficult to follow and decipher at the time. We almost needed the ATC staff to translate their abbreviations and tell us who each person they were talking to was. Even the note-takers around us were flustered and unsure of everything.

I asked what the "Victor 23" they kept talking about was, and they said it was the flight path. Even with some of us in the tower, some on the ground, and jets following the aircraft from McChord, I already had an instinct that there were too many cooks spoiling this broth and that when everyone came to compare notes, we would have a giant clusterfuck fireball of an information file. They didn't know our language, we didn't know theirs, and we didn't know the answers to each other's questions. If we weren't simply staring at one another, we were trying to translate each other's terms and abbreviations, which was an added pain in an already harrowing situation.

Just before a quarter after eight, we got reports of oscillations. We didn't know what that meant, but we knew that something was happening. Something was happening with the stairs, but we didn't know what. The ground was constantly radioing up to the sky, but for some seconds, we heard nothing back. For a few seconds, we thought that perhaps the hijacker had detonated the bomb, and the room fell completely silent until someone said, "He's gone."

Someone behind me shouted out, "Who the fuck is gone!?"

The radio operator, whose chair I was standing behind, turned to us and said, "The flight crew has said that they think their friend has taken leave of them."

We wanted a position of where they were, and they told us that the hijacker had jumped around the area of Ariel, Washington. Already, efforts were being made to set up a manhunt for the hijacker. Our biggest worry then moved on to whether the bomb was still on board, and we wanted to confirm definitively if the hijacker had gone. Understandably, nobody from the flight crew was quick to volunteer to see if the hijacker was still back there. I believe their superiors ordered them to remain in the cockpit for the time being to avoid a mid-air confrontation with a man armed with a bomb.

My gut told me the man was gone, but between Boeing, Northwest, the control tower, and everyone else, the present danger was that their bird was in the air with the stairs down, and it would have to land in Reno. Retracting the stairs from the cockpit wasn't possible, and a nasty landing was the primary concern of everyone around me. I asked how far away they were from Reno, and at that point, I was told they were around an hour and fifteen minutes away in their current configuration.

I went outside to catch some air and smoke some cigarettes. I removed my outer coat and sat on the ground outside with my head in my hands. I couldn't believe what was going on, but I went to the terminal building to call home and tell Charlotte everything that was happening. She told me to be safe and that she was offering her prayers for everyone involved. I couldn't speak; it was so surreal. I was stuttering and stammering to Charlotte because I was apologetic for not being home earlier and for the awful mess I was caught up in. I knew already that whatever was happening tonight would have far-reaching consequences. The foreboding feeling of dread superseded my concern for the flight about to come down in Reno.

We went to first class, and that is where I first heard the confirmation of the hijacker's name. Some agents were already questioning the passengers who had gotten off the flight. An agent was running up to me, and I just said, "Who?"

Then he said to me, "Dan Cooper. The roll call was taken among the passengers in the first-class lounge, and that name was the only one not accounted for."

"Do we have a description of the man from statements any of you have taken with passengers and the deplaned stewardesses? What did he look like?" I snapped back, eager to know who this "Dan Cooper" was and what he looked like.

"Well, sir…"

"Spit it out!" I growled back.

"They said he looked like everybody!" he nervously replied, to the point of whispering.

"What do you mean?" I sighed.

"An average man, five feet ten, mid-forties, with olive skin, a slim build, bootblack hair, loose skin below his chin, wearing a black business suit, a raincoat, wraparound sunglasses, and carrying a cheap attaché case and a paper bag. He had no discernible accent. The stewardesses said he was somewhat nice and that he didn't yell at them or use violence in any way, although one of the stewardesses said he became strange when he got the money bag and asked them to hold it to demonstrate how heavy it was."

I became incredibly frustrated. "Mr. Everybody. That's who we're looking for, huh?"

The stammering worsened from this young agent. "I— It would seem that way, sir."

I assessed that this man could be anybody and matched the description of nearly every middle-aged man in the country. Crooks tend to wield battle scars, tattoos, or any other identifying mark, but this guy had nothing memorable about him. Surveillance cameras and security-based photography were nonexistent, never mind advanced, in 1971, so we had no photographs or footage to look at. I told him to run the name "Dan Cooper" by the nearby field offices, and it was a redundant order because, obviously, that wasn't his real name.

When I returned to the control tower, Northwest

305 was due to land in Reno imminently, and when I looked around the room, everybody in it managed to fit the description of the man we would be hunting for. The tension mounted, and silence shrouded us all as we heard from ATC that the aircraft was coming in to land. My gut was telling me that landing with the stairs down would cause the airplane to explode, and we still weren't entirely confident that both the man and the bomb were gone. We knew the plan would be to storm the aircraft upon landing, but what if the bomb were to detonate?

It is very easy to take an idealistic view of the hijacking, especially with the modern view through today's eyes. At that time, the lives of the crew still aboard were very much at risk, and so many variables were floating around the room and in our minds, making us sick with worry and dread. I would never want anybody to feel what we felt that evening. "Heroes" and "cultural icons" don't tend to invoke feelings like this in anybody, including law enforcement.

The atmosphere of relief came over us when the aircraft touched down safely in Reno while we waited patiently for an update. It was around thirty minutes later when we were told that the flight crew and the stewardesses were safely off the aircraft and taken into the care of the agents from the Reno office. We waited for the call from our counterparts, and I was later told on the telephone that the hijacker was gone. He left behind one backpack parachute and a chest reserve with lines cut from it. I wondered if he jumped with the dud, and when I asked if it was there, the agent I spoke to said it wasn't; the dummy was gone! Then, we were told of the news of a potential smoking gun: a black clip-on tie left behind on the seat.

Part Two

"See him now
As he stands alone
And watches children play a children's game
Simple child
He looks almost like the others
Yet they know he's not the same
Scorn not his simplicity
But rather try to love him all the more"

Phil Coulter

Chapter 7

Merchant Bank, Regina

Dan Cooper, May 2, 1946

The war raged on, and by the summer of 1942, all the men in the Air Division had been shipped out to the RCAF, and I elected to remain in Canada on policing duties. There wasn't a wave of crime, but rather a wave of suspicion. Any foreigners were treated cautiously, both by the Mounties and the general public. We kept lists of foreign nationals from both Germany and Italy, and although we weren't supposed to spy on them, we did. It was quite ironic, spying on people to see if they were spying on us. Yvonne was mentioning marriage, and the first time I wrote to my superiors to request permission in March of 1942, my request was denied.

***

One of the notable annual events that takes place in Regina every year is the RCMP Musical Ride, where we don our uniforms and perform cavalry drills and manoeuvres. I took part in the 1941 and 1942 events, although they were quieter affairs than in the pre-war period. There some criticism that the Musical Ride was proceeding given the war and that Canadians were dying on European soil. However, they decided to move forward with the event in an attempt to try and raise morale for those of us still in Canada. Not that it mattered to me, because on the day of the 1943 Musical Ride, I was on the beat in Regina alone. I had some experience and could handle myself, so I was on patrol alone in an RCMP automobile. There were fuel shortages and rationing, so to counteract this, we could patrol alone in the car or sometimes with up to three others.

That particular day, I was alone and twirling the end of my black tie around my fingers in the car's driver's seat when I heard what sounded like an alarm. It was awfully loud, and I had never heard that kind of noise before. Not all the cars had sirens or alarms on them to alert people to our presence at that time, and the one I was in didn't have a siren, so I drove closer to the sound. I was driving down Scarth Street in downtown Regina when I heard the alarm coming from the Bank of Montreal. Quickly, I loaded my service revolver and grabbed a whistle that I kept in the glove box. Calling for backup wasn't an option, as this vehicle hadn't been fitted with a radio yet.

I stood on the street and blew my whistle, waiting for a whistle response from nearby, but none came. The police coverage was minimal due to the Musical Ride, and of course, that would be a great day to rob a bank in Regina. I ran toward the door, and just as I opened it and stood inside, two of the bank thieves grabbed me, but I managed to push one away, leaving me face-to-face with the other. Out of nowhere, he lunged and grabbed my tie, pulling me to the ground. I dropped the revolver, and it slid across the floor as he moved behind me, tightening his grip and choking me with my own tie. I quickly crouched down and managed to throw the man over my back, and he landed on the floor in front of me. Meanwhile, his accomplice had made a break for it and escaped through the front door, leaving me to arrest the man I had just thrown down.

With one thief handcuffed, I burst through the door and ran down Scarth Street after the other. I slalomed in between shocked bystanders as a flurry of Canadian bank notes flew out of his bag towards me. The man looked quite confused, stopping for split seconds here and there to decide where he would turn—he was clearly not a local. Not that I was one either, but I had lived there for four years. This would not be a battle of wits; it would be one of fitness, and one that I was sure I would win. After around a mile of running, he began to tire, and once I was within three or four feet of him, I jumped onto his back, and we crashed to the ground. I didn't have another pair of handcuffs, but I was able to easily frogmarch the exhausted, breathless criminal back to the bank to retrieve his friend and put them in the car.

When I gave my report to my sergeant, a detail that he honed in on more than any other was the fact that I was pulled to the ground by my tie. This caused his brows to furrow, and I promised to tuck it in in the future. It didn't matter, as he informed me of other incidents where drunkards or brawlers had grabbed a Mountie's tie and other instances where the ties were caught on horse reins after a horse bolted, dragging the man along with it in a thirty-mile-per-hour noose. After this, we were ordered to wear clip-on ties every time we donned any form of uniform, both ceremonial and practical.

This exciting day at work not only earned me recognition for bravery but, most importantly, a favour that I duly cashed in by resubmitting my request to marry Yvonne. This time, it was granted, and I cabled her father to tell him of my intentions. I actually sent it from the RCMP cable machine to make it look more impressive. Keeping cable lines free was essential, and messages had to be short, so all I said was, "Est-ce que je peux épouser Yvonne, s'il vous plaît?" I am unsure if the impressive RCMP-headed message made a difference, but he cabled me back to the station to say yes.

***

I was granted leave for one week to marry and have some form of honeymoon with Yvonne. We travelled home to Fort Smith and got married at St. Joseph's Church on November 1, 1943. My parents were overjoyed. Even my sisters came, and it was a lovely day and evening. We all went back home for a meal, and Yvonne was slightly saddened that the stables were empty after my parents gave up caring for the horses. My mother cooked a wonderful meal, and our home was big enough to accommodate everyone. I know my father found it very difficult not to drink, and when I was outside having a cigarette, he approached me with a bottle of bourbon and a Canada Dry mixer. He poured the bourbon into my glass, followed by the Canada Dry mixer, but poured only the Canada Dry into his glass.

My father lifted his glass and said, "Que le Seigneur tourne vers vous son visage et vous donne la paix," meaning, "May the Lord lift up His countenance upon you and give you peace."

We clinked glasses, and the drink tasted terrible. How my father drank this stuff on a daily basis for years was beyond me. Having been on the beat in Regina around drunkards and whatnot, I knew alcohol was not for me. I drank the occasional drink to be polite, but I have always abhorred drunkenness. After this, my father went back inside, and Yvonne came to join me outside.

"You will make a good father. I am so happy."

"I'm so happy too. I'm sorry it took so long for this day to happen," I told her as I placed my hands around her waist and stared into her big blue eyes.

"We will have a happy family, as long as you don't make our boys join the Mounties!" she chuckled at me.

"Je ne peux pas le garantir," I wryly said back to her, and we just stood smiling at one another. How madly in love we were! It was a lovely time—the happiest I ever was and the happiest I ever will be.

***

The war ended in 1945, and our family hadn't grown at all. We had been so desperate to have a child for the past couple of years since we married, but nothing was happening. Yvonne was terribly upset and felt that it was her fault. I constantly reassured her that it wasn't. We had both consulted a doctor in Regina and were told that the war and my job as a policeman were stressful, and that stress could affect fertility. Yvonne and I told each other everything, and she thought that some love-making pains she experienced could be the cause of us not expecting a child. Upon examination, no problems were ever found, so I assumed that the fault was mine.

I became a sergeant in early 1946, having only been promoted to corporal the year before. While it carried more responsibility, it came with fewer patrols and a higher paycheck. In policing and most other professions, promotions mean less risk to life, less legal liability, more money, and more people to throw under the bus if needed. No sooner was I promoted than we finally found out we were pregnant. We were overjoyed, and we decided to vacate the boarding house we had lived in for years to find our own house. We had stayed in the boarding house for seven years and saved most of our money so that we could buy our own home, which we did.

Yvonne went into labour six weeks early, and I just happened to be at home with a patrol car in our driveway. Although not entirely lawful, I put the light and siren on to get her to the hospital. She was wheeled away, and I demanded to accompany her, but initially, the midwives wouldn't allow me, and I could not understand why. So I paced up and down the hall before asking the nurse at the nearby station if I could go down. My request was denied, but after asking nicely several more times, my request was finally granted.

Yvonne was sweating and looked awfully pale. I knew childbirth was dreadful for a woman's body, but I didn't imagine it being this bad. She passed out several times, and the midwives kept attaching an oxygen mask to her face. She was injected with pain relief and looked at me with a blank stare, squeezing my hand. Eventually, she awakened and yelped more than screamed or shouted. It was very unsettling for me to witness, and I knew immediately that this wasn't a usual delivery. I was trying to read the faces of the midwives, and my initial readings told me that they were not too hopeful but were trying their best to be positive.

Eventually, the midwives backed away and held our baby, but there was no crying.

"It's a boy," the nurse said, and I stood up quickly to look at the little bundle in her arms—he was an awful blue colour. I immediately feared the worst, as did Yvonne when she sprang up again on the bed. However, we could see him moving, and the nurse handed him to us. We were told to massage his airways to get him to take deep breaths. This really helped, and gradually, over the course of half an hour, his colour returned. What a relief! We decided to call our baby Richard, and even at less than an hour old, he was the beautiful image of his mother. It's another wonderful day in my memory, that second day of May in 1946.

Richard and Yvonne were to remain in the hospital for several days while Yvonne recovered and Richard received therapy in an oxygen tent. I visited every available second that I could, and given my new position on the force, I could disappear without being questioned. Yvonne eventually recovered, and we were home together as a family. We doted over Richard and loved him with all of our hearts. When I held Richard one evening while Yvonne rested in bed, I understood my parents' pain when Mathieu, Lucille, and Eric died. It made me think about them and miss them.

***

As Richard grew up, we noticed he wasn't like the other children. He had reached one year old and still wasn't walking or talking. The doctors and people we took him to were quick to ask if he was blue when he was born, and then they would give us their commiserations and say that he was "an idiot" or "slow." I remember when Eric was described like that when we were children, and it was painful for both of us. When this became apparent, my parents moved to be near us to give any support that they could. Yvonne's parents were older and didn't wish to leave Fort Smith. My parents were in their early sixties, and as far as support for us, they were limited in what they could provide, but at least they were there.

Special education schools didn't really exist back in the late 1940s and early 1950s. There were some short-term programs to help Richard learn and for Yvonne to meet other mothers in the same position as us, but we agreed that we would avoid placing Richard in an institution for as long as we could. The difference between young Richard and young Eric was that Richard wasn't eternally tormented. He was happy and saw all the beauty in the world, even if he didn't understand it. He loved animals and would quickly pet dogs in the street if their owners allowed him to.

Richard was tall and slender and had my black hair. However, he had his mother's smile. Yvonne was slightly distant from Richard in his earlier years and descended into a deep postpartum melancholy that nobody could pull her out of. When I returned home from patrol each day, she often closed the door to our bedroom. That was our life for the first twelve years of Richard's life; we were constantly living the same day over and over again. Yvonne had to leave her part-time job because Richard couldn't attend school. Even though he was special, I think if given a chance, he would have been able to complete some aspects of school. He could count a bit, use some words, and express his feelings. Maybe I wore rose-tinted spectacles, but I always had an instinct that Richard was able to understand much more than what Yvonne and I believed.

Sometimes, Richard really made Yvonne and me laugh, and he could pull Yvonne out of her depressive states with his charm. Yvonne used to bake date squares—oatmeal mixed with dates—and I took them to the office. Given that Richard could become excited when he had excess sugar, he was limited to one square. One evening, I was having a cigarette and decided to have a date square with a cup of coffee. Richard stood in front of me with his sad eyes, and given that Yvonne was upstairs, I decided to sneak him a little treat. Richard did his little giggle, and I heard rustling from upstairs.

Yvonne burst into the room and admonished me in her motherly way. "Did you give Richard a date square?"

Richard gulped and looked at me as all of the colour drained out of his face.

"Yes, my love, I did."

She turned to Richard with her arms folded and a strict

look. "Richard, did you have two of those today already?"

Richard didn't really know where to look and zipped between looking at me and looking at Yvonne. He had to lie to one of us, and he just stood in stunned silence for around five seconds before bursting into laughter. His laughter was infectious, and when Yvonne laughed, Richard won the battle. He had some clever streaks, and when I told my mother this story, she became very nostalgic, as Eric was similar in nature and always got an extra cake from Madame Laroche.

Richard and I used to walk in the evenings, and he never seemed to tire. He could walk for miles and enjoyed being outside. I enjoyed reading and started taking trips to the McNally Robinson bookstore with Richard, which was a twenty-minute drive from our home. I loved this particular store because they sold books printed in French and even children's books. I spoke to Richard in French and English to see which one he would pick up, but he mostly stuck with English with the few words he had. It didn't matter what books I got for Richard; he was always more interested in the pictures and pointing out things that he liked or made him happy.

The store clerk was a very kind lady named Margot, and she didn't scoff or scorn whenever Richard and I came in. I had already been used to it with Eric, but time had passed since Eric was alive, and I don't recall things being as bad when taking Richard out in public, although the customary stares, tuts, and downright looks of disgust still remained. It still bothered me, even though I grew up with it. I'm not sure Richard was aware. I have a vivid memory of one of our trips to this store because I purchased one of my favourite books, *Bonheur d'occasion (The Tin Flute)* by Gabrielle Roy. I still have it and have kept hold of it after all these years.

Richard was starting to like comic books, mainly for the pictures, and he started laughing hysterically in the comic book section while I was chatting with Margot at the counter. I was wondering what he was laughing at and decided to investigate. When I found him at the back of the store, he handed me a comic book, and it struck me. On the cover was a man in a green fighter pilot suit and helmet, with a fighter jet behind him in the background. It was almost like a pop Andy Warhol image of the hero of the comic, and it was called *Le Triangle Bleu*. I never saw Richard so happy looking at a book before, and it was very touching for me as a parent to see my otherwise childlike twelve-year-old experience the same joy and wonder from a book as other twelve-year-olds of the time.

I took it from him to flick through the pages and saw that it was all in French and written by Albert Weinberg. It was certainly a European publication that had made its way over to Canada. Interestingly, I caught sight of the hero's name, "Dan Cooper." I remember thinking that it was bizarre for a European comic book to choose such an Anglicized name and to have him be a Royal Canadian Air Force pilot. I pointed at the man on the cover and said out loud to Richard, "Dan Cooper," and Richard was thrilled. Margot also found this incredibly endearing. I found it very gratifying for Richard to have a hero like most other boys, and I remember thinking to myself that I wished the hero was me.

Chapter 8
The Search Area
Clifford Harding, November 25, 1971

Thanksgiving for me was cancelled. What's worse, every available FBI agent in the Pacific Northwest and Reno, as well as military personnel, were called in to comb the search area. The weather had cleared somewhat, and I didn't feel guilty about leaving my family on Thanksgiving. Charlotte understood but was still pissed off at me. After I left home, we went en masse to Ariel, Washington, which was around three hours away from our field office, and we left at 5:30 a.m. Ariel is a tiny little place with not much to speak of. It's very rural, along Washington State Route 503, and I don't think anyone knew where they were or if we were in the right location. The aircraft was supposedly flying overhead of our location at 8:13 p.m. the previous night, which was the noted time "Cooper" jumped. This was noted from the flight records, taking into account the one-minute delay in communications between Flight 305 and the ground.

The first thing I noticed when we arrived was the number of aircraft flying overhead. Special Agent Ralph Himmelsbach, who led the Portland Field Office, is legendary not just for his work on the Dan Cooper case but for his long and illustrious career as a caseman. He was a private pilot and immediately began searching the area in his own light aircraft. Communications were not as instant as they are now, and gaining the facts as they were uncovered was difficult. The search area was colossal, covering almost two hundred square miles on the deck and perhaps one thousand square miles above our heads. I can't exactly recall if the helicopters came on the 25th or the day afterward, but they were there too. Orders for the deployment of resources and manpower went up as far as the oval office, but I was never privy to that kind of clearance. With all the latest manhunting technology and expertise, finding this guy shouldn't have been an issue—if, of course, we were looking in the right place.

***

There were sixty to sixty-six fingerprints found on the aircraft, cigarette butts in an ashtray, and two of the parachutes. On the morning of the 25th, I wasn't sure yet which parachutes were left behind. The details were coming in piecemeal, and often the piecemeal that did arrive was either slightly inaccurate or just completely fabricated and sensationalized. In the Bureau at that time, everyone wanted to get a big break. Everyone wanted to make national news or be the agent who apprehended the bad guy. There were so many agents with so much information that extracting evidential accuracy was pretty much fucked from the morning of day one.

What I had hoped for was that there would be a dead guy dangling from a tree or a mangled corpse with a parachute rig on, being devoured by the bears. We were all mustered by the military and told to stand approximately four feet apart and comb the wooded areas in front of us. Regarding landing zones, it wasn't complete brushland, and the field we were standing in would have made a perfect landing site, with the adjacent woods being a perfect place to flee for shelter and possibly food. This muster seemed to take forever, and we didn't know who was in charge—the military, ourselves, the cops, or the National Guard. There were barking dogs that would scout ahead to try and find a trace or a scent, and because we were so slow to start, I was able to count fifteen dogs and seventy-five men.

Naturally, fifteen dogs and seventy-five men make noise, and if this scumbag was still in the woods, he would have had ample time in which to collapse his camp and simply leave. We spent too much time planning how the search would be conducted, who would be radioed if anybody found anything, who would take control of any evidence, and who would take the culprit under arrest for questioning and charge. I asked Johnson to see if the Reno office had anything else from the aircrew or the evidence itself. I knew if I made the call myself, I would become angry if different people told me different things. Johnson's strength from an investigatory standpoint was being able to sift through evidence and pursue the best pieces of information. We needed to profile this man and do it quickly.

Still, the radio comms between the overflying aircraft weren't reporting any dangling parachutes from above, and I had the sickening feeling that we would lose this big game of hide and seek. There were so many of us that I knew it was going to be a huge waste of time, energy, effort, resources, and manpower if we were unable to find him. We all crunched and slogged through the forest and didn't find as much as a cigarette butt. No camp, no footprints, nothing. So he either landed here and escaped, or the flight path we plotted was off.

After we got out, cleaned off our shoes, and looked somewhat presentable, we knocked on doors in the local area. Of course, we had a grand mixture of people claiming to know the guy, people who had no clue as to why we were there, and others who felt greatly disturbed at their Thanksgiving being interrupted. Nobody gave me anything of any value that I can recall. As a rule of thumb, civilian witnesses are notoriously unreliable, given that they are judgmental. People have their preconceived biases, not just against the suspect in question but against law enforcement itself. As an ex-federal agent, I always get people thanking me for my service, but most of the time, when I was trying to protect and serve the people, they didn't want to talk to me or cooperate in any meaningful way.

Some were even congratulatory in their words about the suspect. One local I questioned was effusive in his praise, saying that this guy "stuck it to the man" and all this other nonsense. Even when I reminded him that he held a stewardess with him for the duration of the flight, that he was armed with a bomb, and that he extorted parachutes and money, I couldn't persuade him to rethink his attitude. There were families worried sick about their loved one being aboard a hijacked flight, but in later literature, the passengers are never referred to as victims. They were victims. This was not a victimless crime, even if they didn't necessarily have full awareness of what was going on at the time.

Anytime people tell me that this was a victimless crime, I pose this scenario. Let's imagine I attempt to poison you. I replace your salt with something highly toxic, and you sprinkle it all over your steak. After some time passes, nothing happens, and the poison has no effect on you whatsoever. Poison can affect different people in different ways due to various factors, such as general health, metabolism, immune system, etc. Is that a victimless crime? I think not. Pointing an empty gun at someone is still a crime, and threatening to kill anyone, even with nothing in your hands, is a crime.

***

Johnson came back to me and had a big notepad full of notes. He wore that familiar cheerful look on his face that meant he had something promising to share about the case. He beckoned me over to a car, and we sat in it to go through everything that he had. He had the easier job of communicating with our colleagues in Reno as well as gathering information prior to the flight from Portland Airport.

"Seems like I was right, Cliffy boy," he said to me triumphantly. "This cat wasn't no jumper."

"Well clearly he was, Johnson, to pull off this caper."

Military men love talking about their military experience, so Johnson was enthusiastic in displaying his knowledge of jumping: "Well, the dummy rig is gone. The two chutes that got left behind were a twenty-six-foot military rig and a cannibalized front parachute with three shroud lines removed."

"So?" I was slightly lost. I've found that skydivers and ex-military jumpers speak in such jargon, believing that everybody speaks their language and knows every minute detail and component of a parachute, as well as their sizes. In the scramble to obtain the cash and parachutes in Seattle, I was unsure at this point where everything came from and what the actual specifics were. We were on the clock; lives were at stake, and we had to move quickly.

"Alright, let me break this down. The two backpack parachutes, they came from a local stunt pilot, Norman Hayden. The backpacks are military-grade and meant for emergencies. Plane gets hit, engine shuts down, you need backpacks to get the fuck outta there. One was a twenty-four-footer, the other was twenty-six. Can't steer those things. He wouldn't have no control over the damn thing whatsoever, and with the wind last night, that sucker could be anywhere. Now, the other chute that was left behind— that one's a whole lot larger and safer. That's what I would've taken. Can't imagine anybody with even the most basic jumping know-how taking a smaller chute over a soft landing larger one. Another important fact: the front parachutes they gave him were straight up useless. They came from Seattle Sky Sports, that skydiving club not far from the airport. They just aren't compatible with those backpacks. So, when this guy got 'em, he would know there ain't no way to clip that specific front chute to the backpack as his reserve."

I just came right out and asked him, "So, what're your thoughts, then?"

Johnson was very quick to say, "This guy is fucking dead, my friend, d-e-a-d. He wasn't landing here and walking away. Period. The canopy he jumped with was a small twenty-four-foot one packed in a military container— obviously, he didn't know the difference. Those rigs came with packing cards, and he went and grabbed the smaller but newer one."

The jargon crept in again, and I had to ask, "Is a packing card the information about the parachute?"

"You got it! When a rigger packs parachutes, they jot down their name, the make and model of the canopy, the date, and everything else. The chutes were packed by a fella called Earl Cossey, a master rigger. These rigs can't be packed by just anybody; they gotta have a license and extensive training. The Cossey name was on the packing cards left sitting on the aircraft after the hijacker escaped. I reckon that the higher-ups will be questioning both Cossey and Hayden."

I didn't speak this language, and it wasn't registering with me. In my mind, a parachute was just a parachute, and it didn't make much difference. Johnson and I argued about questioning local skydiving clubs, but with every exchange we had, I never backed down, and we put that on our list of tasks for the days ahead. Eager for him to move on from the parachutes, I asked, "What else have you got?"

"Well, the folks on the flight crew gave a real detailed description, and it matches what the passengers and crew that got off at SeaTac said too: about five-ten, brown eyes, wearing a raincoat, a business suit, some sunglasses, olive skin, maybe in his mid-forties, carrying a briefcase and a paper bag, a smoker, got some thinning black hair, and a bit of loose skin dangling on his neck. They're making a composite sketch of him as we speak, although I'm downright certain he didn't make it!" Johnson exclaimed.

I was curious to know his demeanor, so from the early witness statements, I wanted to know if there were any defining behaviors or characteristics. Johnson shrugged his shoulders and said, "Well, the stewardess he kept beside him said he was rather cool, man. He didn't raise his voice or cuss at her or nobody else. He wasn't threatening violence toward nobody. He just…sat there."

I just said, "Okay!" but I knew that the guy looked vague, and that description matched at least 80 percent of middle-aged polite and mild-mannered men in the United States. I wasn't too hopeful, but I wanted to spare Johnson's feelings by not relaying my fears aloud to him. This "Dan Cooper" had become something of a phantom; we had no idea where he was, and despite the aerial and ground searches over the day of November 25th, nothing found. The aerial searches were starting to wind down as the cloud cover was restricting their flying time.

Most on the ground seemed to be convinced that with the entire area being covered with airborne and land vehicles as well as dozens of men, we would find the man or the crater, but it was like the man either evaporated after jumping from the plane or we were simply in the wrong place.

"What're your thoughts on him landing in the Lewis River or Lake Merwin? I mean, if we can't find him strung up a tree, a hole in a field, or anywhere else, he could've taken a dip." Even as I was saying this, I thought that his landing in the water was a bit of a long shot.

"Nah, man. If he landed in the water, we'd have a floater by now. Parachutes float, money floats, and bloated gas-filled corpses float and wash up. We got nothing. No fishermen have called in saying they've snagged a bomb on one of their hooks," Johnson sighed. We weren't getting anywhere fast. On this note, we decided to retreat home and return again in the morning.

***

I returned home at 9 p.m. that night, having missed the entirety of Thanksgiving. I ate my cold Thanksgiving dinner, and Charlotte barely uttered a word to me. She just said, "I'm going to bed. I'm sure you will be gone again at first light?" I just nodded and shrugged. Charlotte was able to master closing a door aggressively so as not to slam it or wake the children, yet somehow show her exit was not a happy one.

I left the kitchen and collapsed onto my armchair, which was beside the bay window overlooking our lawn and my mud-stained car. The living room was in darkness, and the house was completely silent—Charlotte had turned the lamps off, and the girls were fast asleep. I had missed Charlotte's parents and my children, and I knew Charlotte's dinner must have been sublime fresh out of the oven because it was still superb six hours later.

For some reason, I didn't feel tired, so I decided to turn

on the television to watch the late-night NBC bulletin at 10 p.m. I was never one for watching the news, but given the number of people involved in this search effort, I believed it likely that even I would learn something new from it. I turned on the news and listened to the anchor speak about the events:

"When he got on a plane in Portland, Oregon last night, he was just another passenger who gave his name as D.B. Cooper. But today, after hijacking a Northwest Airlines jet and ransoming the passengers in Seattle, he made a getaway by parachute somewhere between there and Reno, Nevada. The description on one wire service: *master criminal.*"

Jumping out of the seat, I had my head in my hands. *D.B. Cooper? The man gave his name as "Dan Cooper." How the fuck did they get this wrong?* I then saw the aircraft as the Reno correspondent was talking about the crew being interviewed by the Bureau in Reno. The aft stairs were mangled, and it must have been terrifying for them on the flight deck; they must have made a terrible crash with sparks after touching down because there was no way to retract the stairs from the cockpit. Although, when the flight crew was interviewed, they looked tired and somewhat annoyed. I knew immediately what that look was about; they had probably been interviewed by five or six different agents or cops in such a short period of time after what had been a traumatic ordeal for them.

A senior agent, Harold Campbell, was also interviewed for this news segment, and the reporter asked him if there was a chance that Cooper was still on the plane upon landing and had escaped the aircraft while it was taxiing onto the main runway in Reno.

He said, "A search was made of the plane immediately after landing. We had the airport covered."

Earlier that day, we found nothing, and my thoughts

were racing as I paced up and down my living room after the news bulletin had finished. I pondered into the early hours. *Could it be that this man didn't jump at all? How can all of those men, dogs, and airplanes not have noticed a single thing?* My mind was being pulled in so many directions. Although my gut instinct was certain about one thing: this man was alive and out there somewhere.

Chapter 9
Allan Memorial Institute

Dan Cooper, May 2, 1961

I knew this conversation was going to happen. Yvonne had wanted to sit down and talk to me for several weeks, but I was working late nights and bringing paperwork home. Coming off the streets in the Mounties brings its challenges: compiling reports, making final decisions on recommendations to prosecute, and even interviewing suspects when there was a shortage of men in the station. I worked plenty, and it was a coping mechanism that I had the luxury of having and that Yvonne didn't have.

She was losing weight and seemed gaunt. I knew it was coming. Every evening when I came home, she would have a fresh bruise, a clean scratch, or a large clump of her hair missing. I came home one evening, and she was sitting at the kitchen table, demanding I sit down and have this conversation. So I removed my tunic and left my cap on the stand to sit opposite her.

"Mon chéri," she began, reaching her scratch-riddled hands across the table to hold mine. Initially, I didn't want to hold them, but I knew I had avoided this for so long. "Richard is becoming too much work around the house; you know he becomes upset and violent, and I am now in a position where I cannot entertain him and cater to him throughout the day and night. You get to sleep at night because of your duties, whilst I am awake with Richard trying to comfort him and care for him. I know you love him dearly, mon chéri, but you are now forty years old. I am the same. If something happens to either of us, who will care for Richard?"

I stood up to leave the table because I was not willing to entertain Richard living somewhere other than under my roof, although when Yvonne started to cry, I caved and sat back down.

"But he is such a happy child at times, ma belle; look how happy he is when he gets to look at his Dan Cooper comics and when we go for walks in the evening."

Trying to reason with her made the situation worse, and the crying became so hard that it escalated to shouting at me, "You are at work all day! I am here, alone, with Richard and his temper when I cannot make him happy. You have the good role of buying him those comics and taking him for ice cream or a promenade around the area. You never have to tell Richard he cannot have more chocolate, fight with him to shower when he doesn't make it to the bathroom, or argue with him to eat dinner. Have you seen him choke? Have you seen him throw plates across the room when his food isn't to his liking?"

I just sighed and lit a cigarette. It was tough to contain the emotion, and although I'm not much of a drinker, I poured myself a bourbon and 7UP. It reminded me of my father, and it was my go-to in difficult situations like these, despite it being a very rare occurrence. Richard had been going to a facility near where we lived, but it was only one day in the week, on Tuesdays. But I did know that they were opening residential options for the children who were growing up if their parents could no longer manage them, like us.

Yvonne just came out and said it: "I have been

corresponding with the Allan Memorial Institute in Montreal. I told them of our situation, your role in the RCMP, and that we would be willing to move to be near Richard if they felt he was safe enough to live there."

Not knowing what to say, I just poured another drink and kept smoking. I knew it was the right decision because our parents were becoming older and more frail, so they could no longer assist with caring for Richard, leaving Yvonne completely alone while I was working. Getting a transfer to C Division in Quebec would be easy, given the large-scale societal change across Canada at the time. There would be no financial burden for Richard to go into institutional care, given that our healthcare system is rightfully funded by the taxpayer and free at the point of entry.

My mother was beginning to turn senile and was starting to believe that Richard was Eric. At times, she was starting to forget her words and phrases in English and was reverting back to French. For her sake, Quebec was the right move. Of course, my father went along with it, as he was once in the same position I was in with Eric, although Eric didn't live long enough for this painful conversation to happen between my parents. Richard was placed on a waitlist for the Allan Memorial Institute, and in January 1962, we were told that Eric would be able to go. We had to put our house up for sale, and because we lived in a desirable area, the house sold pretty quickly.

***

We moved to Montreal in April 1962, when not only the house was sold but also my transfer was completed. We drove across the country because we couldn't fly with Richard or take him to an airport. We had a couple of overnight stops along the way, and luckily Richard saw this as an adventure and didn't give us too many challenges. I was able to hold my rank given the retirement of the superintendent of the C Division in Montreal, and my superiors were sympathetic to my situation. Policing in Montreal back then was mainly the responsibility of the Service de Police de la Ville de Montréal (SPVM). The RCMP typically only became involved in cases that involved federal jurisdiction or cross-provincial or international borders.

Richard was blissfully unaware of what was going on in terms of details, but he knew things were changing and becoming different. Although he couldn't exactly talk about it, he knew. He seemed to have an acute sense of change, which would bewilder him initially, but he always got used to it. We moved to Outremont, Montreal, which was only a few miles from the Allan. The night before Richard was admitted, I took him for a walk, and we went to an amazing candy store in town called Bonbons Régal. Richard was so happy, and whenever I couldn't hold in my sadness, he put his hand on my shoulder. I will never forget that—he knew I wasn't myself. I told him that we were taking him to a new place to live tomorrow. It choked me to say it, but he didn't really understand. It didn't make it any easier.

When we came home, Yvonne had all of Richard's trunks packed and all of his Dan Cooper comics in a brown paper bag on top of them. They were already placed at the door, and when Richard saw the trunks, he went berserk. Moving home wasn't easy for him, and we knew that another move so close to the one we just completed would be very painful for him. Richard had been prescribed barbiturates to help him sleep, and that night he and Yvonne slept soundly, but I didn't.

***

The next morning, we arrived at the Allan, and we had to sign a bunch of paperwork. A nurse came to take Richard for a walk around the grounds while Yvonne and I looked after the particulars. The place seemed to have a good atmosphere, with surrounding gardens and a large stone building. It had been in operation since the turn of the century and was mainly a day clinic, but it had opened up for some institutional care for complex folks like Richard. At face value, it was bright and welcoming, with a full program of leisure activities for the patients. There were flower and vegetable gardens and greenhouses at the rear, bright and vibrant paintings hung on the walls, and it achieved its goal of not feeling too much like a hospital.

Luckily, Richard seemed to settle down very quickly and liked his room. He had a room of his own, and though there weren't bars on the windows like those in the cells I've thrown many a man into, it was secure. He seemed to smile, but it was short-lived once I went to get my coat and hat and he went to get his. I sat with him and promised him that I would visit him every day, and even though Yvonne was internally relieved, she held Richard's hands and sobbed. Richard didn't really know how to manage this, despite having seen his mother cry so frequently. A nurse stood at the door and offered to take Richard for a walk so that we could leave. Richard simply stood up and followed this nurse, and as difficult as it was, we took the opportunity to leave and allow Richard to settle in.

The house was so quiet without Richard when we returned home. Although my siblings and I drifted apart over all of these years, I kept in touch with them at times, and they sent Yvonne flowers and gifts to sympathize with us. It helped to a degree. I knew they would have been thinking of Eric and being reminded of our mother, who, by this stage, was completely senile and being cared for at home by our father.

***

As the three years passed, Richard settled well and appeared very happy as we approached the end of 1964. He was enjoying the activities and taking his medications, and he had built a perfect bond with one of the nurses, Jeanette. He used to laugh often in her presence, and he always listened to her. If Richard became uncooperative, she would fold her arms and stare at him until he did what he needed to do, like eat or put his overcoat on to go outside. The staff always greeted me as "monsieur" or "sir" and never by my first name, even though I seldom went to visit Richard in uniform or wearing any form of insignia.

Yvonne missed Richard terribly and had stopped eating; she was almost as depressed as she had been when she was at home with him all day. I couldn't understand her feelings, no matter how hard I tried. It was painful trying to relate to her, and this spilled over into my policing duties when I was becoming irate with the men and those in custody. So much so that Chief Superintendent Bergeron recommended I take a few days off, but we had a very interesting conversation once I returned.

He beckoned me into his office, which was certainly not grand for a man of his rank and stature. He was a huge man at nearly two meters tall. Bergeron was very formal, and although he addressed me by my first name, he would have winced if I called him by his. His office had papers everywhere, and the only thing weighing them all down was his ashtray. He sat behind the desk, and when he ordered me at ease after saluting him, I had nowhere to sit.

"How is your boy?" he asked me. Getting personal was never his style, and it took me aback slightly.

"Bon, Monsieur," I simply said. I didn't want to say too much just in case I broke etiquette or just simply broke down completely.

"I hope he is doing well. The reason I wanted to talk to you was because LBJ is getting the guns out for Vietnam."

"Quelle surprise!" was my reply, and it brought a little chuckle out of him. It had been over a year now since JFK was assassinated, and there were never any real whispers that Canada would become involved in the war in Vietnam, at least not publicly. If there had been a rounding up of troops, I certainly would have known about it, and nothing would have escaped me, even if it was classified.

At that point, he opened his right desk drawer and handed me a document. It had "classified" along the front, and before I could examine it properly, he snatched it back from me.

"I almost forgot," he said. "Before reading this, you will have to sign some papers."

I insisted on wanting to know a little more first, but he told me that he couldn't explain anything without at least having me sign paperwork and that this was in no way an agreement or my consent to do anything at that point.

Another couple of papers came out, and along the top was boldly written, **"Official Secrets Act,"** and my curiosity got the better of me. I signed and printed my name at the bottom of the three pages I had to sign, handed the papers back, and then he continued:

"We are not mobilizing Canadian troops to Vietnam, neither airborne nor land forces. What we wish to do is support the CIA in delivering aid to the southern Vietnamese regions. We have a stellar reputation, and I believe if we are seen assisting in the administration of aid and medical care in the worst-affected regions, it will protect us from attacks both foreign and domestic."

Initially, I expressed discontent at this and felt we should not go to Vietnam under any circumstances.

"I would not be in a position to spare any of my men in C Division," I told him. "This is America's war, and as far as I am concerned, we can allow them to fight and die in it, sir."

Bergeron wasn't initially impressed with my attitude, and he shook his head after I said that. What came next was the original document that he wanted to show me, which had "Air America" printed on the inside page. I took a few minutes to read the introductory notes, which said that it was a non-civilian airline that was founded in 1950 by the CIA. From 1962 on, Air America played a crucial role in U.S. operations in Southeast Asia, undertaking the transportation and extraction of U.S. personnel and providing logistical aid to the Royal Lao Army, the Hmong Army led by Major General Vang Pao of the Royal Lao Army, and armed Thai volunteer groups. The company was also responsible for the transport of refugees, and they conducted photo surveillance operations, which provided vital intelligence on the activities of the Viet Cong. These operations were among the earliest U.S. military engagements in Southeast Asia. Air America's aircraft, while marked as civilian, were regularly used under the jurisdiction of the Seventh and Thirteenth Air Forces to conduct search and rescue missions for downed U.S. pilots across Southeast Asia. Remarkably, Air America pilots were the only known employees of a private U.S. corporation to operate military aircraft not certified by the Federal Aviation Administration in a combat environment.

Vietnam wasn't in my plan, and I didn't want to leave Richard for too long. I initially refused, but Bergeron continued:

"You won't have to go to Vietnam, at least not yet. You

were airborne trained before the war, and we want you to take a leadership role in the distribution of aid if and when you are required. At the moment, there is no desire to go to Southeast Asia, but we felt it was best to be prepared if the government wishes for us to have a role. You have the correct qualities; you can choose your own men; and from now until the day you die, you are protected within that agreement you just signed. This is entirely confidential, and while the CIA's role may become apparent in the future, ours will not. The CIA and FBI are agreeable to our providing expertise and tactical support. Their training and know-how are nowhere near as good as ours, and when asked from above who would be a good candidate for these operations, I thought of you. This will be an opportunity to get some space at home, earn higher wages, and protect Canada from being dragged into this awful war. It will give us a chance to offer some diplomacy because the likelihood of the gooks talking to the Americans is low; they may talk to us."

It was a lot to take in, and I suppose I enjoyed the aviation side of things when I first joined the Mounties nearly twenty-five years prior. It was somehow nostalgic to me to be airborne again, and Bergeron's appeals were very convincing. For all I knew, I was never going to go anyway, but in any case, I agreed.

When I returned home that evening, I told Yvonne about my highly classified conversation earlier. When information is classified, that includes family, but I told Yvonne everything about everything. We never held secrets from one another. She seemed excited and was happy for me. Believe it or not, I missed being at the centre of policing on the streets and in communities. Promotions through the ranks certainly brought more money, but not necessarily happiness. At this stage, I was unsure if I would be going, but it was nice to dream.

***

After getting the exciting project that I didn't even know would proceed, I felt much happier. Senior policing is a bunch of pen-pushing, and I was almost hoping the telephone would ring so that I could take part in this exciting foreign operation. Months went by, and the Vietnam War escalated. I saw the news bulletins every night, but there was no mention of Canadian involvement yet. Richard was well cared for, and we got used to the routine of visiting him in the evenings. He was so happy and did not cry any time we left to return home. He had gained weight, was sleeping well at night, was allowing the barber to cut his hair, was taking his meds for the nurses, and as difficult as it was for Yvonne and I to admit, he was in a much better environment than we could offer him at home.

I spent a lot of time watching the phone and waiting for a call while I was at home. A watched pot never boils, but after almost a year, my watched phone finally rang. It was Bergeron, and he told me that I would need to pack and report to Depot by the end of the week. He made sure to say that it was about the "matter we discussed some time ago," so I knew that this was it. I would report to Depot, and I expected to be gone for at least one week—not overseas yet, but to complete training before potentially moving out a little later. I told Yvonne that I was going to Regina for a week, and she wanted to come with me, but then realized that she couldn't leave Richard with no visitors. I thought it was nice to get out of town for a bit, and I discussed it with Richard's nurse, who reassured us that patient families go on vacation all the time and that she would put some extra effort into occupying Richard while we were gone. We were leaving home to return to the home we once had. Although Yvonne could not stay at Depot, she was going to stay at the little hotel she used to work at.

The evening before we left, she made a lovely dinner at home. Given the grief of losing Richard and how busy my schedule had become, we didn't ever have romantic time together. She decided to dim our kitchen lights and have candles on the table. We laughed and chatted like we hadn't in a long time, and I will always remember that evening.

Just as I was going to light a cigarette, Yvonne told me she had a gift for me and to close my eyes. I closed my eyes as she went upstairs into our room, then descended the stairs to be standing in front of me again. As my eyes were still closed, I heard the sound of two gift boxes being placed in front of me. After Yvonne had taken her seat opposite me again, she told me to open my eyes. Inside one of the gift boxes was a smart black clip-on tie from JC Penney that I loved, and in the other was a set of cufflinks and a tie clip with mother-of-pearl insets.

Chapter 10
The Expanded Search Area
Clifford Harding, December 5, 1971

As time went by, more and more resources were being pumped into the manhunt for the hijacker. When I returned the following day on November 26, 1971, the place was awash with treasure hunters looking to find some fast cash from a crater that dozens of airplanes and hundreds of men couldn't find. It was impossible to seal off such a large area for searching, especially when the search areas included public roads and walkways. There were some false alarms, one being when an airplane or chopper noticed what looked to be a white parachute canopy from above. Upon further inspection, it was just a bunch of kids sheltering under a tarp during a fishing trip gone sideways due to the rain showers and fog.

Senior agents rounded up everyone with the last name "Cooper" and questioned them, which to me was a complete waste of time because who on Earth would give their real name when carrying out this act of air piracy? I knocked on doors close to the Lewis River, and nobody had anything of any note. We had some people say they saw someone wearing black walking down the road at night. This was not helpful because many people walk down roads at night, even in the rain. Of course, nobody saw anybody walking down the road with a briefcase, a money bag, or a parachute.

The search was descending almost into a farce when spy planes were brought in with approval from the Pentagon, but they were not equipped with fog-proof radar, so they ended up being as useless as the private pilots' planes. Reconnaissance photography came of age during the Vietnam War, and the fact that it was being used domestically to find one man was quite extraordinary. Boats were deployed along Lake Merwin by the Cowlitz County Sheriff's Department, but they found nothing after sweeping the lake quite thoroughly. It would be easy to find a floating chute or a corpse, but there wasn't even a hint of a camp or footprints or anything. We spent almost every waking hour combing the area, but it was all a waste of time.

***

On the morning of the 27th, I was called at home early in the morning and told that the first composite sketch of the hijacker had been completed. I was hopeful that somebody would recognize him, and there were copies of the sketch and the description beside the image to make up some form of wanted poster. There were perhaps ten of us in the office, and we all got our first glance. Every single one of us recognized him, and there were even some eruptions of laughter. People thought that it looked like Bing Crosby wearing sunglasses and that the sketch was a joke. The sketches were in black and white, despite many witness statements saying that the man had an olive or darker skin tone.

It was a joke; it just looked like any ordinary guy in his mid-40s. In fact, it resembled two of the people in the room who were looking at the sketch. There was never any hope of anything credible coming from this image, but it was already agreed upon by the powers that be that this was the image being released to the media and local news stations. I was able to obtain a copy of it and looked at it a few times, but nothing came of it. I was waiting for a lightbulb moment where I would somehow recognize this guy, but that moment never came.

Immediately, I knew I wanted the sketch to be redone in color, but it would be some time before that would happen. Of course, whenever that sketch went out, inquiries flooded in because the fucker looked like absolutely everybody's neighbor, boss, mechanic, store clerk, and ex-husband. Some of the leads we were getting were ridiculous, some of them not so ridiculous, but even when questioning potential suspects, we could do very little because there wasn't much evidence to nail the guy.

Probably the most significant error came when we were having a case review toward the end of that year. Several weeks had passed; Thanksgiving and Christmas had come and gone, and someone mentioned the name "D.B. Cooper." There were clippings of newspapers that said "D.B. Cooper" as well, and I wondered where the new name had come from. When I contacted most major media news outlets to get them to change the name back to "Dan Cooper," many of them declined, saying that they didn't want to confuse the public or broadcasters commenting on the case. I yelled to a few of them that the hijacker gave his name as "Dan Cooper" and that was what he should be called, but they didn't care and were more interested in speculating about the case than the FBI seemed to be about solving it.

Going into early 1972, the general consensus among the FBI was that the hijacker did not survive the night for several reasons, the main one being that nothing turned up evidence-wise, and another being that none of the money had turned up in a cash register anywhere. The possibility of hiding the money was real, but to go a couple of months without spending a penny of it gave the FBI leadership enough reason to believe that the money lay at the bottom of the river or at the bottom of a bear's stomach. I still struggled with the idea that nobody found anything and that the hijacker was at large somewhere.

In my experience, people don't just disappear—they are hidden by either themselves or by others who don't want them to be found. A murderous accomplice was out of the question for me too, because there was no way Cooper had comms with the ground to ready an accomplice to pick him up. The original plan seemed to be that Cooper wanted to go to Mexico City, but this was thwarted when the path was set for Reno while they were grounded temporarily at SeaTac.

***

In our possession—and when I say "our," I mean the FBI— all we had were some cigarette butts taken from an ashtray, the Northwest Orient ledger copy of his plane ticket, a front parachute with lines cut from it, an unused back parachute, a hair sample, and a black clip-on tie with a little circular mother-of-pearl tie clip.

At one point, I had everything laid out in front of me in our crime lab, which couldn't do much back in 1971. The Seattle office had what they called a crime lab, but really it was just a place for storing sensitive evidence and examining fingerprints if we were able to obtain any. This room was well-lit and full of boxes, as well as a large slab with a magnifying glass and a light. Johnson and I decided we would examine the heck out of everything we had. Johnson had done his part in questioning people and gathering information from other agents too.

"What will we start with, Cliff?" Johnson chirped to me.

I put on my gloves and lifted the plane ticket. "Dan

Cooper, interesting. Is this his handwriting or the clerk's?"

"Sorry, brother, the clerk!"

At that point, I nearly tore up the ticket and stormed away. "So, what about the clerk? Say anything of note?"

"So, the ticket agent was this dude called Dennis Lysne. He said that around 2 p.m., a white guy in a snazzy business suit strolled up and asked if he could catch that flight to Seattle. Lysne asked if he wanted a one-way coach ticket. The hijacker said yeah, and when Lysne asked for his name, he goes, 'Cooper…Dan Cooper.' The guy didn't check any baggage, and he didn't seem jumpy or nothing. The thing is, he paid with a twenty-dollar bill, and Lysne noted that the man's hands looked more like those of a working man than a desk jockey. Of course, the twenty-dollar bill got mixed up with everyone else's, so there ain't no way for us to track it down."

"Goddammit! This guy really hasn't left any clues, has he?" It was incredibly frustrating for me. Normally, we are the clever ones who catch the bad guys, but the hijacker seemingly had lady luck in his corner.

I sighed. "Alright, the ticket tells us nothing. Let's see the destroyed front parachute." I took it in my hand and was surprised by how small it was. It was in a little olive bag and had the name "Johnson" written across the front of it in black felt marker. The ripcord handle was on the right side of the little rectangular bag, and it had been pulled because the chute itself was found over the seat in front of Cooper's seat. There looked to be three lines cut from it when Johnson counted the shroud lines that help the canopy inflate in the air. It was a twenty-four-foot front chest reserve and was manufactured by Switlik Parachute Co. They made literally thousands of these over the years for the multiple war efforts we were tied to.

"Hey Johnson, this yours?" I joked.

"Shit, ain't no way in hell I'd jump with one of these. You'd be asking for a broken leg at the bottom. These things are pretty much designed to be better than ending up dead on impact. No soft landing with this bad boy. Tina said in her statements that the last time she laid eyes on him before she went to the cockpit, he was tying the money to himself. He pulled this one open, cut lines from it, and then used them to tie the money. The dummy chute still ain't turned up. Maybe he stashed some of the cash into that dummy container or something. That's about all this thing's telling us."

After putting the cannibalized front parachute back, I lifted the back parachute, which was in a tan backpack, and I was slightly surprised at how heavy it was. When 305 landed in Reno, the Air National Guard was quick to examine these two chutes. It was unopened and barely touched, but the manufacturer's stamp on the container bag listed the date of manufacture as 1957.

Johnson snapped the rig out of my hand, saying, "Gimme that!" and then appeared to check it over at eye level. After locating a pocket near the bottom of the container, he pulled out what looked to be two cards.

"What you got there?" I asked him as I stood almost shoulder-to-shoulder with him.

"These are packing cards—you hear that? Cards. Plural!"

"And?"

"There's gotta be one card per rig. This one's got two." Johnson put the rig back down on the table and showed me the card in his left hand. "This card right here's for this rig; there's the same year of manufacture on this card as there is stamped on the chute. Inside that container is a white twenty-eight-foot canopy, which would have been a much better choice than this one." Johnson held up the card in his right hand. "Now, my friend, this here's the card for the twenty-four-foot canopy the hijacker jumped with. The year on this card is 1960, and both the twenty-eight and the twenty-four were packed by the same dude: E.J. Cossey."

I wasn't quite following, so I asked, "But what if the guy who packed the chutes put the two cards inside one accidentally?"

Johnson got on the defense right away. "No way, man! No master rigger or packer makes that mistake. Out of the question. Cooper must've put those two cards into this one and left out his own. These cards are like the gospel, man; you don't accidentally put two inside a rig, and you sure as hell don't just leave them at your ass. They drill this into every jumper from day one."

"Doesn't seem like the behavior of a paratrooper to me," I immediately thought and said out loud.

"Boom! This guy goes for the smaller, crappier rig, dropping packing cards like it's nothing. And I'm right there with you—I can't see this fella having full-on military training and jump experience 'cause he'd have taken the bigger rig and kept that card right in the one he jumped with. This here's evidence, man; leaving this behind is no small thing. It says a hell of a lot about the guy. I've hit up some skydiving schools over the past few weeks; all the dudes there were young hippies in their twenties and thirties who were thinking that a guy in his mid-forties or fifties would stick out like your momma's ass. The oldest cat I came across was a guy in his mid-thirties, and none of them matched the description we got of the hijacker."

Johnson had a good way of lifting my mood when I disappeared inside my own head. When I become somewhat involved in a case, my head sinks into it, and it can be very hard to remove it. He helped me take my eye off the table of evidence for a minute or two, but before long, my eyes were locked on what was in front of me, and I found myself just staring at them without really knowing what I was thinking about. Normally, clues and hints come naturally to me, but in the case of "Dan Cooper," they weren't forthcoming early on.

We couldn't really analyze the cigarettes because DNA testing wasn't invented yet, nor could we swab them for saliva or even fingerprints without destroying them. An ashtray of eight stubbed-out Raleigh cigarettes was all there was to note. We re-sealed the clear bag that the ashtray and cigarettes were in and moved on to the skinny black clip-on tie and clip. It was exactly the same story as the hair sample; we could do very little with it.

The tie wasn't an expensive one. The clip was nice, though, with a little gold clip and a circular mother-of-pearl nestled inside the gold rim. The clip was fixed around halfway up the tie and from the left side. It was a skinny tie, which stood out to me because not many would have worn this style of tie. It was almost like something my father would have worn many moons ago.

The ever-fashionable Johnson chuckled at it and then scowled at it somewhat, saying, "JC Penney. Towncraft Number 3. Sold in the middle of the last decade, but now it's discontinued. Good riddance!"

I replied, "What's wrong with normal ties? What kind of guy wears a clip-on tie?"

"Beats me!" Johnson shrugged.

My uncle was a production supervisor in a textile factory during the war, and I recalled that the workers wore clip-on ties to prevent themselves from being pulled into machines by their ties. When I said this aloud to Johnson, he pondered who else would wear clip-on ties, but we couldn't think of any off-hand. Regarding the physical evidence in the case, what we had in front of us was it. Nothing more, nothing less. The only missing items that could help us nail this case were the parachute, the money, and "Dan Cooper" himself, alive or dead. None of this stuff told us anything of note, other than that he likely used the front chute to tie the money to himself. Dejected and no further forward, we left the stuff on the table and went home.

***

As was becoming the norm at home, I arrived and went straight to the kitchen table with my briefcase of witness statements. I went to give Charlotte a kiss, but she just turned her cheek and went straight upstairs without saying anything to me. I hadn't seen the girls in what felt like an eternity because I was leaving home before they awakened and going to bed long after they had gone, if I didn't pass out at the kitchen table from looking at paperwork and other information relating to the case.

So, I set to work there and then on building a profile of the hijacker at my kitchen table. By this stage, the passengers and crew had been interviewed a couple of times, and some more details were coming to light. Similarities in people's stories and statements were what I needed. The physical description that had already been established described Cooper as a man who was five feet ten, 170-180 pounds, with an olive complexion, aged approximately mid-forties to early fifties, probably brown eyes, wearing a black business suit with a raincoat and brown shoes, as well as carrying a paper shopping bag and a black attaché case. The newer details of the rough hands and the mistreatment of the parachutes and their packing cards convinced me this was not a military man.

Only a handful of the passengers and crew spoke to the hijacker. They described him as softly spoken, with no discernible accent, never using profanity or raising his voice, needing some form of reassurance from time to time, but calm as a cucumber overall, and in complete control of the situation while being able to adapt to deviations in his plan. It was clear that Cooper knew the aircraft reasonably well, beyond the knowledge limits of what one could find in a local library or textbook about the Boeing 727.

When the clock struck 3 a.m., I was becoming angry and frustrated. Nothing was coming to mind, and all I wanted to do was get upstairs to sleep beside my wife, but I just couldn't. The answers were here, and I just couldn't find them. What stuck in my mind was the tie—*who the hell wears a clip-on tie regularly?* With such detailed knowledge of the aircraft, surely he had to be some sort of Boeing engineer or somebody similar. But Boeing hadn't been very quick to point the finger at anyone. Seeing that daylight was beginning to break and realizing I was getting nowhere, I eventually decided to drag myself up to bed. I shut my eyes and tried my best to clear my mind, and just as I started to drift off into sleep, a frightening thought came to my mind that pulled me back into full consciousness: *cops wear clip-on ties.*

Chapter 11

Tacoma

Dan Cooper, May 5, 1969

It was terrific to be back in Regina. We flew from Dorval Airport into Regina over the weekend. I was to report to Depot on that Monday morning. I knew I would have to stay at Depot, but I was happy to stay with Yvonne at the Hotel Norman on that Saturday and Sunday night. We spent that weekend reliving some of the early days of our marriage, including going to the Brown Derby restaurant, which was our favourite place to dine, but we had to stop going once Richard was born. I was slightly concerned, though. Yvonne used to clear her plates whenever we ate at Brown Derby, and she barely touched her seafood casserole. Another thing we forgot about was the smell that emanated from Burns and Company, a slaughterhouse on Winnipeg Street—it was foul yet nostalgic. Yvonne started to become tired and wished to go back to the hotel. I could have walked around Regina all weekend without stopping; when I wish to explore, it would take plenty of time to stop me. I seemed to have boundless energy that kept me awake at night, and when in places of interest to me, I needed to see, hear, and experience every last drop of it.

When I came through the gates of Depot, I took the time to walk around. There were recruits being marched around the drill field, and it reminded me of my first day with the Mounties thirty years prior. Fondly remembering the men I graduated with, I wondered where they all were now. It was only myself and one other man who came to the Air Division with me, and I couldn't recall where anyone else went. A lifetime had passed, and everything seemed to be how it was back in 1939. I held up the palms of my hands in front of my eyes after looking at the stables and hearing the horses. *Those boys' hands are going to be as rough as mine in thirty years*, I thought. A lifetime of holding horse reins and policing will do that to you.

When at Depot, we always wear our red tunics, and it felt good to have mine back on. Some of the men gave me a salute, and firm handshakes were exchanged among old friends. We were in every corner of Canada, and people were eager to hear about how things were with me in Quebec, although I didn't have much exciting information to relay back to them. We stood around, smoked, and caught up with one another until Superintendent Florient beckoned us into the Chapel. He uttered "Salut!" to me and shook my hand as I came in the door. The Francophiles in the Mounties stuck together as much as possible, almost like an unspoken brotherhood.

There were fourteen of us in the Chapel, with Florient addressing us:

"Gentlemen, we have agreed to assist the United States Government in the provision of aid and tactical support in various regions of Vietnam. The Canadian Government is not mobilizing troops on a large scale, but they are keen to have our humanitarian assistance noticed. You are all protected under the Official Secrets Act, and breaching the terms of your agreements could result in discharge from the force and court proceedings. Is this understood, gentlemen?"

"Yes, sir!" we shouted back to him.

"Air America has been in operation for almost twenty

years now, and their operations are kept classified from the public. It is disguised as a civilian airline that takes diplomats, spies, and cargo around the Asian regions. Their role is primarily in assisting U.S. Special Forces, and who better to conceal that fact than their Canadian friends and neighbours? None of you will wear your regular RCMP uniforms; we will issue you with one that will be suitable for flight operations and possible jumping."

At that final part, there were some gulps, but I was very excited. I actually rubbed my hands together and was quite pleased. This was exactly what I was looking for, and just as I was grinning, Florient left the podium at the altar and came down to me. He beckoned me to stand, which I did, and then he said, "You will be in command of this unit, and I trust you will serve with dignity, respect, and discipline."

I was caught off guard, and when I said "Yes, sir!", we both saluted and shook hands while the other men applauded. I wasn't expecting this and was somewhat disappointed because I imagined myself being involved and in the thick of it. What I found peculiar is that our unit didn't have a name, nor did Florient provide us with one. Seemingly, we were going to be lackeys for the Americans, but I wasn't quite sure if I was going to allow that to happen. I didn't want to be a pen-pusher overseas and have to direct operations from the ground. Recognition is nice, but I wanted some excitement.

We were dismissed, and I was in something of a daze with everyone congratulating me personally and inviting me to come for drinks with them. I decided to go for a single bourbon and then go home to Yvonne to tell her my news. When I returned home, Yvonne was sleeping, and she was in such a deep sleep that she couldn't be roused. Normally, Yvonne would have awakened to eagerly hear any news I had.

***

I reported back to Depot the following morning, and all my men were there and ready. I was greeted with a salute from the fourteen men, and when I removed my cap, the men removed theirs too.

"Gentlemen, I am not sure as to what our next instructions are. As soon as I find out what they are, I will be sure to inform you all." Just as I said that, Florient approached us and dismissed us for the day, informing us that we had to go to McChord Air Force Base in Tacoma on Thursday and that we would be flown there from Regina International Airport. We bid one another farewell, and because it was still morning, we had no excuse to go to a nearby bar to talk about what possibly lay ahead of us.

Yvonne was still in bed whenever I got back to the hotel, which again wasn't like her. I shook her, and when her bloodshot eyes met mine, I asked her if she was okay. She nodded to affirm that she was okay, but her pallor and red eyes told me a different story. I leaned down to give her a hug, but her grip wasn't as tight as it usually was, and she got up to use the bathroom. She shuffled through the hotel room and into our ensuite bathroom. While she was in there, I couldn't help but notice three small red spots on the bed where she had been lying down. Even though the bathroom and bedroom were separated by a thick wall, I could hear her coughing.

"Yvonne, look!" and I pointed to the three small red spots on the bed. "How long has this been happening?"

"Mon chéri, I am of the age where my body is beginning to change. This is normal," she whispered back to me.

"Non! We must go and see a doctor right away. I don't have to return to Depot for the remainder of the day, and we are going to McChord Air Force Base in Tacoma on Thursday. We must go at once."

She agreed with me, and I used the hotel telephone to contact a local doctor. When I explained her symptoms, the doctor told us to go to Regina General Hospital instead. Yvonne could barely get into the car unassisted, and I knew then that there was something very badly wrong. I don't recall what our conversation was, but I just held her hand all the way there. Her hand seemed so weak and brittle.

***

When we walked through the door, the nurse at the desk went as pale as Yvonne when she saw her. She took hold of Yvonne's arm, linked it to her own, and walked her to an office down the hall. She shouted to me over her shoulder to take a seat, and when I insisted on coming with them, she just shook her head. I didn't argue back. After around fifteen minutes, the nurse called me from the room at the end of the hall adjacent to the waiting area, and I almost ran up the hall. Yvonne was crying while sitting on the bed in the doctor's room, and the doctor immediately told me that he wanted to have Yvonne undergo laparotomy, an exploratory surgery to assess what was going on.

It was my duty to reassure Yvonne, but she was the first to reassure me.

"They will take care of me here. Go to McChord. They will be keeping me here for at least five days. They want to observe me until Thursday morning, perform the surgery on Thursday, and I will be in recovery for the entire day afterward. You will not see me anyway, but the nurse has agreed to speak with you on the telephone."

Yvonne was stroking my hand, and even with her light movements, it was clearly expending quite a lot of her energy. I didn't leave her side until the nurse requested that I leave. I returned the following day, and because Yvonne was in more pain than she let on, she was full of pain relief medicine and slept for most of the day. She awakened briefly, and I told her I was going back to the hotel as it was approaching 10 p.m. and I had been allowed to stay a full ninety minutes longer than the previous day. I kissed Yvonne on the forehead, and she blew me a kiss by placing her fingers over her oxygen mask as I was going out the door.

***

The flight to McChord was awful. I was incredibly anxious, and one of the men joked to me, "Do we have a fear of heights, sir?" I immediately gave him a dressing-down and reminded him of the correct way to address a superior. He didn't say a word to me or anyone else around him for the remainder of the flight. I was sitting at the rear of the little airplane on the right side and observed the men laughing and joking with one another. Meanwhile, my head was in turmoil. Yvonne would be being prepped for surgery; all I could do was wait. We had been in the air for around two and a half hours, and the time just seemed to disappear. I just stared out the window and detached from the world. The men were looking out the windows and shouting to the pilot to ask what city was below us. It was Seattle, and we were around ten minutes away from landing in Tacoma.

The weather started to turn, and when the wind shook our little airplane, we were told we would have to circle Tacoma a few times until we were able to safely land. I was taking in little details from above, and that image of Tacoma from the air was burned into my brain for many more years to come. Memorizing the space we were flying over was my way of coping and taking my mind off what was happening at Regina General.

We had a turbulent crosswind landing at Tacoma, and when we all deplaned, we briskly made our way into the giant open hangar that had big, bold letters above it: **MCCHORD AFB**. After exchanging some pleasantries with representatives from the CIA, the FBI, and the Special Forces, we were brought to the rear of the hangar, where there were chairs set out for us. One of the FBI agents caught my eye, and when I shook his hand, he gave me an odd look and asked if I was okay, which I said I was. The FBI and CIA representatives were all wearing branded jackets with emblems on them, and all we were wearing were raincoats, white shirts, and black pants. I had never been to McChord before, nor had anyone else from the RCMP, but we were surprised to learn that Canada and the U.S. had partnered during the Korean War to deliver aid and supplies from McChord.

During the period of the Korean War, activity at McChord Air Force Base increased significantly as it served as a crucial hub for the U.S. Air Force and the Royal Canadian Air Force. Their collective mission was to ensure the timely delivery of troops and supplies to the war zone. As airlift responsibilities continued to rise, it led to the need for a more extensive facility. In the war's inaugural year, McChord was instrumental, as the Military Airlift Transport Service (MATS) transported as many as ninety-six thousand passengers from the base, a fact our American counterparts repeated several times to us.

I didn't feel personally affected by the Cold War, but the atmosphere at McChord was tense. The North American Aerospace Defense Command (NORAD), a child of necessity born from a union between the United States and Canada, found itself at the forefront of this battle against uncertainty. Shielding its homelands, the colossal heart of

NORAD pulsed relentlessly, driven by a network of vigilant radars and a constant vigil for nuclear detection, becoming the watchful eyes and ears against the lurking spectre of the Soviet threat.

The Semi-Automatic Ground Environment, christened as the SAGE system, embedded itself into NORAD's core, pulsating with data, amplifying radar tracking capabilities, and bridging the gap to air defence systems. This mechanical brain provided a swift response to the shadowy menace that skulked beyond the borders.

The Cuban Missile Crisis had the world teetering precariously on the brink of nuclear war. Akin to a sentinel in the night, NORAD's systems blazed with an alert, their defences ready to rebuff any inbound terror, standing as a crucial bastion in the management of this high-stakes international roulette. NORAD, not content with merely standing still, sought solace within the sturdy embrace of Cheyenne Mountain in Colorado. A refuge from the fear of nuclear annihilation, this move represented the next level of fortification, safeguarding not just their physical presence but the heart of their operations.

The year 1964 marked an era of newfound responsibility. An agreement inked with the Federal Aviation Administration saw NORAD's wings spread wider, its gaze sharpening to keep vigil not only on military aircraft but on all that dared to venture into U.S. airspace. It was a testimony to their evolving role from merely an air defence shield to a guardian of the entire aerospace. Amidst the tumult and the tension, the saga of NORAD was a beacon of resolve and steadfast readiness.

All these technological advances were overwhelming for us; during our briefing, we were looking at each other and subtly shrugging our shoulders. The Americans were nodding and smiling as if they were up to speed with all the equipment we were being shown. It was exciting and terrifying in equal measure, but I recall not feeling entirely certain how great the nuclear threat was and that all of this seemed to be a huge overreaction.

There was an adjacent hangar that we were all directed to go to. They weren't internally connected, so we had to go back outside into the rain and briskly walk to the other hangar in the pouring rain. We all grabbed the sliding door and pulled it open to be awe-inspired by what greeted us. In all her grandeur stood the Boeing 727. She was brilliant white all the way around, with a black spot on her nose cone. All there was painted on her was a registration number, and I had never been this close to a civilian-type liner. We were all amazed by how big it seemed. From the underbelly of the rear of the plane, we saw that a retractable staircase was down, which would take us inside the fuselage.

I ascended the aft stairs and held on to the handrails all the way up. I led the way, and as the others followed, we were all completely silent, staring around the maze of wires and switches inside the fuselage with awe. All of the passenger seats had been removed, bar a few, and there were two parallel tracks fixed to the floor that led from just in front of the cockpit right back to the airstairs we had just come up. We were told that the 727 would be used for passengers and some cargo, whereas cargo drops with a parachute would be done with the C-130 Hercules. However, there wasn't one available for training purposes at Tacoma at that time, and although the mechanisms and drop procedures were similar, only the C-130 Hercules had a ramp at the rear instead of stairs.

An engineer from Boeing wearing a white coat and carrying a bunch of papers came aboard and asked who was in command. I raised my hand to say that I was, and he directed me to the cockpit. A dull sort, he wasn't very captivating when explaining the aircraft controls and emergency procedures, as he would provide me with a booklet with the information on it and an American three-man crew to fly the aircraft. At the front of the flight deck were two seats for the pilot and co-pilot, then a third behind the co-pilot seat on the right side for a flight engineer to check the electrical and mechanical status in-flight.

The cockpit door was open, and while this dull and boring engineer was explaining the ins and outs of the ocean of gauges and switches, I looked aft to see the men fixing lines to large crates from the ceiling of the aircraft and pushing them toward the aircraft's rear. They were attaching static line parachutes to these crates and having a very pleasant time pushing them out the door and hearing them crash onto the hangar floor. Even though I was completely captivated by the airplane, I couldn't help but think about Yvonne and how she was doing. Eventually, I requested that the engineer excuse me so I could use the phone in the hangar's office. I walked quickly out through the fuselage, always looking downward so I wouldn't trip on the masses of wires, parachute lines, crates, and everything else strewn around inside. I went down the stairs and made my way to the office at the rear. A gentleman was there, and when I asked to use the phone, he vacated.

When I called, I frantically asked the nurse how Yvonne was, and she told me that she had come around after the surgery and would be able to receive visitors tomorrow. So at least she was alive, and I was relieved. When I asked if all was well, she said they were doing some more tests, but Yvonne was out of the theatre and recovering, so that gave me at least some reassurance. I asked that my love be passed on to her, and she agreed that she would. Then I called the Allan to inquire about Richard, but he wasn't doing so well. He had become irritable and upset since he had had no visitors for the past few days. I asked if he could have the telephone receiver so he could hear my voice, but the nurse was quite abrupt in telling me he was asleep, having been up all the previous evening. I didn't argue, and I bid her adieu and asked that my love also be passed to Richard.

I went to venture back up the stairs when a huge crate flew out and shattered right beside me. If the crate had been a few inches to the right, it would have hit me. I gave a burning stare up the airstairs, and one of my guys just uttered, "Désolé," and looked down at his shoes. One of the CIA guys screamed at him to look out below before discharging the crate outward, or else civilians could be killed or property damaged. It saved me from having to admonish, although shouting was never my way of imparting discipline. Anybody can take shouting and screaming, but knowing someone is disappointed in you is much worse and has the more desired effect when wanting men under your stewardship to perform.

Back on the flight deck, the gentleman from Boeing asked me to close the cockpit door quietly, which I did. It was at this point that he said he was going to tell me some features of the airplane that the rest of the men were not to know and that I was forbidden from explaining to them. Before getting into what he wanted to tell me, I interrupted by asking why the rest of the men couldn't know because they were going to be responsible for operating the aircraft and overseeing the dropping of both men and cargo. Of course, I was told that it was a matter of national security and to agree to keep this information to myself. It was explained to me that the airstairs could be lowered in flight, the aircraft could take off with the stairs down, and there was currently no mechanism in the cockpit to override either scenario. I don't know what I was imagining he would say, but I believed I was about to be shown a self-destruct mechanism or something more dramatic. I explained that surely the pilots would know this information, but I was told that in their training, they were told that the stairs must be locked in place before take-off and that lowering in flight was not an option. Boeing had realized the fatal flaw in the design of their aircraft, and it was much too late to cancel the orders for the aircraft now because Uncle Sam had paid so much for them, as had many airlines across the world. Boeing wanted to prevent a PR disaster and keep the value of their shares, so admitting a design flaw was off the table for now.

***

The long day had come to an end, and everyone was in a good mood. We hadn't expected to be shown everything we were shown, and this seemed like a worthwhile effort for us all to belong to. We believed we would be doing a good service on a humanitarian level, and the Mounties would add good value to these efforts. From the get-go, the men saluted me and not the Special Forces command, the FBI, or the CIA, which seemed to irritate them slightly. It was time for us to be flown home that evening, and I couldn't wait to get home to see Yvonne. We would be returning to Regina from SeaTac Airport, and we would split into separate cars for transportation to the airport.

One of the FBI men, who seemed wary and skeptical about our involvement, was our driver, and he took the driver's seat with me sitting up front with him, and three men squeezed into the back. The agent driving us was a young go-getter and reminded me of my younger self. He appeared to be in his late twenties, and I struck up a conversation with him by asking him what role he would be playing in all these proceedings.

He said to me, "We are preparing a field office in Saigon to help us with investigating espionage, counterintelligence efforts, providing security for U.S. personnel like diplomats, and so forth."

"Ah, very good. How long have you been serving?" I asked him.

"Just over six years now. It's much better than being a beat cop, no offence," he said, then he kind of gulped because clearly he had forgotten himself in the moment. I couldn't help but smile—this man was going places. I always had a keen eye for those who wanted to excel in policing. There is no greater burden on any police force than cops who don't want to improve, better themselves, and succeed.

"Today's beat cop could be your captain in ten years, mon ami, and your president in thirty years. Make and keep as many friends as you can." Then I became slightly formal and looked over my left shoulder to the men in the back, saying, "Isn't that right, gentlemen?"

"Oui, Monsieur," they said back to me. I'm not quite sure if it made our driver blush slightly, but it was always nice to give a diplomatic wing clipping when the situation warranted it.

Eager to win my approval back, our chauffeur asked, "So, you have gone far in the Mounties; what advice would you give me?" This was a great question and the perfect demonstration of the American aptitude for flattery, which had always impressed me.

"Well, agent, I tell my men the main things to consider when it comes to good policing. The first is to make sure to look at all the physical evidence; your answers are always there to some degree. The second is to take note of the words your suspect says to you or your witnesses, because one can easily remember things people tell them much quicker than remembering actions they observe. Always remember that civilian witnesses are generally unreliable. Use your intuition and your training, and your gut feelings will almost always be correct. Then, the most important part: never shout at your horse, because they hold grudges for quite some time."

The men in the rear laughed and agreed. FBI agents tend not to break their serious façade, but I could see the smile creeping out from the corners of his lips. I think he saw a different side of policing with us friendly Canadians. It was nice to have some laughter, because as we got closer to the airport, I was becoming more anxious to get home to see Yvonne.

Once the twenty-minute drive to Seattle-Tacoma Airport was complete, I said, "Merci!" to our driver.

"Pas de problème," he replied with a smile.

We got our things out of the trunk, and the men made their way into the terminal building ahead of me. Just as I shook our driver's hand, I said, "I'm sorry, mon ami. I didn't catch your name."

"Clifford Harding, Monsieur."

Chapter 12
Sketches, Confessions, and Red Herrings
Clifford Harding, May 26, 1972

It was clear that we were getting nowhere with the evidence recovered from the case, the statements provided by the victims on the flight, and the many dozens of people being questioned on a daily basis. For all the world, "Dan Cooper" had utterly vanished. By mid-1972, we had come up with nothing, and when the press was asking us how the case was progressing, we were running out of things to say. When dealing with the media, there are some secret codes we use that are designed to promote public confidence. Saying on camera to the nation, "We have absolutely jack-shit; we have no idea who this guy is or where he went," wasn't an option then, and this is the same by today's standards. What we used to say were things like, "We are following up on leads," "We have various lines of inquiry that we are pursuing," and the old classic, "There are certain evidential factors that we cannot release to the public, but we are using those to get closer to apprehending the hijacker."

In the subsequent years, many felt that the FBI was hiding something, and I agree with that. What we were hiding was that we knew nothing, and private investigators seemed to be making more progress than us. What now lies in the public domain is pretty much everything we ever knew. When the case is broken down into numbers, it looks like this: there were seven hours from the time "Dan Cooper" entered Portland Airport at approximately 1 p.m. to when he exited the aircraft with the money at 8:13 p.m. somewhere between SeaTac and Reno. There were thirty-six passengers on the flight in total, with only four people speaking to the man himself during the ordeal. So the evidence was scant, and I wanted to focus on where the man bailed out.

In the months after the hijacking, we were provided with a wealth of aerial photos of the flight path that 305 took after taking off from SeaTac toward Reno. The path was known as "Victor 23," and it was like an airborne highway that aircraft follow between airports. Even back in 1971, the accepted time of the jump was approximately 8:13 p.m. because there was a minute or so delay between comms in the aircraft and the air traffic towers. In a couple of moments leading up to the jump, there were oscillations noted on one of the flight engineer's dials, which indicated some activity or movement after Cooper got the stairs down to prepare to exit.

At that time, the aircraft was moving at a constant speed through this predetermined air highway, so Cooper's drop zone should have been easy to find. Determine the time of the exit, pair it with the location of the aircraft, and there you should have it. In our case, we should have found the guy or his corpse, but we found absolutely nothing in the wide radius we gave ourselves to search. This left me with two deductions: either the flight path was incorrect or Cooper didn't jump at exactly that time. I spent many hours at my kitchen table on a daily basis, passing by my family to set up camp in the kitchen, and then sleeping at the table or on the couch in our adjoining living room.

Exploring the flight path itself, there were

communications between all the major airports in the area in the event the aircraft had to make an emergency landing, and the military jets from McChord were tailing the airplane from a distance. I found it very challenging to believe that there were any deviations in the flight path, given the radar and communications data that we were provided with. Flight 305 was tracked all the way to Reno, and communications between the flight deck and surrounding towers were constant. For a large portion of the flight, they were airborne with their stairs down, which was quite a hazard, and the well-being of the four crew members aboard was the main priority. The aircraft leaving this path and moving too far off course was extremely unlikely to me because the data would have shown it, and seeing as the pilots were obligated to tell us their exact position, it would have been foolish not to, given they didn't know if they still had a real bomb in the back or not. Evidence guides investigations, so naturally, the federal government was going to deploy its resources to where the evidence pointed in terms of the time and location where Cooper jumped.

As an agency, the FBI wasn't a bunch of bumbling idiots who made a rough guesstimate as to where the hijacker landed or jumped—everything pointed to the initial search area we had. The place was as sealed as we could have made it without closing down every road, town, public park, walkway, or nature reserve in a twenty-mile radius. We used every sense we had, including the noses of the hounds, who also combed the wooded and open areas in the proposed drop zone. In my view, the flight path was correct and provable, but where and when Cooper exited the aircraft was not. This was problematic.

The last person to see Cooper was Tina Mucklow, and the last time she saw him was when he was tying the money bag to himself and getting ready to exit, just after he told her to leave him alone and go to the cockpit and close the partition curtain between first class and coach on her way there. This leaves a situation where there are four in the cockpit while Cooper is trying to get the stairs down alone in the aft section. There were no witnesses; nobody actually saw him steady himself and jump from the plane with the money and the bomb. So I wondered if the time he jumped was accurate. Was there a way in which those oscillations could be felt even if he left slightly earlier or later?

I made a point of questioning some airline pilots, and of course, this gave me very little value because not many have the experience of flying a jet with the stairs down, nor could they visualize a situation where oscillations could be felt in the cabin or cockpit without standard turbulence and the stairs closed and in position. The Boeing 727's aft stair design had been a feature intended to be used for remote airports, not for a quick escape by a daring criminal. It had been a flaw that the industry was quick to correct, but for me, it was a frustrating loose end.

I picked up a report about a recent experiment. A similar aircraft, also a model 727, had been used to drop a dummy payload. The plane was set at ten thousand feet, cruising at a speed of 170 knots, and for five minutes, the payload was tracked. The mathematics were precise: in those five minutes, the aircraft would've traveled approximately 14.16 nautical miles, or about 16.29 ground miles.

That was a sizable search area—a swath of land that could hide countless secrets. I sighed, rubbing my temples. The numbers on the paper remained the same, but the answer still seemed just out of reach. Despite the frustration gnawing at me, I was determined to find this guy. The frustration was getting the better of me, and all I could do was sit alone at my table, surrounded by all these reports and photographs that were giving me absolutely nothing.

I wanted to consider angles that the wider investigative team at the Bureau didn't consider—did this man have an accomplice?

The witness statements from the crew were very detailed in that they all corroborated the conversations that took place between the hijacker and Captain William Scott on the runway. The specific configuration that Cooper requested was alarming: non-stop to Mexico City with no fuel stops in the United States, a maximum altitude of ten thousand feet, the landing gear down, flaps down to fifteen degrees, cabin lights off, cabin depressurized, at the lowest airspeed possible without stalling the aircraft, and the aft stairs down. The flight crew felt this configuration was absolutely ridiculous and dangerous, which I suppose it was, but what was interesting was Cooper's insisting that not only would the aircraft make it to Mexico City non-stop, but that the aircraft could take off with the stairs down.

The aircraft refueling seemed to take some time, and 305 sat on the runway for more than ninety minutes before taking off again. That put the hijacker's plan of jumping in the last remnants of daylight down the crapper, along with any chance of an accomplice seeing him. He jumped with a white parachute; clouds also happen to be white, and seeing him from the ground at dusk in drizzly weather was simply a no-go.

After a lengthy exchange between Cooper, the flight deck, and Northwest Orient Flight Ops, an agreement was reached between all parties to have that fueling stop in Reno. Having spent a lifetime with crooks and listening to their demands, requests, and threats, I've observed that not many of them give in during the crime, and they insist on their demands being met. If Cooper had an accomplice somewhere in the Pacific Northwest to either drive him home or fly him out of the area, all he had to say was,

"Listen up, folks. I have a bomb with me, and if any of you dismay me or deviate from what I want you to do, I will kill all you motherfuckers and destroy this aircraft!"

But he didn't do that. He meekly agreed to this fuel stop without any possible way to alert an accomplice. All he had with him was the bomb, which two stewardesses saw, and they didn't mention seeing any form of radio equipment or walkie-talkie in the briefcase with it. The only other way was if he had a radio in that creepy little paper bag he had with him, but with Tina Mucklow sitting beside him for the duration of the first flight and being with him for most of the second flight, he didn't once use it. Going from around 3 p.m. to near 8 p.m. without having any contact whatsoever with an accomplice to let them know what was going on was a clear indicator that this guy acted alone.

Examining the weather that night, it was drizzling and overcast like every other day here. From an altitude of ten thousand feet, I found it extremely unlikely that Cooper knew where he was jumping into. Handheld radar or GPS was far beyond the technological capabilities of the day, and I could see absolutely no way he could possibly know where he was jumping. From any of the airborne hippies we spoke to, none of them would have been comfortable leaping from the back of an airplane at night, with no clear view of the landing area, without being able to pre-determine a landing pattern, while riding down on a non-steerable round twenty-four-foot canopy.

Cooper had a money bag attached to him, and in any skydive or jump, stability is everything. It was explained to me that an arch position is the optimal freefall stance, and he would have to have his hips forward, his chin up, and his legs at forty-five degrees. It was difficult to imagine how that basic arch would be achieved with an additional twenty-one pounds of cash in a cotton bag tied to his waist and possibly a briefcase tied somewhere else on his body. In order to pull open the parachute, he had to be in a stable position for the canopy to inflate properly, and he had no reserve. The functional reserve front parachute was left on the aircraft, and the other was a dud that we couldn't account for.

Resigning myself to the theory that Cooper did not survive the jump was never an option. I knew deep down that this man was intelligent, calm, and determined. He must have been incredibly desperate to pull off this job with all the odds against him. Nonetheless, we couldn't find him, and although the FBI and plenty of skydivers thought he cratered somewhere we weren't looking, the evidence was telling me that this guy simply landed on the ground and walked away.

***

After many months, it was clear that the initial sketch wasn't getting us any closer to the hijacker. Many commented that Cooper had a darker complexion, and the FBI felt it was time to do another sketch and see if it would generate any new leads or open new lines of inquiry. Slowly but surely, the passengers and crew were spoken to again to go through another composite sketch that would be released to the public and to media outlets. Many wanted this new sketch to be in color to demonstrate Cooper's complexion and that he was in his mid-forties or even stretching into his early fifties.

The main issues with the first sketch were that the guy looked like everybody else, it was in black and white, and it was impossible to age. The guy in the sketch seemed to look like a prematurely balding college kid and a middle-aged executive at the same time, which was quite a feat in my opinion. When the second sketch came out, Florence Schaffner, who was the only person to see the hijacker with his sunglasses off, described the sketch as a mere "hoodlum," whereas Cooper was much more refined and polite. I couldn't help but agree because his calm and composed demeanor was well described by Tina Mucklow, and the sketch looked like a pissed-off Cary Grant. After a round of amendments, the sketch was redone and became the color sketch of "Dan Cooper" that everyone knows and has seen.

I took the sketch home, and I spent almost every waking hour staring at it. This sketch wasn't Mr. Everybody—it was Mr. Most People, and it certainly narrowed things down. The sagging lower lip, olive complexion, and steely brown eyes stared back at me, and I would have grabbed the guy by the throat if I could have. My routine stayed the same, staring at this picture along with the statements and photographs that I had gathered. My obsession was unhealthy, but I didn't see it at the time. Charlotte was becoming more distant, and I found my temper becoming short with the girls, so much so that they were left in tears, and Charlotte was disappointed in me.

Although the more I stared at the sketch, which by this stage had circumnavigated the globe, the more I had the sickening feeling that I had seen this guy before somewhere. So much so that the more I stared, the more I started to imagine that the picture was speaking to me. I couldn't hear words or an accent very clearly, but I heard the clear, audible sound of this man's voice—its tone and timbre. Many suspects I interviewed before claimed they could hear voices when committing their heinous crimes, but now it was I who was starting to hear them. It was like this man was taunting me, and I became angry at myself for allowing him to as I fell rapidly into a state of fragility.

Part Three

"Grief, I've learned, is really just love.
It's all the love you want to give, but cannot.
All of that unspent love gathers in the corners of your eyes,
the lump in your throat,
and in the hollow part of your chest.
Grief is just love with no place to go."

Jamie Anderson

Chapter 13
Regina

Dan Cooper, June 15, 1969

On the way back from McChord, I became completely fraught with worry. I don't recall speaking to anyone, but most of the men appeared to nap in their seats after the long day we had and the information overload. When I touched down in Regina from McChord after the few-hour flight, I immediately hailed a cab. I was so out of breath that I could barely tell the cab driver where I wanted to go, but eventually I spluttered out that I wanted to go to Regina General Hospital. The driver was approaching the front door of the hospital, and I opened the cab door before the vehicle stopped fully. I threw a twenty-dollar bill through the passenger window and told him to keep the change, even though the cab ride would have cost three or four dollars at most.

I ran through the door and was greeted by the same nurse that I met a couple of days ago, but she told me that Yvonne was resting and that I needed to go home because it was almost midnight. I had totally lost track of time and suddenly regretted giving the first cab driver twenty dollars when I could have used the change for the fare back home again. Being too tired to argue, I left quickly and returned home. I didn't sleep a wink, but I was never much of a sleeper anyway. I just paced around the house and smoked until it was 9 a.m. I called my office and told them that I had to be elsewhere that morning, to keep messages for me, and to not call me at home.

After burning my tongue and throat on a hastily made coffee, I ran out the door and jumped in the car. One of the perks of being a cop is having a car with sirens on it so that I could violate every traffic law in the land to get to Yvonne much more quickly. Parking at the front door of the hospital was not permitted to allow ambulance access, but I did it anyway. Who questions the Mounties, eh? When I came through the door, a doctor and nurse greeted me at the door and weren't very quick to exchange pleasantries or greet me with a smile—it was just, "Please come with us, sir."

The horrible disinfectant smell and my burnt tongue and throat didn't make the agonizing walk down the hallway any easier, but when we reached the last door on the right, Yvonne was there. She looked so pale and seemed too weak to smile at me. She had her oxygen mask on, and I removed it to greet her with a kiss, but a second after I removed it, she started coughing, so I replaced it. I knew things weren't good, and I was invited by the doctor to sit on the chair beside Yvonne's bed. I knew I had to brace myself for what was coming.

"Yvonne has growths on her uterus that we believe have spread to the lungs. It is very likely that these growths have been accumulating for quite some time, perhaps years, and were undetected even at the time of the birth of your son. I'm terribly sorry; there is very little we can do other than manage pain and for you to help Yvonne stay comfortable at home."

I couldn't even speak. How was I going to tell Richard? Would he even understand? I just sunk my head in my hands, and when I peeked through my fingers at Yvonne, she had fallen asleep again. I eventually built up the courage to ask, "How much time?"

"I'm sorry, but maybe six months at most. We are approaching winter, and any mild infection could speed up that process. I wish I could tell you something different. We will provide you with morphine syrettes that you can administer to her as necessary, and we will give you a letter for the pharmacy to get more as you need them. I know this is incredibly difficult, sir, but we don't see what else we can do. The disease is too advanced to attempt any more surgery or hospital care that will help. We can provide her with a wheelchair and get her energy up with medication, and you must take the short window to fly her home. It will be exhausting for both of you, but go you must."

Yvonne's hand felt so cold and frail. When I used to hold it when we were teens, she would always squeeze mine, and that moment was the first time I squeezed her hand and she didn't squeeze back, even slightly. The nurse and surgeon left us alone, and Yvonne opened her eyes after a minute or two and gave me her little smile. She just nodded at me and was trying to speak through her gasps. The only word she could get out was "Richard." I said that I would take her to visit Richard as soon as she got out, but she just shook her head before falling back to sleep again.

Luckily for us, when I called the airport from the nurse's station, there happened to be a flight to Montreal the following day at noon. Being very sympathetic to our plight, the ticket agent promised to reserve us two seats at the rear of the aircraft to both board and deplane before other passengers. I asked the ticket agent if there was a method of boarding with a wheelchair and with supplementary oxygen provided by the hospital. She told me that, in addition to bringing supplementary oxygen on board, Yvonne could use the limited on-flight oxygen if she needed a couple of breaths to save our supply. She also mentioned that we could board with assistance on the runway via the aircraft's aft stairwell. I was very touched by the effort this young lady put forth for us, and when I told the medical team, they were satisfied.

I was instructed to go back to our hotel to get a good night's sleep, pack up our things, and prepare for the journey the following day. Placing Yvonne's things into her little leather case was painful. Her makeup was placed neatly on the dressing table, and the chair was adjacent to it at a forty-five degree angle, as if she had just gotten up from it. Knowing none of the makeup would be on her cheeks and lips again was a very upsetting thought. Even her clothes would have been large, loose, and sagging on her frail body. I laid out her clothes and shoes, and I packed some make-up and her hairbrush. Yvonne had her own routine, and I used to tell her that her beauty didn't require enhancements in the form of make-up or lipstick, but she always insisted on wearing it. I was already longing to see her sit at that table or the dressing table in our bedroom at home, and I held out every iota of hope that I would one day soon.

***

When I went back the following morning, Yvonne was sitting on her bed and was able to say, "Petit chou" to me. I threw my arms around her, and when I squeezed a little too hard, she let out a little yelp. I was almost jumping up and down because I was so happy to see her conscious and at least talking a little bit. "Allez! Allez!" she kept saying, and she asked me if I had telephoned Depot to tell them we were going back home. When I realized I hadn't, I rushed out to the nurse's station. I can't remember exactly who I spoke to out of the men, but I told him that I had to go home as my wife was gravely ill. After sympathizing with me, he asked me if he could keep me informed of updates from McChord as and when he had them, and I agreed.

He asked if he could tell the other men and the Americans, and I said that he could. Everyone needed to know where I was and for my absence to be explained—I felt the mission and the men deserved to know. I think this man was quite young and relatively inexperienced because he said, "Bonne chance!" at the end of the call, which was no way to address or speak to one's commanding officer, although I thanked him and told him I would need it.

Yvonne was already in a wheelchair, and I raced to the reception area, almost forgetting her bag of meds and the equipment that was in a brown paper bag. I peeked inside and saw around twenty small syrettes of morphine and other brown bottles of pills, notably Benzedrine. When I asked the nurse what Benzedrine was for, I was told that it was a stimulant that could be administered to keep Yvonne awake and alert on her good days. There were seven or eight bottles of it, and the pills all rattled in this little paper bag as I pushed Yvonne's chair through the corridor and into an awaiting cab outside. Even getting from her wheelchair into the front seat of the cab was a challenge, and she dozed off in the car on the way to the airport.

When we got through the door of Regina Airport, we were met almost immediately by a representative from Trans-Canada Airlines, who let me pay for our tickets in cash and escorted us to the gate. Yvonne was drifting in and out of sleep, and when we got to the gate, I looked out of the huge window that overlooked the runway at Regina Airport. I had only just been here on the way back from Tacoma, and despite the melancholy I was feeling for the weeks ahead, I was still captured by the majesty of the Boeing 727 resting on the runway, waiting for us to board

her. There was a hustle and bustle of passengers, and I was
lost in my thoughts just staring at the airplane when I felt a
feeble pull on my jacket from Yvonne. She was pointing to
the paper bag with the pills in it, and when I brought out the
morphine syrette, she shook her head, and she did the same
with the anti-nausea pills. When the Benzedrine bottle came
out, she sort of smiled. I had a water bottle with me, and she
gulped down two of the pills, and as if by magic, she was
as bright as a button again. So much so that she eked out
her depleting energy reserves to get up off her wheelchair
to look at the airplane on the runway. "How exciting!" she
whimpered with a pained smile before shuffling back to her
chair.

A flight attendant came to get us and took us through
the glass door, which led to the runway, and the aircraft
noise around us was deafening. The McChord 727 we were
boarding had the engines off, but she was a loud bird when
switched on. We were taken to the aft airstairs extending
down from the underbelly of the aircraft, and Yvonne
struggled and limped up the staircase, with me holding on to
her and the flight attendant at the rear of us with her hand
on Yvonne's back. One of the baggage handlers followed
behind us with her wheelchair and placed it inside the last
row of seats on the right side, row eighteen. Yvonne went
into the middle seat, and I sat in the aisle seat.

After a few minutes, more passengers came aboard, and
while they were filing past me, I put Yvonne's meds and our
coats in the overhead compartment. The lavatory was right
behind us, and another feature was on-board oxygen, which
was in another compartment just above our heads. I already
learned that the water temperature-regulating apparatus
was just in front and above the lavatory, so it made sense to
keep passenger oxygen there too. The oxygen compartment
was opened by a purser's or flight attendant's key so that a

passenger couldn't open it accidentally, thinking it was an overhead luggage compartment. After unlocking it, one mask was handed down toward Yvonne, and she received it and gasped gratefully from it.

Yvonne rested her head on my shoulder just before takeoff, and when drink service came, I refused for both of us. For the duration of the flight, she slept. Going from the hospital onto the plane had exhausted her, and she was conserving her energy for the trip home from the airport in Montreal. Now and again, the stewardesses would come and ask if we were okay, and I confirmed that she was content and that I was not, sadly. All they could do was nod and continue their drink service.

After landing, we deplaned first, and nobody rose to their feet around us as I got up. It felt like everyone seated in front of us was staring, and when I looked at some people, they just returned a solemn nod or a small smile of sympathy. The petite stewardess wrestled with the handle on the door behind us before leading us into the compartment where the stairs were. On the left side was the level for the stair mechanism, and I was staring at her as she was trying to configure the stairs. She may have been new, unsure, or simply nervous at the fact that I was glaring at her while she tried to turn the lever that deployed the stairs. There looked to be some buttons in there too that were throwing her off, but before long, the stairs were down. Yvonne got to her feet, but when she looked down the staircase, she clung on to me. She had fear in her eyes, and I decided to lift her and cradle her. She clung on tightly to me, and it killed me when I felt how light she was. The stewardess beside us was trying to conceal some tears, but she was failing.

After Yvonne and I touched down, it was a struggle getting from the runway to the taxi outside with Yvonne in a wheelchair, but after an arduous journey, we were both home. It was late in the evening, and Yvonne was completely exhausted. I had to carry her upstairs to bed, and she was in such a deep sleep that I placed her small pocket mirror next to her face to see if she was still breathing, which she was. Although the doctor in Regina said six months, I knew it wouldn't be that long, and I didn't waste a second getting Richard.

***

The drive to the Allan was a blur. It was sundown, and I drove there with my lights and siren on even though it was only a few miles away. I was in a daze when I walked through the main entrance door and stood in the hallway. One of the nurses asked me if I was alright, and I snapped out of it, saying that I was, before she led me to Richard. When I walked into the room and he saw me, he dropped his Dan Cooper comic, threw his arms around me, and started giggling with delight. Richard hadn't been this affectionate since he was very small, but he obviously missed his parents and had some more awareness as a twenty-three-year-old.

"Oh, look! He is delighted to see you. He had a shaky couple of days after you both left, but with some medication and a few more of those comics he likes, he settled back down again. I hope you had a lovely trip."

I asked the nurse to take a seat beside us, and I put my arm around Richard.

"Richard, your mother is unwell. She may not have long until she goes to heaven."

The young nurse gasped and offered her apologies, but Richard was still giggling with excitement to see me. I felt it was right to tell him, and I am glad I did. One of the support staff members came with a tool box and summoned Richard to come with him to the greenhouse, and he quickly left, leaving the nurse and me alone.

"My goodness, I'm so sorry," she whispered to me, putting her hand on my shoulder. "If there is anything we can do, we will absolutely help where we can."

"Well, there is one thing: I would like to take Richard home every day to see his mother. She is dying and would be too weak to be able to travel here. Can this be accommodated?"

She seemed taken aback and gulped slightly before saying, "I am not sure if that is a good idea, sir. What if Richard goes home and does not wish to return? It could add distress and angst to an already heartbreaking situation. I am not sure if the care team would approve of that."

Anger was starting to build, but I was able to compose myself before responding.

"Richard will be coming home at least every other day. This time is precious, and I will take full responsibility for him. If you require me to sign papers to sign him out and in, I will certainly do so. His mother coming here is not an option, and Richard deserves to spend time with his mother."

She immediately agreed with me and asked me to wait while she spoke to the people in charge. In no time, she told me my request was granted, given the difficult circumstances. Remaining calm gets almost anybody anything they want, whether that is leave from a secure hospital or $200,000 and four parachutes. Richard had already gone for his daily activities, but I had achieved what I wanted to, so I told the nurse manager that I would be back tomorrow morning for Richard, and I returned home. Before long, our house wouldn't be the same again.

The difficult phone calls to family inevitably came that evening. Both sets of our parents were well into their eighties, making the conversations on the telephone extremely difficult and fraught with miscommunications. Yvonne's father thought she had died, and my father was so hard of hearing and exhausted from caring for my forgetful mother that it took me two or three attempts to tell him what was going on. My father gave his prayers and sympathy because he couldn't leave my mother, but Yvonne's parents told me they were coming even if it killed them.

***

The following morning, Richard came home after I picked him up. As soon as Yvonne and Richard laid eyes on one another, Yvonne had more energy than an entire bottle of Benzedrine, and Richard was so happy to see her again. I remained close by in the event he tried to escort her out of bed like he used to do when he was younger, but amazingly, he seemed to have some awareness that she wasn't well and just stroked her arm. They were so happy to see one another, and it really lifted Yvonne's spirits, so much so that she didn't require any Benzedrine or morphine for the remainder of the day. Luckily, when it came to me getting Richard back into the car to go back to the Allan, he complied and came with me without incident. He had been there for a number of years now, and it was creeping into my mind that I had lost some of Richard too. Our home was no longer his home, and he knew that.

Richard's coming home was very powerful for Yvonne's spirits, and she loved seeing him. Richard was always coming and going from the Allan, and it was after a couple of weeks that Richard started becoming upset when returning. To overcome this, a care team member was spared to sit in our home with Richard to reassure him if he needed it and help Yvonne too. It was a great help to me, and after some time, I was able to call to the station and get some updates, sign paperwork that needed to be done, and give some briefings to new RCMP recruits who had just completed training and were finding their feet in my station. Even in the first month of caring for Yvonne, I noticed my red tunic was not as tight on my chest and that my boots didn't hug my calves as much as they used to. The leather hadn't loosened, but the man inside them had changed. My hair had seemingly become more grey, and I was finding more hair in the plughole of my shower.

Now and again, my sisters came to visit to provide me some comfort, bringing along the nieces and nephews that I barely knew. They had their own lives, and I had mine. I wondered why they didn't keep much contact with me and whether it might be because I was a policeman. I wasn't a very good host because I was tired, but I felt there was still an expectation of me to entertain those who were coming to see Yvonne, Richard, and me. Yvonne waking during the night to be sick or receive pain relief was taking a toll, and it became more difficult when Yvonne's parents were coming and going intermittently.

Any time visitors called, I took the opportunity to get groceries or visit the station. I didn't want to fall too far behind in developments in town or at McChord. I was lucky in that my superiors were quite sympathetic, but I grew somewhat of a grudge against them because they initially didn't allow me to marry the girl, my darling wife, who was now dying in my house. If only we had some more time as man and wife—time that was non-transferable and that I would never get back. Yvonne's time was now depleting fast.

I was curious for an update on how the men were progressing at McChord, as they had been out a further two times since I started splitting my time between home and the station in Montreal. When I called McChord, Mr. Harding, who had given us a ride to the airport, answered the phone and told me everything that was happening. The men were now well-trained in cargo handling, refugee evacuation, and in-flight emergencies. I stayed on the phone for quite some time because it was a welcome escape from what was happening upstairs, even if it was just for a while. He didn't express any sympathy to me, not that I had expected it, but I still felt somewhat disappointed because there is no doubt the Mounties told him that my wife was dying; I had permitted them to tell the FBI and CIA command at McChord. Harding was winding down the chat by telling me he would send a package to my home address with updates, essential reading, etc.

I asked to speak to one of my men, and Harding handed the phone over without even bidding me adieu. Of course, nobody was filling in for me—the CIA and FBI had taken complete command and would do so until I returned. Nobody was temporarily promoted or stood in for me in my absence, so there was a slightly uneasy feeling in me that Canadian men were not under Canadian command. To lift the mood, I told David, who was one of mine, that he didn't need to develop a love of cheeseburgers or turn into a hippie, and to stay a proud, maple syrup-loving Mountie.

He just nervously said, "Okay...Monsieur. Adieu!" and put the phone down.

***

A week later, the family was appearing more and more, and Yvonne was sleeping more during the day. My father finally came, and I was glad to see him. He was walking with a stick and was clearly tired from the coming and going from the hotel he was staying at to our house. My sister Simone was at home with my mother, and my father was updating her by shouting at her down the telephone because he could barely hear. Yvonne's parents were starting to become distressed to the point of confusion, and naturally so, given they were in the process of outliving their only child and becoming victims of the cruelty of an unnatural order of life. Yvonne was using more morphine and had started to refuse the tiny amounts of oatmeal and soup she had become accustomed to at home. Our family doctor came to examine her after Richard's nurse had noticed some changes in her breathing, and he shook my hand as I greeted him at the door before going upstairs. Before I closed the door, I noticed the mailman outside with a bunch of flowers in his right hand and a package under his left arm. I took the flowers and placed them on the table inside the door while I signed for the box and went back inside.

My men had sent the flowers to tell me they were thinking about us, which was very admirable. The card wasn't signed by the Americans. I lifted the package, and inside was a manual for the NORAD/Air America-adapted 727 aircraft, as well as some reports by and about my men. In my absence, they had all been taught to bail out of the aircraft in the event of an emergency using emergency backpack parachutes, how to drop cargo safely, and how to operate the radios on the ground and in flight if needed. The officers in my command seemed generally good, although the CIA command thought one or two of them were slightly excitable. I knew them; they were just ordinary, friendly Canadians who knew how to smile and take their duties seriously.

The doctor came downstairs, followed by Richard's nurse, and all he said was, "It is time to call the family to be at Yvonne's side, Monsieur. I don't think it will be long now. I believe she has developed pneumonia." Even though I knew this was inevitably coming, it was such a heartbreaking punch in the gut that all I could do was put my hands over my face, and when I removed them, the doctor had shown himself out. I offered Richard's nurse the spare bedroom in our home, and she agreed to stay without hesitation so that Richard could remain at home with us.

That evening, I was putting a wet towel on Yvonne's lips to stop them from cracking and causing her discomfort. Our bedroom had candles lit, and chairs had been brought from upstairs. As my family was weeping and praying around her, I felt bitter that the hospital doctor had said she could have around six months left but, in reality, would only get around six weeks. As I was doing this, our telephone rang and wouldn't stop. It was loud and distracting for everyone, and Yvonne's mother gave me a glaring look to go and answer it. As I stood to leave the room, she took over for me, rubbing Yvonne's face and holding her hand.

I answered the phone, and it was McChord, specifically Mr. Harding again. He told me that he had some urgent updates that he wanted to give me, and I told him it was not a good time. He insisted that it was a matter of national security and insisted I hear him out, so I tried to tell him that he needed to hurry up and keep it short. He told me that we would be dispatched to Saigon in the coming weeks to begin our aid mission, and when I kept trying to interrupt him to stop, he kept going. He told me I needed to report to McChord two weeks from that day, and that my men had already been briefed and knew to come. I started to become frustrated, as surely this could have waited, but he kept rambling on, and I wasn't fully taking it in.

All of a sudden, when I was writing down what Harding was telling me, I heard a shattering shriek from upstairs. I quickly hung up the phone without even saying goodbye and ran up the stairs, almost tripping on the carpet runner. When I burst through the threshold of our bedroom, Yvonne's mother was shaking and crying, and Richard was holding

Yvonne's hand with a look on his face that I hadn't seen before—one of complete devastation and total awareness of what had happened. My darling Yvonne was gone, and I wasn't there for her as she left this earthly plane and crossed over on the fifteenth of June, 1969. She was only forty-seven, and we had been married for twenty-five years. I was completely numb, and from that moment on, my family and friends organized her funeral at the funeral home because I couldn't speak. Those first couple of days were a blur, but I remember sitting beside Richard on our couch and him having his hand on my shoulder. It was no consolation, however, because I wasn't there for him or Yvonne at the moment when it mattered.

When funerals are shown on television, it always seems to be raining, but on the day of Yvonne's funeral and burial, it was a bright and sunny day. I was never overly spiritual, but it was some comfort to think that Yvonne was bidding us farewell with the sunshine she always brought to Richard, me, and everyone who knew her. Even though it was sunshine that I would never have in my life again, it would be how I always remembered her. Some of the men from the station attended, and they formed a mounted guard at the church as they held their Stetsons to their chests. I held hands with Richard as the priest said the final prayers as she was lowered into her grave. Richard lifted his hand and waved to her as if saying goodbye, and upon reflection, that was the very moment I developed quite a serious grudge.

Chapter 14
Chasing a Phantom
Clifford Harding, November 24, 1972

There was a series of copycat hijackings from January to July of 1972 after "Dan Cooper," but the first was exactly a month later, on Christmas Eve of 1971, when Everett Holt commandeered a flight from Minneapolis destined for Chicago. The plan was the same as Cooper's, but the flight crew escaped through the cockpit on the runway in Chicago, leaving the hijacker to surrender because he was distracted counting his cash.

January 1972 saw three separate hijackings, all demanding parachutes and ransom money. The Billy Hurst hijacking happened on January 12, 1972, and he surrendered after the one million dollars he requested couldn't be obtained. On January 20th, Richard Charles LaPoint bailed out of a DC-9 over Colorado, but the feds put a tracker inside the parachute to find him. Then, on January 26th, Merlyn St. George was shot and killed by an FBI agent in an airport in New York after he refused to parachute with his cash.

April saw the hijacking that seems to have gained more airtime than the others: Richard Floyd McCoy Jr. He was a Vietnam veteran who actually brought his own rig, and he got away with the cash only to be caught a little while later. He got a long sentence in court but was shot and killed by the FBI a few years later following a shootout after escaping the penitentiary.

A ton of agents thought that McCoy was Cooper. He seemed to fit certain characteristics, including being a balding parachutist, and he kind of matched the description that had circulated about Cooper. For me, McCoy was very young and an expert parachutist. Johnson was an expert parachutist, and like he said, Cooper taking the smaller rig for his jump certainly didn't align with the behavior of a professional or paratrooper. When looking at suspects, gut feeling always plays a vital role, and McCoy didn't give me that gut feeling whatsoever.

Stanley Speck's hijacking on April 10, 1972 was foiled after he was tricked into leaving the aircraft to retrieve maps. Two FBI agents were dressed as airline mechanics, and they apprehended Speck after he was tricked into deplaning and meeting them. Even then, airlines were somehow reluctant to introduce additional security measures, as flying back then was supposed to be a fun and welcoming experience, almost like a flying café or bar. Aviation authorities were discussing and announcing more security measures, but none seemed to be put in place quickly, despite airlines having always been financial juggernauts with every resource, excluding money printing facilities.

One of these hijackings, carried out by Frederick Hahneman on May 5, 1972, was temporarily successful when he was able to bail out over Honduras. He was on the run for around a month before giving up the game and handing himself over to an embassy. He managed to extort $303,000, a very precise number, as well as survival gear and cigarettes.

Reno came back into the picture again on June 2, 1972, when a hijacking of a plane flying from Reno to San Francisco was done by Robb Heady. He was a young, twenty-two-year-old paratrooper and Vietnam veteran as well. The flight path had been altered by a minuscule fraction, thwarting Heady's plan of where he wanted to land and escape from. He lost the money mid-air after jumping, but it was found by the FBI a couple of days later, and Heady was captured the following day, I believe.

Martin McNally hijacked a liner going from St. Louis, Missouri, to Tulsa, Oklahoma, on June 23, 1972. He got half a million dollars and a parachute that he didn't know how to put on when provided with it. Like Heady, he lost the cash but landed in a cow pasture in Indiana. Funnily enough, after wandering around where he landed, the local chief of police gave him a ride into town, telling him to mind himself because an armed hijacker was on the loose. He was apprehended in Detroit and thrown in jail for forty-five years. Even I have to admit that I've seen murderers and pedophiles get lesser sentences, and I think a certain amount of public sympathy was afforded to these hijackers getting large sentences. This in turn only added to the legend of "D.B. Cooper," the guy who hadn't yet been apprehended and was "sticking it to the man" somewhere.

Interestingly, Seattle and Portland came back into the story when Daniel Carre seized a flight from Seattle to Portland on June 30, 1972. When the jet landed in Portland, U.S. Marshalls captured him, and he was sent to an asylum somewhere.

Three hijackings followed in July 1972: Francis Goodell on July 6th, Michael Green and Lulseged Tesfa on July 13th, and Melvin Fisher on July 13th as well. So prevalent was the issue of jets being taken and airlines being extorted that now there were two separate hijackings being carried out in one day. All three of these hijackings were foiled by the hijackers surrendering after the flight crew simply escaped through the cockpit.

The extorted cash from these hijackings was covered by

insurance. The reluctance to get security measures in place to protect the public was a purely profit-driven decision, in my opinion, and not many other agents would say that out loud. Airlines had both societal and political influence, extending right up to the Oval Office. If we look at losses from these hijackings, the only financial losers were insurance companies, which not many of us would shed a single tear for. Other than that, the only other losers were the ones who hijacked the airplanes, but they lost their freedom and their lives.

Public pressure was growing by the day, and when airlines were starting to lose profits and their share values were starting to deplete, more security measures were introduced. It was not just at American airports, but at those on either side of our borders and around the world. Identification checks were completed, baggage checked, and on Boeing 727 aircraft, the fatal flaw of the airstairs being able to be deployed and escaped from in flight was amended. I don't know if it was Boeing or the media who called them "Cooper Vanes," but they were fitted to all 727 models to ensure the stairs could be locked in place during flight.

Metal detectors were installed at airports, and while they were welcomed by most, the Second Amendment lobby was out in full force to protest that passengers should still be permitted to carry firearms onto airplanes. I am all for personal security and safety, but for passenger safety, nobody should be able to carry a weapon onto an aircraft unless they are an air marshal of some sort. Air travel was always going to be in demand, and after ticket price increases, the profits went back up, and the airlines were all happy again.

Over time, I started to wonder why I was obsessed with this case. I found myself continuously reflecting on November 24, 1971, replaying the whole evening in my head over and over again. I began to question my actions and the choices I made that day, wondering if I could have done something to change the outcome. When Margaret called me to tell me that an airliner was being hijacked in exchange for $200,000 and four parachutes, I could have said, "Please have flight ops tell the hijacker to go fuck himself!"

The passengers, flight crews, and stewardesses involved in these incidents were terrified, and some, no doubt, were traumatized by these experiences. Even some of the hijackers lost their lives, and I started to feel like I was responsible. Was I one of the people who, by meeting Cooper's demands, started a chain of events that led to every subsequent aviation hijacking in the history of our country? Even though there were some hijackings before Cooper, it was hard not to overthink. Sometimes I still feel that, and caring for myself seemed to gradually make it stop. But for many years, I was eating junk food, I was spending less time with my family, I was drinking alone at night, and I was completely absorbed in my work, trying to right this wrong by nabbing Cooper.

Every night when I closed my eyes, I tried to come up with different ways we could have handled the situation differently. When we had the jet in our sights and knew the passengers were free and clear of the area, why didn't we just storm the entrance and exit doors and send the guy to Saint Peter? However, when Merlyn St. George was slain by the FBI in late January 1972, it didn't deter a single one of the hijackers who came after him. If we went on board and made a colander out of Cooper, would it have stopped this series of hijackings? I'm not so sure. Death is never a deterrent to the desperate, whether they are criminals or addicts.

My thoughts became so twisted that I regretted not ordering a machete through one of the parachutes. Then again, hindsight is a wonderful thing. If we put a machete through one of the rigs and he did take one of the flight attendants with him, would I have been able to live with myself? Certainly not.

Then my mind turned to the money—perhaps we should have used one-dollar bills instead of twenties to increase the weight. Or pennies! What if we had gathered $200,000 in pennies? We had a small scale in my kitchen for when Charlotte baked her world-famous banana bread, and I weighed one penny. It weighed 3.1 grams. $200,000 is twenty million pennies, which equates to a total weight of twenty million times 3.1 grams, totaling a ransom of 62,000 kilograms, or 137,000 pounds of weight. *Try tying that to yourself, fucker!*

Charlotte and the girls were trying to comfort me, but nothing seemed to work. If I wasn't actively combing through case notes and evidence, I was thinking about it. The only time I wasn't thinking about Cooper was when I had passed out from exhaustion or when my bottle of whiskey had been depleted. When I drank, I became angry, and when I became angry, I became very difficult to live with and work with.

Whenever I sat in the field office cafeteria, people got up and walked the other way. I was so intense and angry that I couldn't focus on other cases. When it came to interviewing suspects in other cases, I often lowered myself to shouting at them. One evening, we hauled in a bank robber, and when he smirked at me while I was interviewing him, I grabbed him by his collar while his attorney was sitting beside him. Luckily, I wasn't asked to hand in my gun and badge like in the movies, but I was told to take a week off work. The only thing that week off brought to me was a week of my mind being unoccupied at home, and when my mind was unoccupied, my thoughts went to Cooper, and I got angrier.

***

As the first anniversary of the hijacking came up, the Bureau at large was not a single step closer to identifying or apprehending "Dan Cooper." All these other bums were caught, thrown in jail, or killed. So not only was I bringing the Cooper hijacking notes home, I was bringing these other case files as well to ascertain what Cooper had that these people didn't have.

There wasn't a lot of evidence left behind belonging to Cooper other than the unused parachutes, the tie with a clip, and some smoked cigarettes. This man was very cautious when it came to taking the notes and the matchbooks back. To me, that was a very important detail, and it wasn't public knowledge at that time for the imitators to imitate that strategy. As an evidence man, I couldn't help but find this tactic brilliant. Every court in every country depends on evidence, and forensic evidence is a smoking gun in almost every case. There was no evidence of his handwriting, nor were there any fingerprints that we could definitively say were his.

Another detail I latched onto was the request for an unmarked car to come with the money and the parachutes. To most people, an unmarked car is simply a car. It was a very definite word in the vocabulary of a cop. If Cooper didn't have a law enforcement background of some description, I don't think he would have specifically requested a car that had no markings, sirens, or flashing lights on it.

I already deduced that clip-on ties were commonly worn by cops, and to wear a tie like this was a pretty good move because if anyone tried to seize him by it, the tie could dislodge and it would free him. To be honest, if I wanted to look like an inconspicuous businessman, I probably would have made the same wardrobe choice.

There was so much talk that the hijacker had some form of military experience, but this didn't resonate with me. The guy was calm, determined, and didn't shout or scream at anybody. Military men tend to have a plan and stick to it, come what may, even if it involves brandishing a flamethrower in order to meet the mission objective. Cooper was able to be persuaded, like a good percentage of weak policemen, to alter his flight plan, and the jet left Seattle with the stairs retracted, despite Cooper's request that they weren't.

My focus went to cops over the age of forty who mildly matched the description. Any cop who was over the age of forty, had dark hair, dark eyes, an olive skin tone, and weighed under 200 pounds was on my radar. To me, this massively reduced the number of people in the suspect pool, although if I wasn't already unpopular, then this approach definitely affected my standing and reputation in the Bureau. Going after the military men seemed to be okay, but when I turned my attention to cops, it was completely taboo—even Johnson became distant with me.

I got fewer invites to social occasions with the guys. One of the agents, who was a close friend of mine, insisted that his wedding was family only, despite some of the agents in our office attending. Two senior case agents retired, and I didn't get an invite to the retirement dinners. Even on other cases, I found myself working on them alone after Johnson silently went to work in another office. I don't recall us having any particular argument or disagreement, but I found myself without a partner and didn't get another for quite a number of years.

Chapter 15

Saigon

Dan Cooper, July 6, 1969

I arrived in Tacoma three weeks to the day after Yvonne's passing and was keen to leave the country for a while. As I wasn't going to wear my red tunic for our upcoming missions, I wore a white shirt, but I couldn't find a decent tie to match. At the bottom of my wardrobe, I found the skinny black clip-on tie that Yvonne got for me that I used for special occasions. I decided that this was what I would wear, and I took one of the RCMP pins from my tunic and placed it on the tie to the left of the mother-of-pearl tie clip.

The men were quite awkward around me at first, and everyone shook my hand in sympathy, which I was grateful for, but I ordered everyone to keep to the tasks before us and not mention it again. We were flown to Tacoma, and spirits were high among my merry Canadian crew.

I was briefed by Depot the evening before I left that we were going to Saigon to meet with the FBI representatives, establish aid and cargo routes while there, deliver the cargo, and take any passengers we needed to evacuate from the area. We were accompanied by several envoys and diplomats who were set to host discussions on topics that were above my pay grade to know about. All I needed to do was make sure they got there and back home safely, ensure that nobody upset them in any way, and keep the men in check, both

Canadian and American.

We all boarded the 727, and our bags were placed in the baggage hold. On the Boeing 727, one could access the baggage area from outside the plane, where ground-level cargo doors allowed for the loading and unloading of suitcases and freight. This specially designed space catered to both the personal belongings of passengers and commercial goods, often divided into distinct sections for better organization.

Some models of the 727 were equipped with an additional cargo space near the aircraft's nose, expanding the storage capacity for luggage and freight. Within these compartments, careful control of pressure and temperature was maintained to guarantee the secure conveyance of personal effects, commercial shipments, and any animals being transported.

I took a muster as the engines fired up with twenty-two men in total—nine Canadians and thirteen Americans. The captain, co-pilot, and flight engineer were provided to us by Boeing, and although they insisted they weren't briefed on the particulars of any mission, I found that hard to believe at first. I confirmed the flight path with them in that our first stop was Honolulu, then on to Tokyo, then Hong Kong, and finally Saigon. Some of the men asked if we could stay for a short while in Honolulu, but I said no. There were ten seats at the front for the diplomats, all wearing business suits and carrying briefcases, and we all sat on benches along the side of the aircraft in the midsection. The Americans sat on one side of the aircraft, and we sat on the other. As we were all working under a collaborative umbrella, I tried to encourage some interaction between them mid-air. Most of them were in their mid-twenties, and at forty-eight, I was like a fatherly figure to them.

The heat inside the aircraft was unbearable, and we

were all sweating. The hard benches were taking their toll on us as well, and despite initially refusing some downtime in Honolulu, I eventually agreed, and everyone got out to stretch their legs. The tension and division between us and the Americans could still be felt, and I felt they were looking down their noses at us despite our attempts to be friendly. It seemed like there was nothing we could do to bring the bears out of their cave.

We didn't need to be at our next location until a few days later and had already pre-agreed to another rest period when we were to land in Tokyo. Some of my men returned from the gift shop with cigarettes, silly hula skirts, and hats. I found this amusing and thought it would be the perfect way to break the ice on the searingly hot Honolulu airport runway, but the Americans didn't find this amusing and probably thought we were ridiculous.

En route to Tokyo, one of the diplomats broke the tension perfectly. He left his seat, approached us at the rear, and said, "Excuse me, ladies. What has a gentleman to do to get a drink in this place?" before chuckling and lighting a cigarette. He was clearly a man in his late sixties, with greying hair and thick sunglasses. A few of my men had bought themselves bottles that they had obviously planned to conceal from me, and when they were brought out to give this gentleman a choice, he reached for the Jim Beam. He took a hearty swig out of the bottle and then handed it to me. The Americans were starting to crack smiles, and when I took a mouthful, they all nodded in approval. I then handed the bottle across from me to the Americans opposite. There was a refrigerator and a cupboard with glasses behind us in the galley space beside the aft stairs that we quickly made use of. After we finished bottle number four, we broke into song, and everyone suddenly became best pals. What better way to bond a group of young men, eh?

I didn't know that there were meals for all of us—cold chicken salads with a small bottle of dressing in each. I found them when I went to take another bottle from the refrigerator, to the surprise and delight of the men around me. It was food and drinks that won everybody's respect, not my rank, demeanour, or superiority. Like with every other animal, all you have to do is feed them to get them to like you and drop their fear of you. By the time we landed in Tokyo, everyone was worse for wear, and we were delighted to have our prearranged rest.

The following morning, we left at dawn for Hong Kong, and everyone, including the diplomats, was taking their turn to puke in the lavatory at the rear. The heat, hangovers, and Japanese breakfast in the airport hotel made for quite an unpleasant trip. We didn't even deplane in Hong Kong, and we all slept for most of the journey from Hong Kong to Saigon. I awakened the men in the fetal position on the floor with a little nudge from my foot. I was gentler on my men and a little harder on the Americans to make them look lively. Somebody went aft to get the stairs down, and I inspected everyone before they left to make sure their appearance met my standards.

We landed at Tan Son Nhut Air Base, located near Saigon, South Vietnam's capital (now Ho Chi Minh City). Tan Son Nhut Air Base was a hub for military and civilian air traffic. It was home to the South Vietnamese Air Force (VNAF) headquarters and the United States Air Force's 7th Air Force. I deplaned first, and all the men lined up alongside the aircraft while a general approached me, holding out his hand. I shook his hand, and he introduced himself to me as Stanley Taylor. He wasn't in overall command of the base, but he had clear superiority and would be the man I had to report to on site. If there was a stereotypical U.S. Army leader, it would have been him—very tall, with a crew cut, a cigar in his mouth, and his chest so puffed out that he was almost arching his lower back. After introducing himself to me, he ordered some troops to give everyone a tour while he and I walked and talked around the base privately.

"The base was a key target during the Tet Offensive, when Viet Cong and North Vietnamese forces launched a series of surprise attacks. The base endured intense fighting but remained under U.S. and South Vietnamese control," he told me proudly.

The U.S. 7th Air Force was headquartered there, and various commanders would have overseen operations at different times, including Generals William W. Momyer and Lucius D. Clay Jr., neither of whom I ever met or talked to, but I remember their names. It's quite odd, considering that I can't even remember the names of any of my men since all this time has passed. I was shown the radar facilities and the control tower, and I was also provided with a list of their radio codes so that I could communicate with them during aid and cargo runs mid-air. As we came down the steel stairs of the radio tower, a young man was standing there with a mop and bucket, and he had a familiar look in his eye—one of being lost, and it made me think of Richard. I greeted him, and even though he didn't greet either of us back, we proceeded to our living quarters.

The barracks would house all of us. The men were in bunks in the main hall, and I had my own room, which was next door to Taylor's. It was a small room with a private bathroom inside, and the men had to use a large latrine on the other side of the base. I was responsible for ensuring all my men had their boots clean, shirts pressed, and rifles polished. Everyone was issued a rifle in a box at the foot of their bunk, and I was provided with a handgun, which I didn't think I would need. I was still holding my bags when another young man approached me to take them. I told him I could manage, and he gave me the same familiar, perplexing look. This was a look I knew all too well, as Richard couldn't hide his emotions, and it made me miss him. After Yvonne died, it didn't seem to affect him too much, and he was managing well when I couldn't visit him daily. He adapted pretty quickly.

After settling in, we were summoned to the mess hall to eat. We were starving and slightly hungover, so some food was very welcome and well received. I wanted to sit among my own men, but officers had their own table, and I was encouraged to sit with them. I wasn't keen on sitting with them, but I did so anyway. Everyone seemed to be genial, and my men were fitting in nicely, so I wasn't too concerned about sitting away from them. They had to line up to get their trays and get their food slopped on, whereas ours were served to us. As one of the servers was coming toward us, he dropped one of the trays, causing one of the senior officers at the table to start screaming at him, calling him an idiot and other nasty words that were like a red cape to a bull for me. Eventually, the smashed crockery and potatoes were cleaned from the floor. I was fighting the urge to say something about the way this young man was spoken to, but I felt it best not to upset the applecart just yet, and I held my tongue. I didn't initiate any conversation, but when somebody did, I shut it down by saying that I was tired and we had had a long few days. On the inside, I was furious, and I retired that evening too angry and exhausted to sleep.

***

The following morning, I overslept and was awakened by a light knock on the door. I shouted out to wait a moment before throwing on my shirt and clip-on tie, and I must have looked rather shoddy when I opened the door. I was glad to see one of my own, and he informed me that command had let me rest a little longer due to recent events, but that we would be taking off for an aid drop in one hour. This meant I had to do pre-flight checks and inspections to ensure everything was in order. While caring for Yvonne, the men had the opportunity to get to know the C-130, and they learned how to operate the rear ramp and attach the static parachute lines to the cargo boxes being dropped. There were some subtle differences that were pointed out to me, but the overall layout between our 727 and this C-130 was similar. Where we would drop supplies was inaccessible to trucks and other motor vehicles, and the threat of a Viet Cong ambush was high. Some aid convoys were attacked, resulting in casualties, so airborne supply drops were the answer.

The supply drop zones we were tasked with were all within a few hundred miles of the base. In the event of any attacks, we were able to turn around and land quickly. The C-130 felt much more choppy and turbulent than the 727, given that it was a propeller plane as opposed to a jet. Inside the fuselage, I was overseeing the men attaching the parachute lines to the supply crates, and they kept losing their balance and falling over at every jolt. The racket inside the airplane was horrendous, and we had to keep shouting at one another to be heard. I had an earpiece radio system to give and receive orders to and from the cockpit, but it was difficult to hear. I often resorted to using the interphone at the rear of the aircraft because I could hear it much better.

When we reached thirty-five hundred feet, the landing gear was put up, and the pilot shouted to me that we were at altitude and 135 knots of airspeed. This was the time the rear door and ramp were to be opened, and only the four loadmasters and I would take the cargo forward and release it from the lowered airborne ramp. From looking out the side of the ramp, we could see the drop zone area below, as we had aerial photographs on board of where we needed to drop the crates. The warm air was smacking us with all its strength, and at first I couldn't really make out if we were in exactly the right place, so I lay down on my belly and shimmied to the edge of the ramp while the loadmasters were shouting at me to get back up. The risk of falling off the ramp didn't really bother me, to be honest, as my main source of happiness was already gone.

The first mission had gone off without a hitch, and after a few hours, we had touched back down at the base. We were given a debriefing by a visiting general, but I didn't take much of it in. I was starting to grow concerned for some of the troops, especially the ones I had seen being berated the day prior, but as we had just arrived, I didn't want to cause a diplomatic incident with our American friends. However, I knew that some of my men were concerned too.

***

The first week in Saigon was a blur, except when a familiar face and voice came to greet me—Mr. Harding. He held out his hand and welcomed me to Saigon, and I shook it reluctantly, given that the man had prevented me from holding my own wife's hand as she passed. The FBI did not have an official presence in Saigon during the Vietnam War; rather, U.S. intelligence and law enforcement activities in South Vietnam were primarily carried out by other agencies, such as the CIA, and military intelligence branches like the Defense Intelligence Agency (DIA). As much as the feds deny it, they were there.

"Lost a little bit of weight, have we?" he said to me.

"Well, Mr. Harding, if you have had the year I've had, which I certainly hope you don't, you may one day look as

frail as I; stress will do that to you. What can I do for you?"
I snarled at him, although he seemed to respond well to it.
He was someone who liked being challenged and thrived in
difficult conversations, and I suppose I respected that about
him.

"My condolences. Grateful to have you here, Monsieur."
Although it was too late and the damage was done, I
appreciated the sentiment.

"Surely there has to be an easier way to make a living,
Mr. Harding, isn't there? Instead of being out in this
godforsaken jungle, dropping God knows what to God
knows who, surely you must know of an easier way?"

"Well, if you want a quick lump of cash, you could
always hit the Federal Reserve Bank in Seattle. There's a nice
big bag of cash set aside for emergencies, but you didn't
hear that from me!" he chuckled back at me, and it was the
perfect thing to say to lighten the mood. He couldn't say
too much to me about his activities and what he was up to,
and I felt this was because the FBI and the CIA didn't really
see eye to eye on the Vietnam fiasco; I had overheard some
of the CIA people complaining that the FBI should stay at
home and stop taking up valuable office space at the U.S.
Embassy in Saigon.

"Have you come with an update or any idea of when
we are returning home?" I asked him abruptly. I was already
starting to miss Richard somewhat, even though I knew
I would have to be out there for a minimum of ten days.
Harding explained that I would be returning home in two
weeks, which would be the middle of August, and then
returning again in October for three weeks. Even though
the stay was slightly longer than I had anticipated, I looked
forward to getting home. After a few drops, I started to find
it slightly boring. It felt like we were airborne mailmen.

Before the next supply drop, I slept soundly and woke

up before the other men. Craving a cup of coffee with my morning smoke, I left the barracks and went to the mess hall directly opposite. There was an unsettling hum of activity, which remained at an even level until it was punctuated by an awful barrage of shouts coming from a short, stout soldier in the kitchen to what seemed to be two of his subordinates. Unable to hold back any longer, I approached the shouting soldier and asked him to step outside of the kitchen with me.

He seemed awkward because he didn't know if he should salute me or address me as sir, as I wasn't one of his own. I demanded to know who these men were in the kitchen and why he was shouting at them incessantly.

He rolled his eyes and said, "Just a couple of McNamara's morons, sir!"

"Sorry, could you repeat that?" I said as I stepped a little closer to him, enraged by what he had said. That was the first time I had heard that term, and at first I didn't put two and two together in that McNamara was Robert McNamara, the former U.S. Secretary of Defense who had vacated office the year prior in 1968. McNamara's pet project was "Project 100,000." The initiative aimed to induct 100,000 men annually who had previously been deemed unfit for military service due to low aptitude or medical reasons. The program was framed as a social uplift effort, purportedly providing training and opportunities to individuals from disadvantaged backgrounds. However, in practice, many of these recruits were sent directly to fight in the Vietnam War, where they faced disproportionately high casualty rates. This program clearly exploited vulnerable populations, such as those with low educational attainment or cognitive impairments, by sending them into one of the most hazardous situations possible without adequate preparation. "McNamara's Morons" remains a stark example of the ethical complexities and human costs intertwined with military decisions and policies.

"McNamara wanted more men out here and sent us this bunch who ain't able to do much. We're having to take care of 'em and watch their every move. We have enough going on out here without this extra work!" he protested to me, nodding almost as if he wanted me to agree with him. I looked back into the kitchen, and they stopped what they were doing to look back at me. It was almost like I was looking at my own son and late brother, and I was terribly upset. These vulnerable young men were thrown into a war zone they didn't fully understand and were being shouted at and abused by their own.

I somehow was able to keep my composure, and I just said to him calmly, "The more you shout, the more you will frighten them. These men shouldn't be here—we can take some home with us."

The private started stuttering, "But, s-sir…we n-need as many men as we can on the front lines. The Viet Cong are ruthless, and we need to outnumber 'em when they ambush us!"

"These men are armed and sent to the front?!" I whimpered to him, and he nodded in the affirmative. At that point, I walked away and smoked my cigarettes outside. I must have smoked four or five in a row. Young, vulnerable men, not too far from Richard in terms of emotional and cognitive ability, were being sent to their deaths. I started asking around about it, and nobody seemed to want to discuss it. I was stonewalled and ignored, and nobody seemed to care because these men were viewed as less human than everyone else. However, what I always felt about Richard and Eric was that they were more human than everyone else on a deeper level. Sending these young men to be slaughtered—what kind of human would do that?

Chapter 16
The Analysis of Language
Clifford Harding, April 24, 1973

By this stage, most people inside the Bureau had given up on ever locating or apprehending Cooper. It was never mentioned publicly, but it certainly was discussed behind the scenes. The proactivity of the case largely died off, and the strategy shifted focus from being an active investigation to a passive investigation, meaning we would be dependent on a member of the public ratting him out or the guy giving up the game and confessing to it with evidence.

The serial numbers of all of the twenty-dollar bills given to the hijacker were microfilmed and kept on a list. This list has been published by various sources over the passing decades, but in the immediate aftermath of the hijacking, none of the cash furnished to Cooper ever made its way into circulation.

I had cases that involved hot money and counterfeit money. While more rudimentary than today's CSI labs, 1970s forensics could still analyze fingerprints, handwriting, and other physical evidence associated with stolen money or the crime scene. Investigators would scrutinize bank records, looking for large or suspicious deposits that could be linked to stolen money. Large cash purchases soon after a theft could also raise red flags.

Like most law enforcement agencies, we had rats that

were either already working for or had infiltrated gangs, organizations, and families. We called them intelligence officers or other fancy titles to persuade them they were doing the right thing by reporting their organization's activities to us. Without saying too much, some of us made it worth their while. You name any organized crime syndicate, and we had spies in them: the Italian mobs, the Hells Angels Motorcycle Club, the Chinese Tongs and Triads, and various large gambling syndicates. They all converged in operations like racketeering and gambling, where large sums of money changed hands.

I tried tapping into the darkest corners of our intelligence networks, and I provided the serial numbers document to them, with the hope that some of this cash would turn up. After many hours chasing up informants who were most certainly reliable, I came up empty, and none of the cash seemed to circulate through these gangs. Some of these criminal networks were handling much more cash than our local banks ever could. Banks were also provided with the list of serial numbers, and they were instructed to bring suspiciously large transactions or deposits to our attention immediately. This order was extended from local banks to those across the United States.

Every time I received a fax or a letter in the mail, I tore it open to see if there were any leads. I had made a point of personally sending copies of the serial numbers to a variety of banks, and I requested that they report large transactions to me directly, but it was feast or famine. It wasn't unusual to buy a car, a house, or machinery with cash. At one point, I was provided with boxes of documents detailing any transaction over two thousand dollars from several banks, but it would have taken me years to not only sift through them all but to also interview the parties involved in the transactions, go through all the bank-filed bills to look for the Cooper serial numbers, and then detain someone for questioning at the end of it if I was lucky.

If the money was spent, both inside of our jurisdiction and outside of it, it would have come to our attention. So after nearly eighteen months, there were two possible answers. The first option was that the money was lost by either flying out the aft door or falling off Cooper when he leapt off the stairs, but at this point, the money wasn't turning up anywhere we searched. A bag of money should be very easy to find when it is lost; there were loot bags that turned up from other skyjackers who had lost the money in the air during their jumps. However, if the flight path was slightly off, the bag could have landed in water somewhere. Or, if someone found Cooper's loot and kept their mouth shut, they could have spent it in small amounts over the years. I don't think that the local gas station or grocery store owners in the area had a list of those serial numbers. But with the passing years, lots of bills being spent, and lots of people searching for them, some should have been found in circulation. None were ever found in circulation.

This left the other option: that the cash had been taken out of circulation and moved to another jurisdiction. We had contacts in the Royal Canadian Mounted Police and others in the Dirección Federal de Seguridad (DFS) in Mexico. The description of Dan Cooper included that he had an olive skin tone, but he was also described as having a non-discernible accent, which made me doubt he was Mexican. The idea that Cooper wasn't American wasn't really considered by the FBI at any point. I began to think we were missing something, so I decided to look at the language used by Cooper as reported by the flight crew in their witness statements, hoping to find some sort of clue that would bring me closer to revealing his identity.

I started with his interactions with Florence

Schaffner, and I thought that Cooper asking for $200,000 in "negotiable American currency" was odd. If he were American, surely he would ask for $200,000 and omit the negotiable currency part. There is no definitive piece of evidence that Cooper said it himself, but the flight crew certainly radioed it to the ground, and why would they say that if Cooper didn't ask for it? For us, negotiable currency would go without saying, and it just seemed a very foreign thing to say.

Cooper never used profanity or raised his voice at anyone. Tina Mucklow readily described him as polite; at no point was he cruel or nasty, other than getting a bit upset at times when things weren't moving at the pace he wanted, especially on the SeaTac runway when it took around two hours to get back in the air toward Reno after landing on the ground. Other hijackers shouted, swore, and made threats to kill. Cooper was very calm in all that he did, and he didn't put up much of a fight when Captain Scott said no to several of his requests before they took off again.

Another odd comment Cooper made to Tina Mucklow was when he asked her where she was from. When she said that she was from Pennsylvania but was currently living in Minneapolis, Cooper said, "Very nice country." This didn't really sound like the way an American would respond. Some might consider Pennsylvania to be a nice state and Minneapolis a nice city, but they certainly aren't countries. When she asked him where he was from, he got upset and refused to answer. Why didn't he just lie? He could have told her he was from Seattle, Albany, Las Vegas, Salt Lake City, or anywhere else. He didn't even lie to say he was an American. I'm from Seattle, and if I were asked where I was from when I wanted to keep my identity secret, I simply would have picked a random city like Phoenix in order to throw off the authorities.

The entire hijacking was controlled by the flight crew, more or less. If Cooper had his way, they would have headed to Mexico, and he would have had his knapsack instead of a cotton money bag. Bank robbers and extortionists are normally very good at making their demands known and having their every need met down to the smallest detail. I recalled a few bank robberies that I was investigating where the hostages seemingly controlled the heist, and they were ultimately a failure. The reason why was that the robbers were part of gangs and closed criminal organizations where English wasn't the first language, and ultimately, communications broke down. Did Cooper refuse to argue, fight back, or make additional demands because English was not his first language? Under extreme pressure or stress, bilingual people tend to express frustration or angst in their mother tongue. This seemed to be a decent theory as to why Cooper didn't answer where he was from when he was asked, argue with the flight crew when they refused to take off with the stairs down, or express frustration that a fuel stop was required in the USA prior to Mexico.

***

As I was making what I felt were some breakthroughs in Cooper's choice of language, Charlotte got out of bed and came downstairs again, which wasn't like her. I could hear her marching down the stairs, and she came towards me through the plumes of cigarette smoke. She sat in the chair at the head of our kitchen table and leaned into me, pulling her nightgown tight.

"Cliff, you haven't come to bed in months. The girls and I feel like we are guests in your office, which I am trying to pass off as our home. You haven't gone to any social occasions with us, you refuse to acknowledge visitors when they come to our house, and you are starting to drink more, and I don't like it. Yes, you are working on a high-profile case, but it is rapidly approaching two years since this guy took that money, and no trace of him has been found. What is this all about, Clifford? We feel like we are losing you faster than your colleagues are losing D.B. Cooper!"

"His name was Dan Cooper, Charlotte, not D.B. Cooper." Then she started to become irate and was trying to shout at me without waking the girls up, like an overly aggressive whisper.

"You really couldn't give a shit about us, Clifford! Not an apology, not any form of care for us—nothing! You need to get off this case, and the only case you should be working on is reassuring your daughters that they have a father who actually cares about them!" Then she sighed, and her next sentence was interrupted by a croaking sob. I came closer to her, and I gave her a hug.

"I feel responsible, and I was wrong to play any part in making this caper successful for him. I have to find him and put it right." Although I tried to convince her, it wasn't working, and what I was being issued with was an ultimatum. After this reality check, I wondered if Cooper was having a terrible time with his spouse or losing bonds with his children, if he had any. I was the good guy, yet I was suffering, and my family was starting to suffer even more than I was.

***

Nobody was able to locate the cash, and suspects that were interviewed were ruled out as quickly as they were questioned. Everyone seemed to have an alibi, were too young, or simply wanted the notoriety for their own selfish and egotistical reasons. We hauled all these crooks from all over, thinking they were "Dan Cooper," and most people were going by a physical description, which was vague at best, rather than what the guy actually said and how he behaved during the ordeal. If anyone became angry or started swearing during their interviews or questioning, it was a red line for me, and they were out of the picture. Cooper never used derogatory language toward the police or FBI when speaking to anyone, and that in and of itself was hugely validating for me that this man was at some level of law enforcement.

We all know our own, and when in public in other parts of the country, I can sniff out a cop by the way they order their coffee in a coffee shop or how they cross the street. Even when not on the beat, they tend to look around, and any slight noise will cause them to nearly break their necks in order to look in the direction of any potential disturbance. If Charlotte and I were on vacation and I saw someone who seemed like me, I always sniffed loudly, and Charlotte would exclaim, "Bacon!" and then we would laugh. When examining Cooper's behavior, I just couldn't shake that odor, no matter how hard I tried.

I reported to my superiors what my findings were, and I wasn't the only one to draw the same conclusions about the cash. Nobody was able to find it. There were agents who were officially assigned to the Norjak case, but nobody really seemed to mind too much what I was doing. I suppose anyone would be happy if someone was doing their work for them, and I gladly obliged. However, my hypothesis of Cooper being a policeman of some sort, or even that it could possibly be one of our own, was completely shot down. The military angle had gained so much mileage with some factions of the Bureau, and the idea that he was dead was the view of the other faction.

For anyone who thought he was dead, I always asked,

"Well, where is the parachute, the cash, or the body?" My favorite answer all through the years to this question was when an agent told me, "Cooper became bear food, so his corpse and parachute were probably encased in bear shit." The debate on Cooper reached the level of an unstoppable force versus an immovable object. There was just as much evidence, or lack of evidence, to suggest that he cratered and animals ate him. On the other hand, that same lack of evidence could also point to the man landing on the ground and simply walking away.

I got nowhere attempting to question or investigate our own or the cops at the beginning of 1974. What I really needed was to speak to a cop who doesn't speak English as his first language. I decided I would open my old address book to contact someone I knew in the Royal Canadian Mounted Police, but when they told me he retired at the beginning of the year, I thought nothing of it and turned my attention to some others. In my gut, I knew I was getting somewhere.

Chapter 17

Second Air Base

Dan Cooper, April 15, 1971

Throughout 1969 and 1970, I was back and forth between Montreal and Saigon. As the war picked up, more men were killed, more troops were sent in their place like cattle, and NORAD and Air America's efforts had to be scaled up to match. What hurt me most was that I was seeing Richard less, and it was clear that he was missing me. He never forgot who I was, but when I was with him, he would appear sad. When he looked at me with his big brown eyes, I saw the same look as those troubled men in Vietnam; it was a fear of the unknown and a confusion as to what was going on. Richard couldn't understand why I was seeing him less, and when I asked the care staff if they felt he could be taking it personally, they told me they weren't sure.

I was so consumed in grief over Yvonne's passing that when my mother died in January 1970, I couldn't really take it in. What seemed to hit me harder was when my father died in November of the same year. They were both eighty-eight. They were reunited with Eric, Lucille, and Mathieu and freed from the dark abyss that Richard and I were still left in. Yvonne's parents sympathized with me, of course, but they were aging themselves, and seeing me was more upsetting to them than comforting. It was a very awkward interaction at my father's funeral, and after that, I never saw them again.

Juggling regular duties with the RCMP and leaving for up to three weeks at a time to go to Saigon was very challenging for me. I turned fifty in February 1971, and I noticed that I wasn't as youthful and energetic as I once was. Not only was I feeling slightly more tired during the day, but my hair was almost completely grey, and when looking at myself, I thought that I looked old. Everything in life just seemed dull. The only exciting thing that I had to look forward to that year was leading the Musical Ride in March, and I loved going back to Depot, despite the sad memories. No matter how hard I tried, I couldn't fully adjust to life without Yvonne, and I was starting to fear that Richard would soon have to face life without me. After age fifty, the feeling of invincibility and that one's whole life is ahead of them screeches to a halt.

Any domestic murders, bank robberies, heists, narcotic raids, or anything else failed to surprise or interest me anymore. When I spoke of this to command, they concluded that it was because I had stepped on the first step before retirement. For the Mounties back then, if one didn't go higher than my current rank of inspector, it was expected that retirement would happen around the age of fifty-five or after thirty-five years of service, whichever came soonest. I joined in 1939, so I had put in thirty-two years of service and couldn't see how I would continue policing and travelling back and forth between home and Vietnam in a few years.

***

It was April 1971, and I had been in Vietnam for several weeks on the longest trip I had had out there. Some of my men had changed, and around the barracks, the personnel were changing so often that I found it challenging to keep on top of the new names and faces. One evening, I was summoned to a briefing. When I was adjusting my tie and fidgeting with my tie clip and RCMP pin, I remembered Harding's comments that I looked frail, and he was right because my shirt didn't seem as tight on the collar and the skin on my neck had become somewhat looser. I hadn't eaten much, and the little I did eat seemed to disagree with me. I developed something of a fear of food and only ate when I felt I needed to in order to prevent my body from shutting down. My unit was tasked with delivering crucial supplies to a remote village recently liberated from Viet Cong control and to the U.S. troops at a smaller base nearby. As I was in command of the mission, I knew that precision, timing, and vigilance were key.

We weren't using the C-130 but had decided to use the 727 because where we were landing had a shorter runway, and that was exactly what the aircraft was designed for. There had been some modifications made in the preceding years, in that nose brakes were fitted and more seats were added for passenger comfort. This would be the last mission of this mini-tour, and we would be flying diplomats back home shortly afterward. We took to the air the following morning, and we had everything loaded onto the pallets and inside the cargo holds. Where we would be landing was almost an hour away, and normally our flights were between fifteen and twenty minutes, or a thirty- to forty-minute round trip.

We landed on a makeshift runway that seemed short from the air, but the aircraft was able to handle the landing perfectly on the runway. It was a flat, even strip of land surrounded by trees, and we would have to trek through the trees and haul the pallets through the pre-flattened path through the greenery. We were given harnesses to strap to ourselves in order to haul the cargo around half a mile into the little dilapidated village. It was a large collection of makeshift tree houses, complete with bullet holes and char marks, with several water wells or hydrants protruding from the paths adjacent to some of these huts that the locals were using as their homes. The smell was unbearable, as sanitation clearly wasn't up to standard, and I wanted to order everyone back to the aircraft to make a swift exit.

Today's mission was different. It was about hope and assistance, not war and secrets. The cargo plane was loaded with medical supplies, food, and clothing for the village—a small sign of goodwill amidst the chaos of war. Our supplies were greatly received; some villagers even gave us gifts like bracelets or amulets made from wood, feathers, and animal pelts.

However, one of the CIA men shouted to me to come inside the largest hut near the centre of the village. Mosquitoes and flies were attacking us viciously, and the humid heat was unbearable for all of us. I made my way in, and he showed me an unexpected find. They had found evidence there of a makeshift mining operation and what looked to be strange metals and substances in boxes, vials, and wrapped in cloth. This discovery would send ripples through the intelligence community, but at the time, it seemed like no big deal to me. I picked them up and looked at them as the men of the CIA pulled out their radio packs to frantically relay the gravity of what had been discovered to whoever would listen. I didn't know what they were, and neither did any of my fellow servicemen. Could the Viet Cong be tapping into these rare metals for some unknown purpose? We waited around an hour for instructions, and once we heard back, I was ordered to keep them and bring them back with me. So, I took custody of these minerals and wrote down in my notebook the descriptions of what they were. Some seemed shiny and silver, others dull or black, and

I measured them so that they could be catalogued whenever we got back.

We made our way onto the aircraft, and the pilots unlocked the airstairs to let us all in. It was seemingly uneventful, but the pilots told us that our passengers back at base were not ready to leave yet. They asked if we could wait an hour or two until the airspace was clear, promising that our passengers would be ready to leave quickly when we returned, so I agreed. Everyone came on and sat down in their seats, and I took the chance to look more closely at some of these rocks, metals, or whatever the hell they were while I took my position in the jump seat in the cockpit. While examining some of the samples, a fine metallic dust got onto my hands, and I unwittingly transferred some of it to my tie, leaving something of a stain that I was licking my thumb and trying frantically to get off. The particles clung to the fabric—a tiny testament to a discovery that could change the course of the war. When I realized that Yvonne was no longer here to admonish me for leaving a stain on my black tie, I stopped, and a tiny wave of grief came over me.

Back at base, the intelligence officers were astonished by what had been found. Someone had taken my notes and was describing them to an officer on the radio, but I wasn't paying attention to the conversation, despite being in the cockpit where the communications were taking place. If these metals were as rare as the intelligence officers thought they were, they would be vital for advanced technology. If the Viet Cong had been mining and processing them, it could mean that they had external help, possibly from a world superpower. The implications were enormous, but I was more concerned about the stain on the tie and consumed with my thoughts of Yvonne.

Suddenly, a shriek came from beside me, which pulled me out of my rumination. It was the pilot, and he shouted,

"Monsieur! Monsieur!" while pointing towards the nose of the plane, and I leapt out of my seat to see what the fuss was about.

At first, I didn't see what on Earth he was pointing at; all I saw were trees, shrubbery, and birds soaring off from the treetops, until I looked down to the end of the runway and saw what looked to be a leather briefcase sitting there about fifty yards in front of our nose. It was a small case, so unassuming and unthreatening to look at that it was very concerning to me.

I yelled into the cabin, "Men, there is a briefcase on the runway."

One shouted back, "Sir, it could be a bomb!" which was exactly my thought. Everyone was looking at me with a fear I'd never seen in them, waiting for me to order someone to go and check out this suspicious case. After a ten-second or so pause, I told them I would go. Everyone shouted at me that I was crazy, but I didn't care. If I were blown to smithereens, I would be with Yvonne again.

A couple of my men offered to come with me, but I said, "Non, asseyez-vous!" and they did. I went back down the stairs, and when I looked back into the fuselage from the last stair, the men were gathering at the door, and I pointed at them to go back in and remain seated.

I turned left around the aircraft and headed toward the briefcase. I didn't want to give anyone hiding in the trees the satisfaction of raising my hands above my head, so I just kept going toward it with my hands down by my sides. In all my years, I had only dealt with a threat like this a handful of times and wasn't sure what to expect. The little briefcase was at my feet, and the clips were open. I knelt down in front of it and took a deep breath. Opening the lid could be my last mortal action, and I whispered to myself, "Paradis avec Yvonne," before throwing open the briefcase.

After tensing my whole body, nothing happened, and my suspicions were confirmed. There were six rust-coloured dynamite sticks bundled together, wires, a cylindrical battery, and an alarm clock with a timer that was showing seven minutes. Immediately, I thought that it would take about ten minutes to fire the engines, get the oil pressure and temperature right on the aircraft, and retract the stairs for takeoff. I turned and started frantically waving my arms to the pilots who could see me, and I roared for them to start the engines to prepare for takeoff. I sprinted back to the airplane and ran up the steps, almost tripping on my way up. The men were buzzing around the empty fuselage, wanting to know what was going on, and I yelled out again to the pilots to prepare for takeoff.

The flight engineer shouted back, "Sir, please retract the stairs, and we can prepare to go."

"No! Go! Now! Allez! Depressurize the cabin, keep the landing gear down and the flaps at fifteen degrees. Allons-y!" In times of stress, I fluctuated between English and French.

"Sir, we can't take off with the stairs lowered because sparks could cause an explosion. We will need to get clearance from base and set the flight configuration."

"We have about five minutes; get us in the air NOW! We can take off with the stairs down—let's go! These are our lives we're talking about. Come on! Allez!"

The young men in the cockpit were starting to get frightened, and as the engines were firing up, I told all the men to sit down. I was looking at my watch after taking my seat, and the plane wasn't moving. Before I could roar at them to go again, the aircraft burst forward, and as it did, a horrific hail of gunfire descended on us, and we all threw ourselves down on the deck. It was pandemonium, and when we felt the plane lift off the small runway, we held onto one another as the pings of bullets were still smacking outside the aircraft.

I crouched, moving toward the cockpit, and through the exit door window, I could see smoke billowing from the port engine on the left side. The pilots shouted that the port engine had caught fire and shut down; alarms were going off and buzzers were going. They looked at me and were awaiting orders. We shook from side to side, and the men shouted at me from the rear, asking what we should do. They held on to each other, stopping objects and each other from falling through the aircraft and out the open rear door. Our altitude was around ten thousand feet, and the pilots felt that with the loss of an engine and the starboard engine leaking fuel, we wouldn't make it back. The aircraft was never fully fuelled due to the shorter nature of our flights, and it was clear that we wouldn't have enough fuel to get back.

I went back into the cabin and shouted, "Bailing out, all men and cargo. The pilots need to decrease the weight to bring her home!" The men got up and took the parachutes down from the overhead storage spaces, with the main parachutes in the overhead lockers on the left-hand side and the front-mounted chest reserves on the right. Everyone was bumping into one another, and the backpacks and chest packs fell all over the ground. Some men were jumping on them to avoid the parachutes rolling down the cabin and out of the stairwell. The noise was deafening, and we were losing altitude. I wasn't there whenever the men had done the bailout procedure in their training, but luckily everyone knew how to put their rigs on and clip the chest-mounted reserves onto their harnesses. I had to be shown how to do it by two of them, making sure that the leg loops went on first, then the shoulder straps, with the chest strap fastened and loose material tucked away, the front reserve clipped and fastened to the D-rings at the front of the harness, and then finally the goggles and the helmet fastened and secured.

As everyone was shuffling toward the exit door, we

jolted slightly upward, sending some of our personal belongings zipping down the fuselage and out the door. Among the items hurtling out the door was the little black bag of metal samples that had been on my seat.

The pilots said to me, "Godspeed! We will radio base with your exit coordinates to get you all picked up. She will be just about stable, and the load will be lightened enough to get back," and then they all shook my hand individually as quickly as possible. The backpack and front reserve parachutes were so heavy, and it caused some pain even just standing there with them. Everyone was standing far away from the rear door, and one pointed down to the stairs, as I had to go and dispatch them.

On the way down, I opened the overhead compartment near the door to get the oxygen supply, which was switched on. I stood at the top of the stairs and beckoned the men forward, and they shuffled down in single file. I made them take a mouthful of oxygen to steady their nerves and said, "Jump, arch, then pull after a few seconds!" Then they all nodded. One by one, they were going out the door, and peeking down, I could see their round white canopies making their way to the ground. Some were praying and saying aloud that they hoped we wouldn't be landing in the middle of a Viet Cong stronghold, which was a fear I also held.

Eventually, it was just me, as I had to go last. I trembled down the stairwell, and as I got halfway down, I removed my tie and rolled it up before putting it inside my left pocket. I didn't want to lose the tie or the pins, so I kept them with me. I stared out the door for a moment and could see the green wasteland below, and I realized I had to go because I couldn't drift too far from where everyone else had landed. I jumped as far forward as I could and pulled the ripcord, with the opening shock jarring me in midair. I looked up to see the big nylon dome above my head. Such was my depression that I was almost disappointed that it opened because it meant I would have to wait longer to be reunited with Yvonne. I could see a small clump of canopies the closer I got to the ground—I wouldn't be landing too far from them. Under the canopy, I turned my head to my left and saw the aircraft hurtling back toward the base. By my reckoning, they were around thirty minutes away, and we were far from the base.

I landed hard on the ground and removed my helmet and goggles before gathering up the canopy and carrying it in both of my hands. I walked around a quarter of a mile, and within an hour, we were all reunited. A few were hobbling and had obviously sprained or broken their ankles, so they sat on the ground. Twenty-two men had jumped, including myself, and there were twenty-two of us together on the ground. We seemed to land in a neutral area, and there was silence all around. We still had no idea where we were, but before long, a truck came to meet us. We went to a nearby base, the name of which I can't recall, and rather than worrying about our welfare, the leadership debriefing us was more concerned at the loss of the metals we had recovered.

We were due to fly home anyway in the coming days, but after that escapade, I knew I was too old for this game. I told the men that after we got home, I was contacting Depot and resigning from the project. Interestingly, the Americans seemed somewhat miffed; perhaps I had won them over in the end, but I knew I didn't want to go back or continue with the project any longer. As soon as we were back on Canadian soil, I typed out my resignation letter, which was accepted. Any further involvement in Southeast Asia would need to be led by someone who had youth on their side. After all the heavy lifting, the hot weather, the grief, and everything else, I had to start thinking about retirement.

Part Four

He who possesses virtue at its best,
Or greatness in the true sense of the word,
Has one day started even with that herd
Whose swift feet now speed, but at sin's behest.
It is the same force in the human breast
Which makes men gods or demons. If we gird
Those strong emotions by which we are stirred
With might of will and purpose, heights unguessed
Shall dawn for us; or if we give them sway
We can sink down and consort with the lost.
All virtue is worth just the price it cost.
Black sin is oft white truth, that missed its way,
And wandered off in paths not understood.
Twin-born I hold great evil and great good.

Ella Wheeler-Wilcox

Chapter 18
Homecoming
Dan Cooper, July 30, 1971

As soon as I was home, I went to see Richard. Ever since his mother had died, he had changed quite rapidly. Richard seemed to settle quickly enough when he first moved to the Allan, but as time went by, he changed. Of course, when anyone goes into institutional care or an asylum, they aren't going to present as well as they would when they are at home. There seemed to be a high turnover of staff, and anytime I went in there, there were new staff and nurses. Richard couldn't keep on top of it, and I didn't blame him because I couldn't either. Richard was always someone who needed to be won over, and with time and patience, it was easy to do. As the years went by, I felt I was losing him more and more, and I worried that I would be left with nobody. One evening I visited him after leaving the station, and I sat on the bed with him. I brought some of his favourite oatcakes from a bakery he loved, but he didn't eat them. Even when I tried to sit closer to him on his bed, he shimmied further up the bed, almost as if he was fearful of me.

I discussed my concerns with the staff, but they just told me that he was now institutionalized and that this was the way he would be from now on. I didn't want to accept that, and I made a point of visiting him more and more, even during the day when I should have been in the station. No matter what I tried to do, Richard wasn't as close to me as he once was. Richard was now twenty-four years old, and in time, he would have spent more time in a facility than he did in our home. I would bring him his Dan Cooper comics and picture albums, but he seemed to lose interest in them. I told him that I had jumped from an airplane and pointed to one of the pictures of Cooper himself under a canopy, but Richard was disinterested and turned the other way. I just wanted to connect with him and gain some form of closeness to him, but anything I tried to do just made the situation worse.

***

I was at home alone on a July evening when my phone rang. It was a staff member at the Allan asking if I was available the following morning to meet with Richard's care team. I told them I was and asked if I could hear what the meeting was about so that I could be somewhat mentally prepared, but I was told that all would be explained to me whenever I got there. I had no choice but to accept and await the meeting. Every so often, there would be meetings about Richard's progress and healthcare plans that I was obliged to attend. Typically, they were every quarter, but his quarterly meeting had only taken place a week or two before being called to this second meeting. The only other occasion I remember having an additional meeting regarding Richard was when he was having frequent choking episodes and Yvonne and I had to authorize a mashed-up diet for him.

When I got to the Allan at 10 a.m. the following morning, I was taken into an office that I had never seen before. It was at the rear of the building and up a flight of dark wooden stairs. Usually, when I went to see Richard, I went in and turned left down the hallway to the rooms where he was, and I had never ventured up to the second level of the building before. I was sitting in front of some doctor in a white coat, who, without even introducing himself, said to me, "I am afraid our program of care here for long-term patients has come to an end."

Initially, I didn't know what this meant, and as I was trying to process what had just been said, a nurse who was standing at the door pulled up a chair and sat directly beside me to my right.

"I'm sorry, what does this mean?" I asked.

"Unfortunately, it means that we will have to find somewhere else for Richard to live. This facility is going to be for day patients only, and those who have been residing here will no longer be able to stay past November thirtieth of this year," the unnamed doctor said to me coldly. He didn't have the slightest concern, ask me my name, or even give me his throughout the conversation.

"Well, Richard's mother passed almost two years ago, and we both know there is no other place like this for miles. Caring for him at home would be beyond what I could afford. What would you suggest I do?" Then he pointed at my RCMP lapel pin with something of a grin on his face before responding.

"Well, with the cost of private nurses and a lack of options nearby, would early retirement be an option?" His grin widened as he said this in a way that disgusted me. The nurse beside me started rubbing the palm of her hand on her neck, and she was obviously feeling as uncomfortable as I was.

"So, why all of a sudden has this decision been reached without consulting other families first?" I inquired.

"Well, there were trials of care and medication that have now reached their conclusion. This place is moving on, and unfortunately, the few long-term patients like Richard who are still here must also move on. There are only five patients still living here."

This was very puzzling to me, as during visiting hours I had gotten to know some other families visiting their child or relative. I asked where some had gone because Michel, a boy around Richard's age, had been in the room next door for a few years, but I noticed he wasn't there after I came back from Saigon.

"Some of the patients here have moved to other facilities, and some have even gone overseas."

"Overseas?" I stood up from the chair in complete horror. "You mean like Southeast Asia, that far overseas?"

"Monsieur, I cannot break the confidence of other patients here, but I can assure you they are being cared for. Some of the residents either had no living relatives, or the living relatives they had did not wish to take responsibility for them." I was quickly becoming uncontrollably angry, and when I took some deep breaths, I sat back down again, and the nurse reached for my hand and clasped it tightly.

"Let's say I was dead—what would happen to Richard then?" I snapped across the desk.

The doctor lit a cigarette and told me earnestly, "It would be the responsibility of the state to have him placed in a similar facility to this at its own expense. We wouldn't be able to discharge him onto the street, given his lack of mental faculties."

I was in total disbelief. "I am all Richard has left in this world, and you are telling me it would be better for him if I was dead? What about Saint-Jean-de-Dieu Hospital or Mont-Providence? Surely, they would be able to admit Richard as a patient?"

"Unfortunately not, Monsieur. Given Richard's high level of need, they would be unable to offer him the appropriate supervision and care that he requires." Not once did this doctor apologize, not only for dismissing my son but for basically holding me over a barrel and telling me I had a few months to either move or somehow gain enough money to get Richard the care that he needs.

I couldn't believe what I was hearing, but I asked, "How many days do I have to organize a move elsewhere or to have Richard cared for at home?"

He said, "Well, today is July thirtieth, so that would mean one hundred and twenty-three days until November thirtieth. That's not a lot of time, so I suggest you try and put whatever plans in place that you can."

All that was left for me to do was bid them adieu, but before that, I went down to see Richard, who was still in his room. Even if he didn't understand everything that I was saying to him, I still told him everything. I told him that he would have to move again, and I promised him that I wouldn't allow him to go so far that I would never see him again. I would never allow him to be transferred hundreds, if not thousands, of miles away from me, and I assured him that if the situation became desperate, I would take him home. Normally, when I told Richard anything negative, he just kept his same blank stare, but I felt that this time was somehow different. Although if one stares at a cloud long enough, they can make any shape they want out of it. Maybe I did that with Richard's expression.

***

Moving Richard again would kill him and likely kill me too. Whenever I had difficult days, I used to go to Yvonne's graveside. I never spoke to the grave marker or greeted her like I heard other widowers do in the cemetery. I wasn't going to leave town, and neither was Richard. Back in those days, life insurance wasn't as common as it is now. I didn't have any additional funds from any insurance payouts, nor did I decide to take legal action to seek compensation. I didn't need it because I was well enough off. Luckily, I had a decent salary that came with my inspector rank. I had my own insurance, which I signed for when I became a Mountie, but Yvonne wasn't included in it because we were not married at the time of my joining, nor did we ever discuss adding her to the policy. Attempting an insurance scam was going to be impossible because I would have been easily caught, disgraced, fired, and had a lower pension.

I decided to request a meeting with my superintendent to discuss early retirement. To say the conversation didn't go very well would be quite an understatement. In short, I was only fifty years old, and I had to either meet the minimum retirement age to get my full pension plan, which was fifty-five, or I had to have served for thirty-five years. Both were a few years away, and I didn't have that much time. If I had cashed out my pension and retired, I would have received a golden handshake of $10,000 and a monthly pension payment of $175, which was an insult after everything I had done for the force up to that point. I didn't say yes or no to this offer because I needed to calculate what Richard's care costs would have been if I brought him home. I brought up being transferred to wherever Richard might be sent to, but a transfer could take quite a long time, and in Montreal, I was very unlikely to be spared to go to another district.

***

Before delving deep into my finances and the costs of caring for Richard, I pleaded our case with both Saint-Jean-de-Dieu Hospital and Mont-Providence, but both said they were already over their patient limit and a vacancy to care for Richard was not likely to come up before the November 30th deadline. What they did agree to do was place his name on a waitlist, and they would call me if availability came up. I'm not sure if they said this to shut me up, but in any case, it worked.

There were several nursing agencies that I contacted, but when I explained Richard's needs, they told me they were unable to help. Most nursing agencies back then were only for the elderly and infirm, not intellectually disabled adults. Absolutely nothing was going my way, and after spending what felt like only a few days constantly on the phone, I looked at my calendar and found that it was already August 30th. Time had gone by so quickly, and I decided to ask around the station to see if anyone could help. One of my officers recommended a nursing agency out of town, and he had positive things to say about them. He and his siblings had hired a live-in nurse to care for their late father so that he could pass at home. After outlining honestly what Richard's needs were, they promised they would do all they could to help. It was a great help and relief to me.

Richard's mind requires routine and familiarity, so a live-in nurse was recommended. However, given that Richard was as tall as I was, at just under six feet, and over 200 pounds, he would require two nurses to care for him at all times for safety reasons. If Richard had a fall or accident, it would require two nurses to ensure he got up off the floor safely. When Richard needed bathing or showering, it also required two nurses to do this. Plus, mealtimes needed to be entirely supervised to ensure that Richard didn't choke or throw his food on the floor. Our house had four bedrooms, so Richard could have his room, and two of the other rooms could serve as sleeping quarters for the nursing staff. Moreover, two nurses couldn't just live in my house full-time. They would need to be swapped out regularly to allow them to go on vacation, and if one got sick, another could slot in easily. What I ultimately needed were four nurses working in pairs, with one pair replacing the other on alternating nights. Then the painful question of cost came up, and I calculated that it would cost me $1,200 a month, or $300 a month per nurse. The agency owner was very warm and reassuring, and she told me I could call her back when I reached a decision and to take my time, although time was running out as August bled into September.

**

Although I hadn't spoken to my sisters in quite a long time, I decided to call them to tell them of my situation. I asked them if they could loan me money to keep Richard stable at home until a bed at a local hospital came up for him to be cared for, but they didn't show me any sympathy or offer any assistance to me. My siblings and I had drifted so far apart, and we had barely spoken since Yvonne passed. After my parents died, the land and farmhouse were sold off, and because the farmhouse had become dilapidated and in need of major renovations, it was auctioned for a paltry amount, and my inheritance was just about enough to buy myself a new car. Turning to my family wasn't getting me anywhere, and I called the hospitals back again only to have them tell me that there were still no vacancies and that they were unlikely to have any imminently.

I only had four thousand dollars in savings, and I was getting desperate. Given my rank, I wasn't low enough on the food chain to be offered bribes because the beat cops arrested criminals, and staff sergeants or staff sergeant majors interviewed or dealt with organized crime bosses. I was never above having people followed, spied on, or their phones tapped, but I never would have considered bribery up until now. October came very quickly, and the last resort for me was going to be selling Yvonne's jewellery. She kept all the anniversary, Christmas, and birthday presents I got her in her jewellery box, and having itemized some jewellery store heists in the past, I would say her collection totalled maybe three thousand dollars, which was still nowhere near enough.

More people were starting to comment that I looked feeble and tired, and I was. The only solace I ever had was visiting Richard, and even if we sat in silence together, I loved his company. Now and again, the nursing staff would ask how things were progressing, as some of them genuinely cared about Richard and our situation. Some even told me they had given other hospitals a good word of recommendation in the hope it would accelerate a move, but by the beginning of November, there was still no word. I was reminded as we got into the second week of November that I had less than three weeks to either accept a transfer to a hospital in God knows where or to make alternative arrangements of my own. I wasn't going to admit defeat and have Richard sent to an impossible location.

***

In the early 1970s, commercial flights worldwide faced the looming threat of hijackings. One particularly notable incident occurred on November 13, 1971. On that day, an Air Canada Boeing 737 flying from Vancouver to Toronto with a scheduled stop in Calgary became the scene of a dramatic event. The culprit, a 27-year-old man named Paul Joseph Cini, armed himself with a sawed-off shotgun and claimed to have a dynamite bomb. As the plane cruised at altitude, Cini made a series of demands. Among them was a staggering request for $1.5 million in ransom from the

Canadian government. What made this heist quite interesting was that Cini planned his escape with a makeshift parachute he made himself. He claimed to be a member of the Irish Republican Army (IRA) and that he wanted safe passage to Northern Ireland.

The flight had an unscheduled landing in Great Falls, Montana, where Cini was given US$50,000 by Air Canada and the passengers were released. Cini ordered the aircraft to head toward Canada so he could parachute over the Alberta wilderness. His makeshift parachute became tangled, and when he requested something to cut his tangled parachute lines with, a member of the flight crew brought a fire axe. When Cini placed his shotgun gun down, he received a swift knock on the head with the axe handle, bringing the hijacking to a close, and Cini was apprehended.

This case came to my attention the following day, and the preliminary notes made for some very interesting reading. The United States was facing a growing problem with hijackers taking control of passenger planes and taking them to Cuba, often for political reasons. I was consulted as to what we could do to protect Canadian passengers and airliners for future reference, so I decided to get to work on how that could be achieved, even just to take my mind off Richard's situation for a short while. Cini asked for $1.5 million, and the pilot and a crew member were able to foil that plan. I remember thinking, *If the passengers and crew were kept calm at all times, and he asked for professionally packed parachutes instead of bringing his own, opened the door, and left, he could have been over a million big ones richer.*

Would I call it an aha moment? Maybe. I examined security protocols for air travel that were valid in both the United States and Canada. Passports were not required for internal flights or those between the United States and Canada. I recalled that when Yvonne and I travelled from Regina to Montreal, our bags weren't checked. I gave our names to the ticketing agent, and we could have called ourselves anything as we didn't have any other identification checks. This seemed to be the same in the U.S.—no passport or baggage checks when flying within American airspace. Given Cini's attempted hijacking, Canadian airports would have been much more vigilant, but perhaps American airports wouldn't be as vigilant. I was a policeman long enough to know that policemen can make excellent criminals; I arrested several and saw them put away for a long time for quite sophisticated crimes like money laundering and corruption.

Needing cash quickly, and with all other avenues failing, I had some fragments of a plan. All I had to do was demand money and a parachute without passengers being alerted. I knew from experience that Boeing 727 aircraft were able to facilitate an emergency bailout or skydive via the aft staircase, and not only could it take off with its stairs down, but the stairs could also be lowered in flight. It was a risk-free plan. If I made it, Richard could be cared for. If I didn't survive, he would have premium hospital care anyway, and Yvonne and I would be reunited.

Chapter 19

Closing The Gap

Clifford Harding, March 10, 1974

My efforts on the case had eased somewhat after Charlotte and I had our discussion in the kitchen. The ultimatum that she gave me was my family, or Cooper. Ultimately, I chose my family, and I was able to strike a healthy balance between trying to find out Cooper's identity and being at home with the girls. There were certain terms and conditions imposed on me, one of them being that I was no longer permitted by Charlotte to bring case files or notes home. Additionally, if any mention of the case came up at home, I would have to find an apartment of my own and a divorce lawyer. Although I was allowed to work on the case between office hours, if I found myself facing the temptation to stay in the office late, I had to immediately leave and come home.

In truth, when I stepped away from the case somewhat, things improved for me. We went on our first family vacation to Miami in March of 1974, and the girls were only five and three years old. They absolutely loved the beach, and we ate at some amazing restaurants. It was the best thing we had done in our turbulent marriage. Charlotte and I were sitting on our towels on the beach, and watching the girls laugh and build sandcastles together made me feel wonderful. Helen was full of mischief, and at one point, she tipped a bucket of sea water over Charlotte's head. She gasped and looked straight at little Helen, and when Helen giggled, we all laughed.

After drying herself off, Charlotte said to me, "You know, this was what you were missing when you imprisoned yourself in the Cooper case. You missed Helen's first steps. You missed Celine's first day of elementary school. Of course, if you had missed our wedding anniversary or my birthday, I would already be on my second husband, dear!"

"I know. It is a little easier now, but I still struggle sometimes, knowing he is out there somewhere, not giving the slightest damn about anything or anyone. I was just so anxious to locate him. One evening recently, on my way home, I picked up a book about anxiety and dark thoughts, and I read it cover to cover in a single sitting. It describes a scaly, tentacled monster that can live inside and latch onto people. It can control your thoughts, and any time a bad thought enters the mind, you should acknowledge that it is the monster flexing its tentacles. It resonated a lot with me. I've had to learn to accept that it was there and that any time I was experiencing obsessive or anxious thoughts, it was just the monster. Nothing else." I have never been a fan of woo-woo self-help stuff, but I did find this very interesting, although I can't recall the name of the book as it was probably thrown in the trash after a number of years.

Over time, I didn't find myself being as bitter, and spending time with the girls helped to rid me of the tentacled monster. Charlotte didn't really understand it, and it was hard to explain, but it helped ease some of my anxieties over the years. It really stuck with me. I realized that was what Cooper had become within me—a festering parasite that would feed on every ounce of happiness I had. Within a couple of years, he took the experience of seeing my children in their early formative years from me, and I would never forgive him for it.

After a refreshing vacation, I was slightly more pleasant to be around in the office, and people started interacting with me again. Within our office, it was widely accepted that Cooper was dead or that he had successfully left the United States. The case was very much open from an investigative point of view, but people of interest were dropping off, and overall activity on our end was quite low by this point.

I had always wanted to turn my attention to suspects outside the United States, but it was always a risky move because that would come under the purview of the CIA, which didn't play a role in the investigation to this point because it was a domestic hijacking and not a foreign one. During a meeting with a special agent in charge, I asked if I could contact our Canadian and Mexican counterparts to see if they could offer any leads or anyone they felt could match the description or profile of Cooper. When contacting law enforcement in other countries or jurisdictions, I had to have the blessing of a deputy assistant director, and I was promised that my request would be passed up the line, although it could take a while for them to respond.

***

Throughout the hijacking, Cooper displayed extensive knowledge of the aircraft. The configuration of having the jet fly at ten thousand feet with the flaps down to fifteen degrees, the landing gear down, the cabin depressurized, and the stairs down was very precise. Surely he knew the aircraft well, and in the early days, some pilots were questioned as people of interest. But like the skydiving community, the airline pilot community is also very small, and there were no pilots or stewardesses who were quick to call us and tell us that they believed their captain, co-pilot, or flight engineer could be the hijacker. I called a few pilots that I had connected with over the years and asked them some questions, but I reassured them that they wouldn't require a lawyer, nor would anything be recorded. A common theme was that until November 24, 1971, they didn't seem to be aware that the 727-100 could take off or land with its stairs down.

Based on additional information about what Cooper actually said during the hijacking, which I became aware of while in the tower as these events unfolded in Seattle, he insisted that the aircraft could depart SeaTac with the stairs down, saying, "It can be done—do it!" There was one suspect, Kenneth Christiansen, who was a purser with Northwest Orient Airlines. The purser would have been a lead flight attendant, and he was forty-five years old at the time of the hijacking. Although he resembled Cooper a little bit, witnesses couldn't conclusively identify him, and from an investigative point of view, commandeering an aircraft from his own airline where it would be likely for someone to know and recognize him was madness. He had experience as an aircraft mechanic after the war, but very likely wouldn't have had the specialist knowledge Cooper displayed. He was ruled out in my eyes.

Another interesting suspect was Robert Rackstraw, a former paratrooper, helicopter pilot, and Vietnam veteran. He had a colorful criminal past, and several people were quick to put him forward as someone capable of carrying out the heist. Of course he was; however, this man was a pro and wouldn't have taken the wrong parachute. Did he look like Cooper? He did a little, but he was only twenty-eight years old on November 24, 1971. He looked a little older than twenty-eight, but not old enough to be in his mid-forties to early fifties. Although a few amateur sleuths articulated compelling hypotheses implicating Rackstraw as the culprit, I never believed that Rackstraw was Cooper. But some circumstantial evidence at the time and more contemporary digging made him a very interesting suspect.

Ted B. Braden, a former U.S. Army member with deep parachuting expertise from his time in elite Airborne divisions, has been occasionally spotlighted in the Cooper case discussions. His known criminal activities, including a trucking scam and instances of going AWOL, combined with his military acumen, paint a picture of a man capable of such a daring feat. However, no concrete evidence ties Braden to the crime. Richard McCoy, who orchestrated a similar hijacking, once alluded to the fact that if anyone could've survived Cooper's jump, it would've been someone with Braden's skillset. Despite this, discrepancies in Cooper's eyewitness descriptions and Braden's appearance cast doubt on this theory. He wasn't officially named as a suspect, but he certainly was. Again, this was not the guy. He had already served time, and his prints were on file, so he would have been busted by this stage.

My attention then turned to the possibility of an insider at Boeing, which led me to Sheridan Peterson. He seemed to fit the profile, with the correct age and a close enough physical description, although he had blue eyes. Peterson had experience as a smokejumper, which involves parachuting into wildfire zones, so he had the airborne skillset that many associated with Cooper's audacious escape. Additionally, Peterson's time as a technical editor at Boeing in Seattle gave him potential knowledge about the plane used in the hijacking, which added another intriguing layer to an already suspicious character. Yet, while these facts may stir curiosity, it's important to underscore that no direct evidence has solidly connected Peterson to the hijacking. He wasn't in the country on November 24, 1971, and he seemed to have a solid enough alibi. Despite his fascinating profile, the FBI never definitively pinpointed him as the elusive Cooper.

None of these guys were cops, and English was their first language. My profile of Cooper seemed to vary wildly from the generally accepted one. Typically, when someone exclaims that everyone around them is crazy and that everyone is wrong, what that person requires is a mirror held up in front of them to see who is crazy and wrong. Over the years, many people would try to hold up a mirror to get me to see my own reflection, but I was never going to accept a mirror being held up in front of me.

After exploring the possibility that Cooper could have been associated with Boeing, I realized that an insider within Boeing would have been ratted out the same way a pilot or a flight attendant would have been ratted out. Nearly three years had passed, and unless the airline industry had the most sophisticated wall of silence in the history of criminal investigations, Cooper was not employed in the airline industry in any shape or form, despite having specialist knowledge of the aircraft itself.

***

At the end of 1974, after waiting months for my request to communicate with the authorities above and below our northern and southern borders, I got called to meet with one of the deputy assistant directors who came to the field office to meet with me. We exchanged pleasantries, had a cup of coffee, smoked a cigarette or two, and went through the rigors of small talk before he eventually told me that he couldn't authorize me to communicate with authorities in either Canada or Mexico. I was told very firmly that any investigative work outside of our national borders would have to sit with the CIA, and if the Bureau set a precedent of its agents investigating foreign nationals, it would cause a diplomatic incident with the CIA and would be difficult to both justify and reverse later on.

I fell just a yard short of telling him that his reasoning was complete bullshit and that the FBI had frequently liaised with authorities outside of the United States. In the tumultuous landscape of the 1960s, while the FBI's primary mandate was domestic, the intricacies of international crime and espionage often saw its reach extend beyond American shores. The shadows of the Cold War necessitated robust counterintelligence efforts, with the Bureau actively delving into espionage matters that spilled over international boundaries. Additionally, the U.S. carved out extraterritorial jurisdictions that permitted the FBI to pursue investigations related to crimes committed against American citizens or interests abroad, such as terrorist acts. To enhance our global footprint, we established liaison roles, fostering collaboration with allied foreign law enforcement and intelligence agencies. This was further cemented by the presence of FBI legal attachés, known as "Legats," who were stationed in U.S. embassies and facilitated crucial cross-border communication and cooperative investigations. Even so, while the FBI's international involvement in the 1960s was undeniable, it's important to note that it largely played a supportive or intermediary role, distinct from the more overt international operations of the CIA.

Despite my pleading, it all fell on deaf ears, and I was told that I should keep my focus on other cases and more pressing priorities. The little tentacled monster was writhing, squirming, and spreading throughout my body. This answer felt completely off, and considering we were dealing with a skyjacking in American airspace that nobody was near solving, this aroused huge suspicion in me. I knew it was time to take matters into my own hands.

Chapter 20
Planning

Dan Cooper, November 21, 1971

When I had only nine days left to prevent Richard from being sent across the country, I called to visit him. He was unaware of what was going on, but he seemed to be glad to see me and was happy for my visit. As I was leaving, one of the staff members stopped me and told me a tiny bit of good news: I had gained an extra week of time, which wasn't much but was still appreciated. However, I was also told that if arrangements were not in place by December 7th, Richard would be transferred to Huron Park Hospital in Ontario, as that was the only facility that had availability and could meet Richard's needs. Huron Park Hospital was at least a six-hour drive from where we lived, and I told them that I was doing my upmost to get better arrangements in place. I already told them my plan was to take Richard home with nursing care rather than have him transferred to an impossible location away from his only visitor. I knew that I needed to move quickly with the limited time I had left.

When Richard and I were together for his visit, I held his hand and hugged him. He hugged me back, and I said, "Au revoir, mon chou!" It suddenly occurred to me that this could be the last time I see Richard. When I walked out the door, I looked back in, and he smiled at me. I was happy knowing that my last memory of Richard would be his smile as I left.

***

When investigating a crime, there are always the five w's: the who, the what, the where, the when, and the why. I needed to not only answer all of those questions for myself but also remove any clues that would allow the authorities to answer them. The who was me, yet it couldn't be me either. Changing one's appearance isn't too much of a challenge, and I decided I would dye my grey hair black and pick up a new black suit that I had never worn before. Most men of that era wore black suits and were more formally dressed for travel, so it was an easy choice. What I wanted to do was get a suit and raincoat that were slightly too large for my frame. One thing I noticed when trying to catch criminals was that their weight and build were always a deciding factor when deciding if someone matched a description, so if I wore a baggier suit, I could look like I weighed anything from my true weight of 165 pounds right up to 180 or 190 pounds. Another advantage would be that a slightly larger suit would be easier to move in if I had to crouch down, scale a fence or tree if I had to flee the airport, or evade capture after parachuting to the ground. Eye colour is always a defining feature, so I got a cheap pair of horn-rimmed wraparound sunglasses. I think the suit, shoes, and sunglasses cost me around forty dollars.

What was I going to do? In the roughest terms, I wanted to extort $200,000 from the airline and then escape using a parachute. If I were alerted that a hijacker wanted $200,000 and a parachute, I would make sure that the parachute was faulty or wouldn't open so that the money could be returned to its rightful owner. I considered bringing my own parachute, but a man carrying a parachute would have been both suspicious and noticeable. Parachute containers are very obvious, and I may not have been able to bring one on board in a carry-on bag. Canadian and American airports had cops—it wasn't completely lawless back then, so I needed to avoid attracting their attention at all costs.

One of the most bizarre hostage situations I encountered during my time on the force was when two kidnappers were holding a family hostage in their home in Montreal about five years prior, and the kidnappers wanted two pizzas delivered to the house. Initially, I wanted to lace the pizzas with barbiturates so we could lift the kidnappers and have their prosecution paperwork completed by the time they woke up. Doing this was ruled out, just in case one of the hostages had eaten a slice and came to harm, because then *we* would have been prosecuted.

So that was the reason why I was going to ask for two sets of parachutes—two back parachutes and two front parachutes—to imply that I was going to take a hostage. The authorities wouldn't know which parachutes I would take or which the hostage would take, so they could tamper with neither. All of this had to happen without the passengers noticing, or if they somehow did notice, I had to make it so that they couldn't approach or corner me. Overpowering someone with a gun is straightforward. A firearm is a one-directional weapon that can only harm the person directly in front of the barrel or the person holding it. An explosive device had me covered from every direction, and it was likely to incite more fear than a pistol, especially in the United States, where people bring their shotguns to church on Sundays. I decided to take my revolver anyway as a backup.

Dynamite would be easy for me to get a hold of, as the station had plenty of seized dynamite that was confiscated under the Explosives Act. If anyone didn't store or handle their dynamite correctly or didn't have the appropriate licences and permits, we seized it and kept it securely in the station before having it disposed of. This was part of my role—signing off on evidence or dangerous substances to be disposed of. Getting my hands on explosives was easy, as I had the key to the secure holding area of hazardous evidence and weaponry, and it wouldn't arouse suspicion. We had had some explosives training as well, and I was well enough versed in improvised and home-made explosive devices. All I needed in addition to six sticks of dynamite were wires, a cylindrical battery, and a glass saline vial that could work as a tilt sensor. I went down to the station and simply lifted them without any difficulty.

After grabbing the explosive materials and a pair of confiscated motorcycle goggles, I took myself down to the infirmary and grabbed two first aid kits. They were plentiful, and I knew they would come in handy. I also managed to find some antibiotic medication, which I took on my way out. Satisfied that I had everything I needed, I walked out of the station and drove home. It was that simple. I happened to have a cheap attaché case at home that I barely used, and all it needed was some dust wiped from it after I pulled it out from the back of the wardrobe in my bedroom. In this attaché case, I could easily carry the components for the bomb and connect everything together on the morning of my flight.

Where I was going to do this job was a tough choice, but I knew that the when needed to be immediately. Given my position in the RCMP, I had appeared at press conferences and on television to comment on high-profile cases, so being recognized was somewhat of a risk factor. I decided that this would have to be done in the United States, where nobody was likely to recognize me and where I could flee back across the border into Canada.

Any heist that was time-sensitive meant that the authorities would have to act quickly. Flying from San

Francisco to New York would give the authorities ample time to plot my demise, so I needed a short flight. The only area I was familiar with in the United States was Tacoma and the surrounding area. I already had access to aerial photographs of the area to establish a drop zone, so it would be ideal if I could land around there.

The only route I could see while looking at a map of the area was a short flight between Portland International Airport and Seattle Tacoma. I called Portland International Airport from a payphone in town and asked if there were any upcoming flights to Seattle, and I was told that there was a flight at 2:50 p.m. on Wednesday, November 24th, three days later, which was the eve of Thanksgiving. This suited me perfectly, as I figured there would be plenty of people travelling home for the holiday to blend in with or hide behind.

All I had to do was hand a stewardess a note with my demands and inform her that the passengers weren't to be notified. Upon landing in Seattle, after the money and parachutes were on board, I could ask the jet to take off again toward Mexico and jump soon after takeoff between Portland and Seattle. The aircraft could take off with its airstairs down, or they could be lowered in flight if the pilots refused to lower them for takeoff. The early flight time was perfect because if we landed at 5 p.m., which would be the worst-case scenario, fuelling would take between twenty and twenty-five minutes, and so we would hopefully be back in the air while there were still faint glimmers of daylight.

I double-checked the rules of entry into Canada from the United States and vice versa. I needed photographic identification or proof of citizenship, so what I decided to do was wear my citizenship. I would travel to Vancouver, British Columbia in my red tunic uniform under my real identity. Everyone knows that one can always trust a policeman, and I would be seen as trustworthy by airport security. The route I was going to take was flying from Montreal to Vancouver and then from Vancouver to Portland, where I would test out using an alias with the suit on in order to have a practice run without a functioning bomb on board. Come what may, after landing with the money when the job was done, I needed to get to Portland to fly back to Vancouver and then back to Montreal, wherein I could travel in uniform and hope that American authorities would not be harsh on an ID check on the way back if all went to plan. My travel plans were confirmed in that I would fly to Vancouver the following morning at 8 a.m., and my flight to Portland was at 6:30 p.m.

Entering the United States did not require me to have my passport, but I needed an alibi as to why I was in the Pacific Northwest on November 24, 1971. I decided I would call into the RCMP station in Burnaby, Vancouver between the two flights and tell them I was going around the stations over the next couple of days to carry out inspections. Then I would slip over the border, and the paper trail would only ever have me going from Montreal to Vancouver and back again. The flight time to Vancouver from Montreal is about six hours, giving me a little time to stop at Banbury, which isn't far from Vancouver Airport. Then I would return to the airport for the ninety-minute flight to Portland.

I had frequently travelled to Tacoma, but my problem was that I had resigned from NORAD earlier in the year and would have no reason to be there. The only option was to show paperwork from the Canadian Secrets Act if I were ever questioned. I had an ID card, plus my RCMP badge and rank insignia pin, which Canadian and American border patrols at the time would have recognized easily. My identity was easily verifiable, and even if my "Sorry, I can't tell you—that's classified" excuse was to fail, it would at least buy me some time to go on the run. The only thing would be to create a contingency plan for telling Richard's nurses to work with the authorities to get Richard placed in a hospital nearby.

Given that I was so short on time, I gathered my things that evening and made sure my uniform looked pristine and that my insignia badges and medals were pinned to my tunic. I took a look at the first aid kits that I had picked up at the infirmary but noticed that they didn't contain any pain relief medicine. I still had Yvonne's stock of morphine syrettes at home, along with her Benzedrine; I could never bring myself to throw them out after she passed. So, I decided I would take those with me. I polished my boots, put some clothes in a small suitcase, and put the other materials in the attaché case.

***

My biggest worry was somehow losing the courage to follow through with the plan. I awakened at 5:30 a.m. on the 22nd and put on my uniform and Stetson. I looked as if I were going to some form of ceremony, and I ensured I had all my medals pinned and arranged in a neat row on my left breast pocket. I called for a cab to take me to the airport, and like I predicted, everyone was cordial to me. I purchased a return ticket for Vancouver, which would return me home on the 29th of November at noon. For the flight, I was given a complimentary upgrade to first class after checking in my small suitcase, but I kept my attaché case with me.

I was offered martinis that I wouldn't drink in uniform, and the food was okay. I put my head back and was surprised to fall asleep for around an hour because I was tired. I was awake the night before, tossing and turning and trying to think of contingencies if my plan were to take a left turn. I kept the briefcase on my knee for the entire flight, even though an explosive device hadn't yet been created. When I got to Vancouver, my suitcase was first on the baggage reclaim carousel, and I went straight into a cab to the Banbury RCMP station. When we were just pulling up outside the station, I lied to the driver and told them I forgot something at the airport and that we needed to go back after I informed the men in the station. The taxi driver agreed and waited outside with my suitcase still in the trunk while I calmly walked inside, holding my briefcase.

The men at the desk stood to attention immediately, and I told them I was in town for the next few days and to have records in place as well as the common areas scrubbed to prepare for inspection. One asked me if I wanted to take a car or get a ride to another one of the three stations, but I said no. The reason I got a cab in the first place was because cruisers and patrol vehicles were for emergency response only—not for picking people up from the airport, not for leaving one's wife at the hair salon, nothing like that. I was offered coffee, but I said no because I was in a rush and had to leave quickly. The men bid me farewell, and I got back into the taxi to return to the airport.

There were bathrooms inside the departures terminal building, and I took my suitcase into the bathroom to remove my uniform, hang it on the stall of the bathroom door, and change into the black business suit before packing my uniform back in the suitcase. I sat in the bathroom and stared at my folded uniform inside the still-open suitcase, and I was quite amazed at the shame I was supposed to feel but didn't. To me, it was just a red tunic, boots, and some shiny pieces of metal with ribbons attached. I saw the glint of the mother-of-pearl tie clip on my clip-on tie but decided not to wear it for now, opening the top buttons of my shirt instead.

I left the bathroom and went to the Hughes Airwest ticketing desk for the flight to Portland International. I checked my suitcase, and the ticketing agent asked for my name for the baggage tag and the ticket. The name I gave was "Frank Martin." When I received my one-way ticket, I said goodbye, and that was that. In those days, Hughes had big yellow airplanes, and when I got on board, I sat at the front of the aircraft in the front row near the cockpit. I kept my briefcase and raincoat over my knee, and I never once thought people were staring at me—I seemed to be blending in just fine. I read a magazine through the duration of the flight, and before I knew it, I had landed in Portland.

When I got my baggage back in Portland, I asked one of the airport staff where I could stay the night as I had to come to town suddenly. She recommended the Benson Hotel in downtown Portland, describing it as the crown jewel of Portland. It sounded pricey, but I didn't care as I had five hundred American dollars with me, and a nice hotel would be something of a treat. It was pouring rain when I got outside, so I put on my raincoat, zipped it all the way to the top, and closed all the buttons. When I got outside to the line of yellow cabs lined along the curb at the front of the airport, I decided to speak only in French with some broken English so the cab driver would know to take me to the Benson without asking me too many questions.

The Benson was simply stunning. The lobby was very bright, with a huge overhanging chandelier, dark wood reception desks, and immaculate cream floor tiles with black glinting speckles. I checked into the hotel, gave "Lucien LeClerc" as my name in broken English, and paid with cash. When I handed over $210 for seven nights in the hotel, I wondered what Yvonne would have thought of spending that kind of money for a short hotel stay. Interestingly, the lady behind the desk was a fluent French speaker, and we conversed for a few minutes. She told me her name was Suzanne, and she was originally from Baie-Comeau but was now living in Portland. I told her I was from Quebec City and was here to join my in-laws for Thanksgiving. This put me at ease and settled my nerves somewhat. She gave me a key with a cream enamel keychain with the number 333 embossed in green on it. I gathered my belongings back into my hand, and we bid one another adieu.

I took the elevator up to the third floor and walked about half-way down the hall on the left to find my room door. When I entered, I placed the briefcase on the dressing table, removed my dripping raincoat, and hung up my suit in the wardrobe. I stood in the room wearing only my underwear and looked out the window to the street below. My room had a front-facing window, and I could see an ocean of fast-moving umbrellas below. I felt hungry because I hadn't eaten all day, but I didn't want to eat just in case I threw it all up. Things got very real all of a sudden, and I felt it would have been easier at that point to just go home.

***

The following morning, I was walking to a pharmacy that was located near the Pioneer Courthouse, about half a mile away from the hotel. The courthouse was a beautiful building, and there was a tourist sign outside that described it as the oldest federal building in the Pacific Northwest. There were iron railings surrounding the building on either side of the entrance steps to the building, and there were a few posters and signs fixed to the railings petitioning to save the courthouse and prevent it from being demolished. I paused to look at it and gulped for a moment, realizing I could be here another time in the future in a very different capacity.

The pharmacy was a small family store that had a

stack of hair dyes on the rear wall. I picked up a semi-permanent black dye, and the only other things I needed were vitamin C and two bottles of expensive shampoo. One evening, Yvonne had decided to dye her hair, but when she shrieked at the colour of it, I was ordered to purchase shampoo and vitamin C. In this state, I knew not to ask too many questions, but after several hours of scrubbing, she had managed to strip the dye from her hair by mixing the shampoo with the vitamin C. To my amazement, it worked! So if and when I got back to the hotel, I would wash the dye out of my hair using this method. I had considered using boot polish instead of dye, but it would be too hard to get off of my scalp and fingers. I spent decades polishing boots and making others polish their boots, and I was well aware that the stuff is designed to stick to skin and that too much could go wrong.

After returning and sitting in my hotel room for a while, staring at my briefcase and paper shopping bag from the pharmacy, I decided that getting something to eat was a priority, and for whatever reason, I was in the mood for seafood. I showered and put on my shirt and raincoat before going downstairs to hail a cab. I asked the cabbie to take me to a seafood restaurant, and he took me to Dan & Louis Oyster Bar.

The inside of the restaurant had a family feel, and it was nautical themed. It had life preserver rings and black-and-white vintage photos all over the walls. There was an alcove on the left of the entrance door where I had a table by myself. The food was terrific, and I was surprised by how much I ate. For a while, I forgot about what was coming up the following day and sat at the table for a long time, ordering half-shell oysters by the half-dozen and quietly slurping them. I must have sat there for a good two hours until it was approaching closing time and I left. It was nearly 10 p.m. by the time I got back, and I went straight to the elevator. As I jolted upward toward the third floor, I wondered if I was deep inside the last twenty-four hours of my life.

Chapter 21
The End of the Road
Clifford Harding, January 26, 1975

I was finding it very hard to accept that the Bureau didn't support me in pursuing leads or suspects that were outside of the United States. Plenty of the circumstantial evidence I uncovered indicated that there was at least a fair chance that the hijacker wasn't an American but rather a foreigner who seemed to know the Pacific Northwest. After a while, I thought the tentacled monster within had left, but slowly it was starting to grow back. I was never one to take no for an answer, and I needed to try and speak to any contacts I had in the RCMP or the DFS. I didn't have that many, but I decided to make some calls here and there. Given the time difference, I had to get some clearance from Charlotte to make some of these calls from home or to stay in late.

After around a month, Charlotte put an end to me making calls at home because I would get frustrated, shout and swear down the phone, and ultimately upset the children. The DFS were actually quick to get back to me, and a couple of people they sent me as potential suspects were very interesting. Some of the cops they sent were either accused or internally found guilty of collaborating with the then up-and-coming drug lord, Pablo Escobar. The Columbian and Mexican drug cartels had already established some entry points into the United States, both with the help of easily bought U.S. officials and those at the Mexican borders.

The narrative in my head was making some form of sense. Drug cartels and operations involving large amounts of cash and piles of drugs often needed the cash to be laundered or transported through different means. There was one suspect of interest, Guadalupe "Lupe" Torres, who lived near Guadalajara, Mexico, and I wanted to talk to him. He seemed to fit everything in the profile: he was in his late forties, had dark hair and dark eyes, had done jail time for assisting a bank robbery while still employed as a police officer, and up until recently he had been living in a run-down apartment but somehow managed to buy a nice new house in the suburbs of Guadalajara in the summer of 1972. He was on probation, and through someone I trusted in the CIA, I managed to get a contact number for the office of his probation officer.

Telling them I was in the FBI was a no-go, so I decided to come up with a new identity of my own. When I spoke to the probation officer, I told him that I was an investigative journalist who was investigating the hijacking of Northwest Orient Flight 305 and looking for D.B. Cooper. I made an offer in that I would send him a cashier's check for any information that he had on the guy, and I asked him to name his price. The price provided to me was five hundred dollars. So, I agreed to send the check in the mail and was told that upon receipt, any paperwork or information that could be sent to me would come. I told him to mail the information he had to Hotel Sorrento in Seattle, an old boutique hotel where Charlotte and I used to go for drinks and music in their famous Fireside Room. The name I gave for the mail was "Brian Taylor."

My contact in the CIA was solid. I'll call him "Peter." We became friendly when I was assisting in the running of the FBI liaison office in Saigon between 1967 and 1970. We used to smoke our cigarettes and complain about our superiors. At that time, the CIA didn't really understand why we were in Vietnam, and to be quite honest, I didn't really know either. It was mostly a bureaucratic nightmare that prevented me from being with Charlotte for large portions of our two pregnancies. Some colleagues in both the CIA and FBI were wary of Peter, and some believed he was a Russian spy. He was of Russian descent on his mother's side and had a sneaky, rat-like face. I knew keeping a guy like him on my side could be beneficial to me, and I didn't distance myself from him when most others did. I asked him to check into death records, public records in relation to land ownership, and anything else he could find. Of course, he had a price too, and I had to write another check for two hundred dollars.

After waiting a few weeks, I called the probation officer again because I had checked at the Sorrento a few times and nothing had arrived yet. I didn't show my badge or anything during my visits, but I still feared that going in a fourth or fifth time would arouse suspicion. I was promised that the information was on its way and that I would need to be patient because the snail mail from Mexico to Seattle was especially slow. I was anxious at home, and when Charlotte asked why I was going to the Sorrento without her, she started to become suspicious of me. When I went to bed at night, she would turn the other way, and when I asked her one night what was wrong, she just said, "Go to sleep, Clifford!"

She knew I was pursuing Cooper again, and by the time I wanted to claw my way back and get back on the wagon, it was too late. I was awake at night, tossing and turning, wondering if what would arrive in the mail would be enough to finally unravel Cooper's identity. Without the widespread availability of information on the internet that we have today, there wouldn't have been much public information about the case other than the description of Cooper and the fact that he had bailed with $200,000 by parachute from the back of a Boeing 727 jetliner. Finally, when I checked at the Sorrento again, the package for "Mr. Taylor" had finally arrived, and I took it straight to the office, but wouldn't brandish anything in there for fear of being caught and reported.

Inside were two photographs: one mugshot and one military photograph with the suspect in his parachute gear. It was a black-and-white photograph and had 1950 written on the back of it in ink. The mugshot depicted a middle-aged and haggard man with shame in his eyes from his former colleagues having to take his mugshot. The picture was from 1964, and the man was released in 1970. The one detail that jumped out at me right away about Torres was that he didn't have loose skin on his neck. One young passenger on Flight 305, William Mitchell, who sat on the other side of the aisle from the hijacker and stewardess Tina Mucklow, was adamant that Cooper had loose skin on his neck like a turkey wattle. He was close enough to get a good look at him, yet at a distance that allowed him to absorb more of the hijacker's features, and that was gospel to me. Sitting too close to someone can be more of a hindrance than a help when it comes to a description. The height on the mugshot was six feet one, which was close enough to five feet ten. I wasn't convinced, but I had a telephone number that was provided to me, and I decided to call the man, but I would need to do it from a public payphone somewhere and not at home or in the office.

I knew I would need a small fortune to contact this guy, so I went into a phone booth at the Northgate Mall in downtown Seattle and had around five dollars worth of quarters to call Guadalajara. I wasted two or three quarters dialing the number with the call being disconnected, but after some attempts, I heard a muffled voice answer the phone.

"Hola!"

"Ingles?" I asked him.

"Yes, who is calling?"

"My name is Brian Taylor. I am a journalist investigating the case of the hijacking of Northwest Orient Flight 305 and am on the trail of D.B. Cooper, who is still at large. A former colleague from your days in the army provided me with your telephone number."

"Is that so?" he said in a skeptical tone, because he could smell the horse shit from Mexico. "Well, for a journalist, you sound like you would make a very good cop. Not many journalists immediately open with a case they are *investigating,* but rather a story they are *researching.* I know why you're calling, and I'll have you know that I've been out of the army for twenty years and only purchased this home three years ago from money I inherited on my father's death. Would you care to tell me who you really are and what this is really about?"

No matter where in the world cops are, we always know our own. "Okay, Torres, you got me. I am from the FBI, and clearly you know I shouldn't be talking to you. I am not giving my real name, but I wanted to ask you some questions if you'd be willing to speak with me."

"Well, if the hijacking of Northwest 305 is being investigated by the FBI, you are clearly from the office of either Portland or Seattle, am I right? Next time you speak to someone behind your employer's back, tell them you are from the Sheriff's Department instead. More offices, and more for you to hide behind, amigo!" Then he burst into laughter. We both knew he was right, and if the shoe were on the other foot, I would have laughed at his pathetic lies too. Then I topped the payphone up with some more quarters.

"Well, you know the case, and you're a jumper—what is your take?"

"Cooper is dead. He was given four parachutes, and the newspapers said that he took the NB6 bailout rig over a civilian steerable canopy. If he tied a cotton bank money bag to himself and jumped at ten thousand feet while tumbling, the parachute wouldn't open. The only way Cooper will be discovered is when a hunter realizes he is pissing on his bones in the forest!" Then I heard the phone's dial tone and knew he had hung up on me.

I slammed the phone booth door on my way out, and some passersby started staring at me, so I lifted my hand to apologize to them. I took my glasses off and just sat on a metal bench beside the phone booth and stared blankly around me for about fifteen minutes. He wasn't the guy. He had a very distinctive accent, and there is no way that a Mexican accent would be able to be described as a "non-discernible" accent. I went back into the phone booth afterward to call Peter to see if there was any update on the information I had requested about this man's father dying and being left a large sum of money. Everything checked out just fine, and Torres was out of the game. The black hole of this case had chewed me up and spat me out yet again. It seemed that every promising lead over the past few years had just led me down a rabbit hole of hope, only to get a slap in the face and the door slammed on me when the person of interest being investigated had alibis or didn't match the evidence.

***

I was working late nights and found myself sleeping at my desk, and I often stayed at motels to avoid going home and feeling Charlotte's wrath. The case had completely taken me to a level of corruption that I had no idea how to stop. I was completely powerless, like an addict. I was never going to accept that this fucker was living a happy life somewhere while my life was falling apart at the seams. Work on other cases was starting to suffer; I was falling behind on paperwork, and other agents were asking me what I was doing. Anytime someone asked me, I either refused to answer or told them menacingly to back down. I took no crap from anyone—the only documented person that I had taken crap from was Cooper on November 24, 1971.

On August 1, 1975, I returned home late from the office to a sight I had been expecting for quite some time. On the other side of the front door were two suitcases and a large manila envelope. Inside the envelope was a handwritten note from Charlotte telling me that she had taken the girls out of town for a vacation of their own and that I needed to be gone by the time they returned on August 3rd. She ordered me to find somewhere of my own to live, explaining that the girls could visit me on the weekends. Behind the handwritten note were divorce papers that I had absolutely no intention of signing until I at least talked to Charlotte again. She had signed her portions of them, along with her lawyer's countersignature, and cited the reason as irreconcilable differences.

The only coping mechanisms I had were alcohol and making telephone calls to Peter to see if there was anything else he could get for me. When I sat that night on the phone with him, I had a brainwave and asked if there was any information he could get from the Mounties. He told me that he had tried in the past but had received little to no response from them. The Mexican authorities were somewhat slow to respond, but they did suggest a few people. The Mounties seemed to have suggested nobody, and I ordered him to see what he could get, and another check would go in the mail on Monday morning. He agreed, and we left the conversation at that for now.

***

When Charlotte and the girls returned and got out of the cab outside our house, I went out to them, and Charlotte held her hand up and took the girls past me through the front door and closed it behind them, leaving just the two of us outside. She told me it was over and that it would be better for the girls if I left. I was pleading with her in full view of the cab driver, but her mind was made up, and there was nothing I could do about it. I decided not to cause a scene in front of the girls and went back inside to collect my suitcases. I went to hug the girls, but they just retreated and walked slowly backwards up the stairs, staring at me like the stranger I was. This hurt me much more than when the love of my life told me she wanted me gone and that she would rather raise the girls mostly on her own, with me being more of a passing visitor in their lives. I loaded the suitcases into my car before driving to the Marco Polo Motel in Fremont. Charlotte didn't even say goodbye to me.

When I got out of the cab, I lifted my suitcases and brought them inside to check in. I got a ground-floor room that was adjacent to the parking lot and immediately went inside to hang up my clothes and make myself at home. There was a phone inside the room, and I called the office to tell them I couldn't make it in that day as I had a situation at home, but I didn't get much sympathy. I can't recall who answered the call, but I told them I was at the Marco Polo and could be reached here. I then called Peter, and he told me again that he could get no response or interest from anyone at the RCMP in relation to any suspects they felt would meet Cooper's profile. I had a flashback just then, and I went silent on the phone for a few seconds, prompting Peter to ask me if I was still on the line. I recalled to him that I had taken a group of RCMP who were recruited into NORAD from Tacoma to SeaTac airport one evening and asked if he could get me a list of names of NORAD recruits who came from Canada and that met Cooper's description. There was one man in particular that crept into my head, but he had graying hair instead of the dark black hair that Cooper had. I thought he could easily have been in his mid-50s even by then, and I had the sickening feeling of being led to the entrance of a rabbit hole once again. His name escaped me, and he wasn't very memorable, quite like Cooper. I tortured myself trying to recall this man's name, but it was gone.

***

A few days later, I had a knock on the door, and it was the receptionist from the motel telling me that a call had come through for me at the front desk. When I got on the phone, one of the deputy directors came on the line and told me to come down to the office immediately, and then slammed the phone down. I knew even then that I was caught and had to face the music. When I walked in the door, everyone stopped what they were doing and seemed to stare at me. Nobody even acknowledged me, and I went straight for the office at the end of the hall, where I was directed to go by the front desk. There were three of them there, and without greeting me or making small talk, one of them cut to the chase.

"So, going outside of your jurisdiction, are we? Your rat in the CIA has been flushed out, and he's flushed you out with him. What the fuck were you thinking, Harding?"

I sunk my head into my hands. "I thought I had some good leads, sir."

"Good leads? The only thing you have accomplished is getting the CIA's backs up and pushing everybody away. Look, I know you have gotten involved too deeply in this. We all make mistakes; I get that. We all have cases like this, but you have gone too far! This is your last chance. If I ever hear that you are getting involved with this case again or are as much as in earshot of people talking about D.B. Cooper, your badge is gone. Understood?"

"Understood, sir!" Then their looks told me to get the fuck out of that office without them actually having to say it. I should have been fired or suspended, but somehow I got to cling on to my position, and I knew I would have to keep my nose clean from then on. I went straight back to the motel to call Charlotte and ask when I could see the girls, and she said she would bring them to see me the following day, and I could take them to the movie theater or to the park. I tried to convince her that I was done with the case, but she didn't believe me. I had already said it a few times before to her, and she was at the end of her patience.

I never really knew what I wanted to achieve in this pursuit, but I knew one thing. I'd lost everything because of it.

Part Five

Once a man of honest trade,
Now a phantom, a renegade,
He sees a chance to steal some gold,
A gambit risky, a tale untold.

The moon above, a witness cold,
He creeps into the rich man's hold,
His heart aflutter, his hands a-shake,
One desperate chance he has to take.

Jude Morrow

Chapter 22

PDX

Dan Cooper, November 24, 1971

My eyes fluttered open at 6:45 a.m., and it was a freezing cold morning. When I opened my curtains, it reminded me of the classic Canadian fog, and my initial fear was that all flights for the day would be cancelled. I stayed at the Benson Hotel, which was known as one of the most upscale hotels in Portland, and from the miles of dark wood panelling, crystal chandeliers, and the luxurious room I had, I could see why. After an hour or so, I looked out my window again and saw the fog lifting, which gave me mixed emotions because if the flights were grounded, I wouldn't have to proceed with the plan and I could just go home. However, I had already come this far and needed to keep Richard at the forefront of my thoughts.

I picked up the cheap, black Clairol hair dye that I had bought from the pharmacy and massaged it through my greys and on my eyebrows. I had to wait an hour for the dye to take effect before washing it all out in the bathtub. After rinsing it out, I quickly dried my hair with the bathroom hairdryer, and I was surprised to see myself looking a little younger, and if I do say so myself, quite convincing. The bathtub looked like an old pool of tar, and I pulled the plug and scrubbed the bathtub so it came up like new. I scrubbed my hands in the sink to ensure all the black dye was gone before opening the wardrobe to put on my suit. I pulled on my new brown shoes and my black suit, which, upon looking in the mirror, seemed a mismatch to me, but it was too late to change.

I sat on my bed with my clip-on tie in my hand. The clip was already on it, and I noticed a small hole in it where my RCMP pin used to be. It was getting close to 9:30 a.m., and I decided to go downstairs for breakfast. I barely ate, picking at some ham and eggs while sipping a cup of white coffee. A server asked me if everything was okay, and I said in French that I was feeling slightly "malade" and rubbed my stomach before smiling at her.

I decided to go outside for some fresh air and a cigarette. Standing beside me was a lady with a little dog, and I bent down to pet it, which the lady seemed to find endearing. It felt comforting to me for whatever reason—I never owned a dog, but I still felt compelled to pet this dog to expel some of the nervous energy I was now starting to feel inside. I bid the lady and her little dog farewell and looked up toward my open bedroom window, knowing what I would have to do next.

Even going up in the elevator to my room felt nauseating, but I just closed my eyes and took deep breaths. When the elevator dinged at my floor, it startled me, and I walked out. Luckily, nobody was there waiting to get in; otherwise, someone would have instantly known I was sketchy.

I've always been methodical, patient, and cautious. That's how I found myself in this dimly lit room, preparing for the heist that would make history. I started by taking everything I had gathered out of the case and laying it on the dressing table in a row. I had the explosive components prepared and lifted out the remaining items from my shopping bag to make sure I had everything else: goggles, a first aid kit, a revolver with two rounds, a flashlight, wire cutters, morphine syrettes, Benzedrine, some strong electrical tape, two lighters with fuel, and some aerial photographs to spot potential landing zones from the air.

My hands worked slowly but surely, twisting the wires together as I recalled the basic bomb disposal I had been taught and some improvised explosive devices that had been left in evidence at the station. I had six sticks of dynamite, a 9-volt battery, and an assortment of wires and switches. It was a simple setup, but it had to be convincing.

I positioned the dynamite sticks in a row inside a custom-fitted compartment in my attaché case. The dynamite was old but still potent. The nitroglycerin-based explosive had a sensitive nature, and it required a careful touch. I knew the chemistry; I knew the physics. I had to be delicate.

The detonation circuit was simple but effective. I connected the wires to two metal plates on either side of a small compartment. Inside that compartment, I placed a glass vial filled with a saline solution. *A basic tilt sensor,* I thought to myself. I also attached a command wire that I would tape to the right side of the case. The dynamite was placed on the left side, along with the battery, so there was a small distance between the command wire and the metal plate. If the command wire was secured in place, and the case was resting on my knee and held with both hands, the chances of accidental detonation were reasonably low.

The battery's positive terminal was wired to one plate, and the negative terminal was wired to a blasting cap, which was carefully inserted into the dynamite. The other plate was connected to the other side of the blasting cap, completing the circuit. If the case were tilted or shaken violently, the glass vial would break, allowing the saline solution to bridge the gap between the two plates, completing the electrical circuit. The resulting surge would trigger the blasting cap, igniting the dynamite and causing a devastating explosion.

I double-checked my connections and reviewed a mental checklist, ensuring everything was in order. It was a psychological tool as much as it was a real threat. The sight of the red sticks of dynamite and the hastily rigged wires had to be convincing.

My plan was set. My escape was plotted. All that was left was to board the plane and make my demands. As I closed the case, I took one last look at my creation. It was a thing of simple yet deadly beauty, constructed with precision and care. It was a symbol of my determination and cunning. I picked up the briefcase and headed for the door, a small, almost invisible smile playing at the corners of my mouth. My name would soon be known across the nation as a symbol of audacity and mystery. I ran my hands along my RCMP uniform hanging up inside the wardrobe and was filled with hope that I would wear it home again.

I took the briefcase and held it under my left arm instead of by the handle to keep it more secure, with my raincoat over the top of it. I put my right hand across my pockets to ensure I had everything: my wallet, pocket knife, wraparound sunglasses, and my shopping bag of extra supplies I couldn't put in the case or check on as luggage. When I pulled my hotel room door closed behind me, I expected to feel some sense of impending doom, but I didn't. When I got back downstairs, I looked toward the check-in desk for Suzanne, but she wasn't working, and I slipped outside.

I got into character by exaggerating my French accent on the way to the airport. For a taxi driver, if law enforcement were to ask about any suspicious passengers, an inconspicuous businessman in a black suit speaking broken English on the way to the airport is a needle in a haystack and very common. I just kept breathing steadily, staring out the window, and counting down the miles until Portland International Airport. Ten turned to eight, eight turned to four, and then four turned into an arrow pointing towards the exit to approach the airport.

When we got there, the taxi driver was speaking to me like I was deaf and stupid, trying to explain that he would have to go to the long-term parking lot and that there was a shuttle bus to the terminal. I just agreed, gave him a five-dollar bill for the fare, and got out of the car with the case and raincoat in hand without waiting for my change. What good would coins or money be to me anyway if it all went wrong?

The little shuttle had a double sliding door in the middle of it, and it looked like a train car on wheels. It didn't look like any bus I had ever seen, and I found it very odd. I was debating in my head whether to get on this bus, which would take passengers up to the second-level entrance gates, and I decided that I would. I was edging ever closer to the point of no return, and I knew it. There were plenty of empty seats, and I was surprised that there weren't more people, given that it was the day before Thanksgiving. I started to feel that by trying hard to blend in, I was standing out even more, as nine or ten seats on this bus were empty and there weren't a bunch of people to hide behind or blend into.

After we took the few-minute drive to the second-level entrances, I gathered everything, having to move somewhat unnaturally and slowly due to the nature of my cargo. I placed the briefcase flat on the ground and pushed it against the wall beside the entrance door with my raincoat over the top of it while I stood in front of it and blocked it. It was a big beige building with the control tower attached to it, and there was a big green glass walkway right in front of me stretching across from the entrance doors to the other parking lot on the other side of it. It seemed quiet here too, with not much going on. I truly thought there would be more people wishing to go home or travel over the Thanksgiving holiday, but clearly, I was wrong.

This began my series of lasts. I took in the scene outside briefly, possibly my last time standing on solid ground. Inside the terminal building, I harboured some nerves, but deep down, I wasn't too concerned if it was my last day on God's earth or not. The state would have to take care of Richard if I didn't come back alive. Either way, he won.

***

The terminal building was slightly more busy, and I gave myself something of a wide berth from everyone. I consciously avoided clusters of people but tried not to stand out too far on my own. The electronic arrivals and departures board was overhead, and my flight to Seattle-Tacoma Airport was departing in fifty minutes. There was overhead Northwest Orient Airlines signage pointing downstairs to where their ticketing desk was. United Airlines was upstairs, and there were some others downstairs too. I don't recall there being an escalator to take passengers down to the lower level, but I certainly recall holding the briefcase in both hands with the paper bag on top of it just in case I slipped or somehow fell down the stairs.

Just at the bottom of the stairwell was a row of ticketing desks to the left, and to the right down an open corridor were the baggage carousels and the lower-level exit doors. Of the row of ticketing desks, Northwest Orient was the first desk immediately to my left, with Pan American Airlines being slightly further down. There was a line, and I joined the back of it. I didn't talk to or acknowledge anybody there; I just stood still and looked straight ahead until there were only two people in front of me. It wasn't too late to turn around, but I had come this far. I took the briefcase by the handle with my left hand's index finger and thumb and used my other free fingers to hold the paper bag. I had my raincoat underneath my arm, concealing the briefcase slightly.

Quickly, the two people in front of me purchased their tickets, and when it was my turn, I asked, "Is this the right desk for your flight to Seattle?"

The ticketing agent, who wore the name Dennis on his name badge, said, "Yes, sir, it is. Would you like a one-way coach ticket?"

"Yes." Then I put my hand into my right pocket to produce the twenty-dollar bill for the fare and handed it over.

"May I take your name, please, for the ticket?"

It was there and then that I felt, even if just for a moment, that I could be Richard's hero, and I said, "Cooper...Dan Cooper."

"Thank you. Do you have any baggage to check for the flight?"

"No."

"Okay, sir. The departure area is at the end of this hall and to the right. Have a nice flight and happy Thanksgiving!"

After receiving the ticket, I just nodded and walked toward the departure gate, and on the way, a bar caught my eye. Not because I was in any mood for eating a large meal, drinking, or anything else, but because of the décor. I stopped to look at its art-deco furnishings and tilework. It immediately took me back to the last restaurant meal Yvonne and I had together in Regina, at the Brown Derby. I wanted to go inside, but there were only a handful of people there, so I decided not to. Passengers were congregating around the departure area, which was midway down the large hall with massive windows to look out onto the runway. I looked out the window and saw a covered gangway being attached to a United Airlines aircraft, and passengers were able to board through this gangway from the second-floor waiting areas.

I watched the United Airlines bird take to the air after zooming down the runway, and after seeing the airplane put its landing gear up, I knew we were next to board, and suddenly I felt the urge to go to the bathroom. There was a bathroom at the end of the waiting area at the very bottom, and I went into one of the stalls. I clipped open the briefcase and noticed the electrical tape around the command wire had loosened slightly, so I applied the last piece I had to it to secure it. I had an envelope, a small sheet of unlined paper, and a felt pen that I removed from my inside jacket pocket. I pondered what to write down on the note that I would give to the stewardess and how I should write it. I started writing in capitals, "MISS—," then I stopped and continued with normal handwriting: "I have a bomb in my briefcase; please sit beside me." I didn't know whether to write more or not and decided I wouldn't. I folded the note in half, placed it inside the envelope, and put the envelope back into the inside right pocket of my jacket.

As I sat in there, I heard the boarding call for Northwest Orient Flight 305 to Seattle. Just as I was about to stand up, I heard the bathroom door open, and I didn't want to go out while someone was in there. I listened intently to his flow, and he took forever and a day to wash his hands afterward. After I heard the door close, I left, and there were a few people standing at the departure gate door, which led out onto the runway. I was either last or second to last in the line, and through the window, I could see stewardesses assisting passengers over and holding umbrellas for them, which was slightly amusing to me. I debated whether to put the sunglasses on now or wait. I chose the latter.

I went straight up the aft airstairs and was again surprised to see so many empty seats on the aircraft. The 727-100 passenger liner was equipped to hold ninety or so seats, and I estimated that the flight was only one-third full at best. I could see down to the cockpit door, and I didn't see many in first class either. Immediately after the lavatory door on the right side as I entered the cabin, I noticed the empty back rows. I quickly sat down in seat 18E, and the memories came from our flight from Regina to Montreal.

While staring out the window at the terminal building, I was taken out of my daze by a flight attendant asking me if I wished for a drink, and I ordered a bourbon and 7UP. The drink was given to me, and I handed the stewardess another of my twenty-dollar bills. She asked if I had anything smaller, and I apologized because I didn't. She told me that I would get my change back once the rest of the passengers were served refreshments. I needed the drink to settle my nerves, and I thought to myself that it would likely be my last glass of bourbon. I can't recall what brand of bourbon it actually was, nor did I look at the drink menu protruding from the little pocket on the back of the seat in front of me. I wanted to give a toast to my father, and just as I did, the plastic glass slipped from my hand and onto the floor around my feet. I didn't get any on me, thankfully, or onto the briefcase. I took this as some form of disapproval from him and my mother and decided not to order another after it was cleaned up.

After the oxygen, safety, and escape demonstrations were given, the wheels started to turn. This was it.

Chapter 23
Sea-Tac to Reno
Dan Cooper, November 24, 1971

After the aircraft came to a halt and the engines stopped, an announcement came over the intercom system, advising all the passengers to remain in their seats until further instructions were given. I looked out the window, and the pickup rig with the stairs attached was making its way toward the aircraft to plug into the front portside exit door, along with a large car or van following slightly behind around the nose of the aircraft. At that point, it didn't matter to me if the FBI or the cops stormed the aircraft. I thought I was a dead man, but nobody else ought to die. So, I told Miss Mucklow that I was going to the bathroom and to wait until I returned.

I put the paper bag on top of the briefcase, holding it horizontally, and I went inside the lavatory directly behind my seat. I put the toilet seat down and set the briefcase on top of my knee to open it. I felt somewhat exhausted and drained from the two and a half hours in the air, so I opened the paper bag, took one of the Benzedrine from its bottle, and gulped it down without water. I rummaged through the paper bag, bypassing the first aid kit, flashlight, goggles, and morphine syrettes, before finding and grabbing the wire cutters. My hands were shaking, and I knew that with one wrong clip or mishap, the bomb would detonate. I clipped the command wire and disconnected the battery from the wires going into the terminals. I removed the saline vial, gripping it tightly in my hand, and put it into my jacket pocket. I considered flushing it, but I didn't want to leave any evidence in the aircraft waste holding tank. Knowing that the bomb was now disarmed, I breathed a sigh of relief and closed the briefcase before exiting the lavatory.

Returning to my seat, I noticed that the steps had been attached to the front exit door, and I sat back down. The passengers were still seated, and Miss Mucklow walked forward and out the exit while the fuel truck approached, and the truck's hose was attached to the fueling port just underneath the starboard wing. The passengers didn't seem to be too annoyed, and from what I saw, they all remained in their seats, save for perhaps one or two who may have retrieved something from an overhead storage compartment.

The front exit door was wide open, and I could see no flashing lights, which was very unsettling. Plus, it was dark, and visibility out the aircraft windows at night was far from optimal. We were on a dimly lit part of the runway as it was, and for all I knew, the cops could come aboard at any time. For the entire plan to be foiled, all that was needed was one SWAT team at the airstairs and another to come through the front entrance door. All the passengers were moved a few rows down, which left me feeling like I was a sitting duck. A single marksman's shot to the forehead would have finished me, and the bomb was already disarmed.

Before long, Miss Mucklow walked up the aisle, carrying a large cotton bag with a drawstring. Amazingly, none of the passengers stopped her, and when she sat the large bag beside me, I glanced inside it and saw the stacked bundles of twenty-dollar bills. I put my hands on either side of the bag to shake it slightly to see if dye packs were in there, but there weren't any. The bag was not a knapsack like I had requested, and I told her, "This isn't what I asked for."

She didn't seem to panic and said, "Can the passengers get off now?"

I paused for a second to ponder if I should let the passengers off the plane or send her back into the terminal building for a knapsack, because jumping with this cotton bag would mean tying it to myself or otherwise securing it to my person somehow. We couldn't wait any longer, and I didn't want to arouse suspicion amongst the passengers, so I told her the passengers could go. She looked at the bag as the passengers were getting up and commented that there was a lot of money there. Given what I had put her through, I reached into the bag and handed her one of the bundles of bills. It was easily a few months wages, but she immediately returned it and told me she wasn't permitted by the airline to accept tips.

The other two stewardesses approached me as the passengers shuffled off the jet. All was seemingly going to plan, and I knew we would be taking off momentarily. Instinctively, I lifted the money bag up to near my eye level and wondered how I would escape successfully with the money in this bag. The stewardesses were gathered around me, and I don't know why, but I wanted to break the tension like Miss Mucklow had earlier by asking the ladies to hold the bag to demonstrate how heavy it was. The ladies in turn held the bag, almost like a bag of trash, and nodded to agree with disapproving looks.

I then requested that the parachutes be brought aboard, quietly hoping to myself that they were ones I knew how to put on and operate. Miss Mucklow asked me if I would rather the pilots get the parachutes, and I reassured her that they weren't that heavy and she would manage just fine. I remembered that the pilot and one of the male crew members finished off Cini during his attempt, so I was not going to permit the flight crew to leave the cockpit.

Just before Miss Mucklow left again toward the front exit door, I asked for meals to be brought aboard for the crew in the event we were in the air for a prolonged period yet again. I think she just nodded and walked off. I shouted down, "Get me two maps too! A flight path map and one of the local area," but she didn't reply.

The first parachute came on—a tan backpack—and it was handed into my two open hands as I stood in the aisle. I inspected the front of it and saw the pull handle on it. At least this parachute seemed right, and I laid it on the seat in the row in front of me. Miss Mucklow stopped as if to wait for me to complain or raise concern, but when I looked at her again, I asked her to put all the shades down on the windows in our section, which she did before turning on her heels and returning to the exit door again. Next came the two front parachutes, and one was marked with a red X. I had no idea why that was there, and it filled my belly full of dread.

Going with the front reserves was no longer in my plan because, upon inspection, they were unable to clip to the harnesses of the backpacks. They were totally incompatible due to a lack of D-rings on the backpacks that the fronts could clip on to. I thought I could use the front parachute bags as a way to transport the money, and that shroud lines could be cut from the front canopies to secure the money to myself. I pulled the ripcord on the reserve, and it was a functional model. It had a pink or salmon canopy, and all the lines were neatly bundled and packed inside. I retrieved my pocket knife, cut three lines from the underside of the canopy, and laid the canopy itself over the seat in front of me. I was hesitant about opening the other reserve with the X on it in case, upon deployment, there was some form of smoke grenade or something that could sabotage the jump. Curiosity got the better of me, so I opened it. There appeared to be only the remnants of a canopy inside it. It looked like a store display model or a demo model.

Finally, the other backpack parachute came on, and it was in a green container. I sat this one beside the tan backpack and had the two front parachutes on my own seat. Miss Mucklow had a piece of paper and explained it was a printout of instructions for operating the parachutes, but I said, "No, thanks. I don't need them." With the open front reserve bag, I lifted out some of the bill bundles to see how many would fit, but it couldn't fit many. Miss Mucklow stared at the two backpack parachutes and sat in the aisle opposite where we were sitting on the way to Seattle, in seat 18C. I took the money bag out into the aisle and started wrapping one of the three lines I had cut around the neck of the money bag in an effort to secure it and make some form of loop to secure it to the harness. I was up to speed on knots and tying cargo, but my mind seemed to go blank, and I was getting frustrated. I started complaining that I should have had a knapsack, and Miss Mucklow just shrugged.

The phone rang, and she went quickly to answer it. She told me that the meals and maps had arrived and asked if she could go get them. I agreed, and she sighed as she got up to leave yet again. I loosened the knot at the top of the money bag and brought out some of the bundles of bills to put them in the briefcase. Ten of the bundles totaling twenty thousand dollars could fit in there, with room for perhaps another fifteen bundles to total fifty thousand inside the briefcase.

I went to the two backpack parachutes and saw that each rig had a pocket with cards labelled "packing data." I took the two cards out, and I didn't really know what they meant. The green rig seemed to be newer as its card had a more recent manufacturing date, and the chances of this being the same kind that I bailed out with earlier in the year were relatively high. I stepped into the harness's leg loops, tightened them slightly, and then put the shoulder straps on. My choice was made. I forgot to put the packing data card back inside the parachute on my back, instead stuffing it inside the tan parachute's pocket.

One of the ladies asked me where we were going, and I told her Mexico City. They asked if I wanted them to come along as well, but I wasn't sure and just turned away toward the money bag and stared at it. When I didn't answer, they asked if they could leave, and I just told them they could do whatever they liked; it made no difference to me at all what they wished to do. Miss Schaffner and Mrs. Hancock walked toward the curtain when Miss Schaffner quickly returned to say that her purse was in the cubby above my seat, and she asked if she could retrieve it. I told her that she could and that I wouldn't bite her. She let out something of a nervous laugh, grabbed her purse, and went to freedom beyond the dividing curtain between coach and first class.

The cabin started to get eerie and quiet after the passengers all got off, and at one point it was only me in the aircraft, except for the flight crew in the cockpit. From the paper bag, I took the revolver out and kept it in my hand. The door to the aft stairs behind me was closed, so I would have been alert to the noise of the aft stairs being opened or being taken by surprise from the rear. I got down on my hands and knees to look forward from underneath the curtain, which didn't go all the way to the floor. If a troop of boots came aboard, I would put the gun in my mouth before they reached and pulled across the curtain.

When I saw Miss Mucklow's shoes, I sprang back up again, and she gave me the two maps. I asked if she had something to eat, and she said that the meals had come aboard. She then mentioned that she felt a little tired and

wondered if we would be in the air for long. I told her I had
some Benzedrine with me, and if she felt tired or lethargic,
she could have one, but she just raised her hand to wave in
the negative, and I backed down. She retook her seat, and
if she was afraid, she certainly didn't show it; it was both
admirable and concerning in equal measure. At this point,
wanting to take as much evidence as possible away from the
scene, I requested all the written notes back as well as the
matchbooks. When Miss Mucklow handed them over, I put
them in the side pocket of my jacket.

It was time to give the flight instructions, and I gestured
to Miss Mucklow to write down what I needed. She frisked
herself to see if she had a pen or paper, and after finding
one, she pulled out what looked to be a time sheet from
somewhere. I gave the instructions as follows: "We are going
non-stop to Mexico City. No fuel stops in the U.S., cabin
depressurized, cabin lights off, flaps down to fifteen degrees,
landing gear down, ten thousand feet of altitude, low air
speed of one hundred and fifty knots, rear door open, and
the stairs down." As she was writing, she was shaking her
head, as if she already knew what the captain's answer would
be in the cockpit.

She called the cockpit from the telephone behind us,
and after listening to the captain's reply, she said, "Hold on,
sir. I will tell him now," before turning back and addressing
me. "They said they can't take off with the stairs down; it
isn't safe, and they are unable to close them afterwards."

I spoke up so the cockpit could hear me and told them
quite abruptly, "It can be done—do it!"

"Also, because of the drag on the aircraft, there will
need to be a fuel stop along the way. Even with full tanks,
we won't reach Mexico City at ten thousand feet and
at low speed. The jet needs more fuel to remain in the
configuration you requested, and we will be out of range and

will need to land in San Francisco."

"Tell them they can land in Phoenix."

After speaking with the cockpit for a few more minutes, Miss Mucklow told me, "They can make Yuma or Reno."

"Reno. Although, Miss, you will have to help me put the stairs down when we are up." There was no protest from her about remaining on board, and perhaps she had already resigned herself to staying aboard anyway.

Landing in Reno or Yuma wasn't my concern, because I was hoping to be gone long before reaching the airspace over the state line of Nevada, never mind the border with Mexico. I knew Tacoma and the general area from the air, so bailing out quickly was going to be the order of the evening. Given my history, it wouldn't be suspicious if I was noticed in the area around that time and could have been explainable with a semi-convincing lie. My patience was tried when a second fuel truck came by, and after staring at it for a while, I couldn't understand why they were there.

Fuelling should have been finished by now, and I felt as though it was just them stalling. One truck and one employee can fuel a 727, no matter what the public manuals say. The aircraft wouldn't have been completely empty, despite circling above the airport, and it takes an awful lot of fuel and flight hours to drain the aircraft. Civilian airline pilots are hardwired to think that the fuel tanks are empty, even if they have 30 percent of their fuel remaining. At one stage, Miss Mucklow lifted the interphone to ask what the delay was all about, and when the pilots said they were waiting for Instrument Flight Rules (IFR) clearance, I told them they didn't have to wait for that and they could get that in the air.

When I noticed yet another fuel truck approaching us, I threw my arms up in frustration before throwing myself back down into my seat with my head in my hands. I landed in my seat with such force that I worried that I had damaged the parachute on my back. I took it off again and re-inspected it, but if anything were wrong with it, I wouldn't know without pulling the ripcord. I supposed I would find out soon enough anyway, so I quickly put it back on after donning my raincoat.

A few minutes later, the interphone rang again. Miss Mucklow picked it up and quickly put it back down again. The captain was adamant that we couldn't take off with the stairs down, and I resigned myself to the fact that I would have to somehow open the door and deploy the stairs myself or with Miss Mucklow's help while in the air. I knew for a fact that the jet could take off and land with its stairs down with minimal damage, but insisting that I had this knowledge would have come to the attention of investigators and could potentially expose my identity. To argue was to incriminate myself. Like any good defence attorney will tell you, their job often involves preventing their clients from arguing themselves into prison or the electric chair.

I started getting snappy and said, "Let's get this show on the road!" I said it loudly in the hope that the flight crew in the cockpit could hear me, but they probably didn't.

The front exit door was closed from the outside and sealed, and after this, I had some glimmers of hope that I might just pull this off. That was the monster of Dan Cooper; I had terrified these young ladies, and likely the men in the cockpit, but in those moments I didn't have any care or concern for them in the slightest. The meals, attempts to break the tension, and offering of tips were all just empty and hollow gestures for relieving my own nervousness rather than a true display of concern for them.

Our taxiing onto the runway to prepare for takeoff had commenced. I sat in the aisle seat, and Miss Mucklow had taken her seat in the aisle seat opposite. Again, it felt like an eternity just sitting there, especially since there were no flashing lights and the fear of being surrounded, stormed, hauled to jail, or killed was gone, at least for now. When we were zipping down the runway, the lights went out in the cabin, and our wheels were off the ground. After stuffing some of the bill bundles into the reserve parachute container, I pointed to the rear door to demand that Miss Mucklow open it, but she became hesitant, and I stepped forward to do it myself.

The rear door had a large lever on the centre of it, and it was a heavy handle to pull down. After a few attempts, I was able to force it open with the stair mechanism to my left. When I asked for the stairs to be lowered, Miss Mucklow became upset and fearful that she would get sucked out of the aircraft. I already asked for the cabin to be depressurized, so that was never going to happen; otherwise, I would never have planned to escape this way. Not taking my word for it, she went back to the interphone, where the captain advised her to put a seat cushion on her front and tie one of the shroud lines to herself, attaching the other end to one of the floor-bolted seats. She left the aft compartment and went back to where we were sitting, and she seemed to consider it for a moment before taking a few paces down the aisle away from me. As we were climbing upward, we jolted slightly, and my briefcase fell off the seat, which alarmed us both, but it didn't open.

At this point, Miss Mucklow started waving her arms frantically as the roar of the engines got louder as we were climbing up to ten thousand feet. She started shouting to me or at me; I'm not quite sure what she was saying, but after seeing that she was pointing to my seat, I shouted back that I had disarmed the bomb and was taking it with me. She obviously couldn't hear me well, and I came closer to her before repeating myself. I then said that she could go to the cockpit, asking that she close the partition curtain behind her and ordering that she and the rest of the flight crew in the cockpit not come back again. I would get the stairs down myself and go. She spoke back to me, and the only word I heard her say was "oxygen," but I told her that it was okay and I knew where it was, pointing to the compartment that I was eye-level with, which I knew contained emergency oxygen supply masks.

In the heat of the moment, I had figured out that if I could make a handle loop out of the lines cut from the front reserve parachute and attach it to the money bag, I could then secure it tightly against my front with the parachute chest strap, so I started looping and tying as she was walking away. I watched her as she got to the curtain, and I don't know if she waved goodbye to me, but I certainly waved goodbye to her. I went out through the door and opened the stair mechanism control panel, which looked a little bit different from the one I had seen before. The one I was used to just had a lever and one button, but this one had three buttons and another switch. I thought the switch was a power button, but when I pressed it, nothing happened. I pulled the lever, and again, nothing happened. I looked out into the cabin to see if someone was coming, but I was alone. I shouted through, "I can't get the stairs down!" But nobody answered or came to my assistance.

There seemed to be some form of combination or procedure to get the airstairs down, and it just wasn't coming to me. I suppose it made sense to have a procedure to try and prevent unhinged people like myself from just going back there in the middle of a flight and throwing themselves out. I was just pressing buttons at random, and when I put my hand on the lever, it went all the way down this time, and the wind noise billowed through the cabin, but the stairs didn't go all the way down. The hydraulic hinges clunked, and the hatch opened about two or three feet, meaning I would have to use my body weight to get the stairs down fully. A red flashing light went on above my head, and I knew that red flashing light going off would indicate to the flight engineer on his instrument panel that the airstairs were down.

All I had to do now was get to the ground in one piece. The noise was so distracting, and to make matters worse, the open door would have badly affected stability, meaning the pilots would have to fly manually with the steering yokes and without the autopilot. There would be nothing stopping them from dipping downward or climbing, and I would have no way of knowing. I rushed back into the cabin, removed my clip-on tie, and placed it on my seat to stop it from ripping off after jumping. I pressed the large money bag against my chest, looping the shroud line around the top of my hips three times and tying it tightly at the front. I jumped up and down a few times, and the bag didn't seem to loosen. With the briefcase, I took the second line and put it through the handle after stuffing more bills into it to hedge my bets. I got forty-six thousand into the briefcase, and it was flattened and fastened against my backside. The third shroud line had the front reserve container attached, and I tied it to my right leg. I only got fourteen bundles into it, along with everything that was in the shopping bag except for my goggles, which I put on in place of the sunglasses. This left me with $126,000 in the bank bag, $46,000 in the briefcase, and $28,000 in the front parachute bag.

I had wanted to see if I could fit some of the money into the reserve container with the red X on it, but I had run out of places on my body in which to secure it. I lifted it off the seat it sat on, took it through the aft door, and threw it away into the abyss along with the paper bag and the sunglasses. All I had to do was go—this was it. It took me around twenty minutes or half an hour to secure everything, and when the interphone rang, I answered. One of the pilots asked if I needed them to do anything else, and I just said, "No!" before putting the phone back down. The galley was right opposite me, and I hesitated, wondering if I should bring food and drinks with me. There were no bottles of water, only cans of lemonade and soda. There were crackers, cheese, nuts, and a few apples. So I took some of them and put them in the front reserve bag on my leg. I think I got three cans of soda, two bags of crackers, a bag of nuts, and a packet of soft cheese.

After this, I rushed back out and took a breath before putting my foot on the first step. The stairs seemed to jolt down, and the handrails deployed from the sides, and I grabbed on to them to stop myself from losing my footing. My stomach went up into my mouth with each passing stair, and the wisps of clouds were becoming visible, as well as the faint blinks of the aircraft lights. I turned on the stairs and faced back into the cabin, pulling the various knots for the cargo I had secured to myself and reassuring myself they were tied tightly enough.

Looking down, I could see nothing beyond the thick rainclouds, and the aerial photographs I brought were completely useless. The engine noise was deafening, and I could feel the drizzle on my face as the wind battered my raincoat. I said aloud, "Paradis avec Yvonne," before stepping off the staircase.

Chapter 24

The Day the Penny Dropped

Clifford Harding, February 10, 1980

Adjusting to life after the collapse of my marriage was a very challenging time for me. I had tried several times to reconcile with Charlotte, but each time I was rebuffed. We didn't argue or fight in front of the girls; in fact, we barely fought at all. Things were mostly cordial, but the girls needed a lot of reassurance and time of their own. I stayed in the Marco Polo Motel for a couple of months until I was able to get an apartment of my own, which was downtown. It was a nice enough place in a nice enough building, although it never felt like home to me. I lived in some form of denial for at least two years after we separated, and every time my phone rang, I always wanted it to be Charlotte telling me I could come home. That call never came.

I worked on other cases, and between late 1975 and 1980, there was very little mention of Cooper anywhere. He had already gained folk hero status by sticking it to the man and getting away with his cash. His not turning up confirmed in the Bureau's eyes that he was long dead, and although the case was administratively open, there were very few top-notch leads or pieces of evidence that brought the case any closer to being solved. After plenty of time, I learned to let go, and solving the hijacking of Northwest Orient Flight 305 was just another girl that got away. By 1980, I had fully healed from my divorce and my obsession with Cooper. The man responsible for my marriage breakup and misconduct wasn't Cooper—it was me. I matured a lot in those years, and my vanity drove my decision-making. For periods of time, I imagined myself being interviewed on television as the man who located and apprehended D.B. Cooper, and it was this vision and destructive drive that dragged me to dark places. When I was free of that, my mind and body thanked me for it. I decided to quit alcohol but remained a smoker for the time being.

Setting personal boundaries was always a challenge for me, so I promised myself and swore on my daughters' lives that I would never get so deeply involved in a case again. For the most part, I didn't. I started dating again at the end of 1979 and the beginning of 1980, but decided that it wasn't for me and just wanted to focus on keeping on the straight and narrow within the Bureau and coparenting with Charlotte, even though she had gotten engaged again and was set to remarry. I learned many years later through therapy that I have a dismissive-avoidant attachment style, meaning that I don't prioritize relationships and push my feelings so far down inside that it would be almost impossible for me to connect with anyone or have a meaningful connection that would ever last without doing some serious work on myself. Apparently, those with the same attachment style as me can become too involved in their work and have other priorities in life than letting people get close to them.

***

Everything changed on the evening of February 10, 1980. I grabbed some Chinese food on the way home from the office and switched on my television. The first thing that flashed up onto the screen was the FBI composite sketch of Cooper, staring at me again to let me know that he still hadn't gone away completely. I should have switched the television off, but I couldn't help but watch and see what was unfolding. The picture then transitioned to a video showing a pile of rotting twenty-dollar bills sitting on a table and a bunch of photographers taking pictures. The anchor told of how eight-year-old Brian Ingram and his family were on a camping trip, and while on a beach preparing a campfire, young Brian unearthed three bundles of bills buried just underneath the sand where they were about to set up camp. The bills all had rotten edges, and some were blackened. However, on all the bills with visible serial numbers, they matched those retained on the list as the ones provided to Cooper on November 24, 1971. This was a massive breakthrough and came just as the last embers of the case seemed to be dying off completely.

A total of fifty-eight hundred dollars was found—just three bundles of bills. They were buried with the rubber bands still attached to them, and I immediately wondered where the rest of the cash was. If Cooper cratered, then the whole amount would have been found if nobody looted his corpse. Then again, the money was red-hot and never turned up in circulation anywhere that anyone knew of. Nobody had found a penny of Cooper's money up until this find at a tiny beach in Tena Bar, Washington.

One common theme among criminals is that they like returning to the place of their crimes or nearby. I knew of killers who actually attended prayer sessions or candlelight vigils in disguise on anniversaries or even soon after the events. My mind was in overdrive yet again. He must have returned within the past couple of years to plant that money. I have never known paper, not even money, to remain buried for almost a decade and still be in the condition that the

Cooper cash was found in. The television pictures and the investigative pictures were completely clear, and many of the twenty-dollar bills were in remarkable condition. Not only that, but the rubber bands were intact as well when they should have disintegrated.

When I saw this, everything just came rushing back: all the late nights, the cost of losing Charlotte, and how low I had sunk to get him. Seeing his face again made me so angry that I launched my box of noodles at the wall beside my television. It only took a moment to completely relapse and think of all the pain the investigation had caused me. I couldn't help myself, and after learning of this discovery, I knew this man was definitely alive somewhere. This money find completely validated every hypothesis that the hijacker had survived the jump and eventually went home to his own bed. The search areas of 1971 and 1972 certainly didn't go as far as Tena Bar, but when this cash was found, the entire beach was dug up to try and find more cash, a parachute, a bomb, or a skeleton. None turned up. I couldn't get involved in the case; I couldn't do anything, as to do so would have meant serious repercussions for me. There wasn't a single soul that I could discuss the case with, and my priority was keeping my nose clean and moving forward in my personal recovery. After my outburst, I felt like an alcoholic who had just taken a shot of whiskey, and I pledged to ignore everything from now on and keep my focus on being a good father.

Around the office, nobody dared ask me about the case, nor did I mention it to anyone else. The cash came to our field office, and I didn't even look at it. I had nothing to do with any of it, and when people started talking about it nearby, I switched off and disengaged. It was seriously hard to do, but as the days crept into months and eventually years, I thought I had finally closed the door on Cooper.

The money only added to the mystery, and I didn't want to relapse completely to the point where I would lose what little of my life and sanity I had left. The newly discovered cash created a little bit of a media storm in the short-term but did not bring the case any further forward at any point. I decided that I would set myself a new goal to save money for a few years and buy a new place of my own instead of continuing to pay someone's mortgage on the apartment I was living in. I just needed to keep distracted, and I was offering to take the girls more, which both Charlotte and I appreciated. The girls grew up between two loving parents, and by the end of the 1980s, they were both in college. I made sure that I refrained from purchasing newspapers or watching any form of television as much as possible in November 1991, the twentieth anniversary of the hijacking.

***

I was promoted to deputy assistant director in 1993 after having served thirty years in the Bureau. It was a long time to wait for a large promotion, but my behavior prevented me from climbing the ladder at the rate I wanted to back when I was an ambitious twenty-something in the 1960s. I had a different outlook after my promotion and felt some duty of care toward young agents, whom I saw a lot of my younger self in. The hot-headed agents were the ones I took under my wing, and I often told them the story of how getting too involved in a case cost me my wife and large quantities of my girls' upbringing. I felt I had a good influence on them, and I enjoyed the mentorship role, plus the pay check and benefits weren't too shabby.

In 1995, both of my daughters were married—Celine in February and Helen in August. Charlotte and I got pictures together with the girls, and nothing made me feel a sense of pride like walking them both down the aisle on their wedding days. Nothing gives more joy in life than grandchildren, and when my two little granddaughters were born in 1997 and 1998, I felt a love inside that I hadn't felt before, and I swore from that day on that I would be there for them like I wasn't for my own daughters. From 1991 on, I avoided all media as much as possible to prevent me from seeing anything to do with the Northwest 305 hijacking. However, I neglected to do this in November 2001, when I caught a glimpse of some coverage and documentaries talking about D.B. Cooper, who was still at large. When news anchors and documentaries mentioned his name, I sometimes shouted at the television that his name was Dan Cooper! It was only a few weeks post-9/11, and it was impossible to stay away from the media or television around that time.

In December 2001, I gave the Bureau a written notice of my intention to retire in May 2002. This was accepted, and I felt a sense of relief. Not because I was retiring, but for another reason: I could have one final attempt at solving the case before bowing out of service. My children were grown up, I had money in the bank, I was in a position of authority, and I could act pretty autonomously and outside of prying eyes. Most of my colleagues from the early 1970s had retired, died, or moved on by 2001, so nobody raised any eyebrows when I asked for access to the Norjak case files.

At this stage, I didn't need any authority to contact the RCMP; I could do it myself. So, I contacted their headquarters in Regina, Saskatchewan, and I asked to speak to an inspector. I asked for a copy of the names and addresses of all the men they sent to Saigon from 1967 to 1971. I was told that my request would be considered and that I would have to wait. After around a month, I was rebuffed because of the Canadian Official Secrets Act, and I was told that they wouldn't give me any information. This set off a huge alarm bell for me, and when I looked up some former colleagues of mine to call them, they couldn't recall many of their names. One gentleman who a few seemed to know, a man called David Rochford, who was RCMP and definitely in Saigon, provided me with some other names, including that of their commanding officer. He didn't exactly know if the man was alive or dead, but if he were alive, he would certainly be in his eighties now.

From the moment I saw the name, everything flooded back to me. The hijacker knew that the Boeing 727 could take off with the stairs down, as well as other information about the aircraft that wasn't public knowledge, even to the flight crew. Asking for an unmarked car and asking for negotiable American currency would have made sense given his background. This man was pretty close, but when I found more information on him from public records, his date of birth was February 27, 1921, which would have made him fifty years old on the night of the hijacking, which sits just outside the mid-forties estimate. I was breathing rapidly when I remembered some comments the hijacker made on the aircraft, ones like, "Looks like Tacoma down there," and "McChord is only a twenty-minute drive from SeaTac Airport." He knew that because I drove him there. I was almost laughing at how obvious this guy was, and I felt extremely resentful that I hadn't realized sooner.

I remembered this gentleman having gray hair and not black like in the sketches that were informed by the passengers and crew, but hair can be easily dyed. The circumstantial evidence was building, and I remember the crestfallen feeling of getting close to a person of interest and coming up empty-handed. I dug around for a few days to see if the man was dead, and there was no death record that I could find.

Although, when I searched some databases and public

records, his address seemed very familiar to me when I read it. When traveling to and from Saigon, we were instructed to keep any notebooks or information that we wrote down just in case we needed them later on. I never threw them out, and I managed to dig out a box with all the information I kept from those missions. After flicking through some notebooks, I found the address in the notebook that I had written down in order to send a package and updates to him, as his wife was ill and he couldn't be in Tacoma for the time being. He had lived in Montreal at the time. I was feeling how agonizingly close I was getting, but I didn't feel the dark feelings I had felt thirty years prior. I wasn't doing this for accolades or praise; it was for me, and that made it all the more satisfying.

The money found in 1980 meant that the hijacker had returned to the scene of the crime, and as he would have had to cross the border from Canada into the United States, I was able to request if the man had entered the United States after November 24, 1971. As it turned out, he did! He crossed the border into the United States at the crossing into Washington State using his own photographic ID in June 1979. This proved very little; many Canadians cross into the United States all the time, although why, if he lived in Montreal, did he cross into Washington many thousands of miles from home? He needed to get back to the Pacific Northwest for whatever reason. If I brought this to a prosecutor, I would get laughed out of town. I needed more—everything I had was circumstantial, and I didn't have anything yet that placed him in the area on or around November 24, 1971.

All I had to do was place him at the scene of the crime somehow. I sifted through dozens of pages from reports made by the Bureau, the National Guard, and the Clark County Sheriff's Department. Patrol cars are always the eyes and ears of society, and surely a patrolman would have seen somebody walking around. I read every report and document from November 24th and 25th, thirty years ago, and nobody was jumping out. Nobody considered looking at November 26th because it was assumed the hijacker was long gone from the area by this point. Then came what to me was the smoking gun: a deputy from the Clark County Sheriff's Department wrote a memo that I must have overlooked all those years ago, and I was stunned when I read it. *Fuck! Fuck! Fuck! It's him! It's fucking him! I know it is. He was Cooper.*

There was no doubt in my mind, and in the telephone directory for Montreal, his number was listed. I had to do it; I had to lift the telephone and call. I dialed the number, and my fingers were shaking as I was doing it. All he had to do was report me, and I would have gotten into serious trouble. I had second thoughts about contacting him and briefly considered passing the information on to someone else in the Bureau before pressing the last digit of his phone number. I needed to talk to the man myself. If the Bureau fired me, I didn't care. The dial tone was an ominous sound, and after four or five rings, I heard a voice on the other end of the phone.

"Bonjour!"

"Good morning. I'm not sure if you remember me, but my name is Clifford Harding."

"Oh yes! Good morning, Mr. Harding! What a pleasant surprise; I am happy to hear from you."

This took me completely aback because he didn't deny remembering me or hang up the phone. This gave me serious second thoughts and a sinking feeling that perhaps I was wrong.

"Yes. I was looking through some old notebooks and memories from Saigon, came across your address, and decided I would seek you out to talk to you."

He hesitated somewhat, and his voice became subtly different, taking on an almost somber tone. "Almost thirty-five years ago now, isn't it? A lifetime ago. How have things been with you?"

"Well, I just happen to be visiting Montreal next week and thought I would invite you to lunch if you'd like." My heart started pounding at this point, and I was starting to sweat.

"I am eighty-one now and cannot leave home much. But if you would like to visit me, I would certainly welcome that."

This plunged me into even more doubt; the man that I was 99 percent sure was Dan Cooper was now inviting me into his home. I wasn't expecting this to be the behavior of someone guilty of the only unsolved case of air piracy in American aviation history. I instantly regretted giving him a week's notice of my arrival, as the guy could hide any other evidence he had in that time. This was someone who had potentially evaded capture for decades, and he was extraordinarily careful. He was either completely innocent and suspected nothing or was calling my bluff. Although I hesitated before responding, I had already told him I was going to be in town and knew that it was too late to turn back now.

"Definitely, it would be nice to catch up. I will be in town on Saturday and could visit you in the afternoon, perhaps?"

"Certainly. I don't get out much these days, and it would be nice to have a visitor," he said as he sort of chuckled to himself.

"I'm looking forward to it very much." I tried to hide the anger in my voice, but it was almost impossible.

"Oh, I'm sure you are. Adieu, Mr. Harding."

Chapter 25

?

Dan Cooper, November 24, 1971

The winds blew me all over the place, and despite tumbling and being completely disoriented, I could feel the bank bag across my chest loosen. I arched as hard as I could as I plummeted downward. I fumbled frantically for the ripcord and managed to pull it open. As the canopy opened, I jolted violently, and in what felt like slow motion, the money bag on my chest loosened itself from its knot. I was terrified of losing it, but I was able to cling on to it between my thighs. I looked up at the white dome canopy, and with my free hands, I felt the briefcase and the front reserve bag still secured to me.

It was a cloudy night, and I was getting very wet and cold from the rain on the way down. My hands were starting to become numb holding on to the parachute risers, and I felt like I was falling very quickly, much more quickly than I had fallen before because of the weight of the extra cargo. The ground was rushing up to me; it was dark, and with the rain on my goggles, I couldn't see anything and would have to wait until I landed. I wiped my goggles and was about one hundred feet from the treetops. I dropped down between them and felt a thunderous shock and a snap as I hit the ground. Immediately, I thought the briefcase handle had snapped, but after a few seconds, I realized that it was my left ankle.

The throbbing pain in my ankle became sheer agony very quickly, and I cut the briefcase and money bag off of myself and opened the case to grab the flashlight and locate one of the morphine syrettes. I plunged it into my leg and expected to pass out, but I didn't. Amazingly, I felt clear and calm. The briefcase had taken the brunt of the fall and appeared to be undamaged when I untied it and laid it beside me on my left side. The rain and drizzle stopped, and I felt a warmth come over my body. I shuffled myself to sit with my back against a tree, with my damaged ankle elevated slightly off the ground on the cotton money bag. The parachute was still attached to my shoulders, and using the hand-held risers, I reeled it in closer to me from the treetops above and wrapped myself up in it. From the small cone of light from my dim flashlight, there looked to be massively tall trees, and among them were what looked like Christmas trees, all spaced about seven or eight feet apart.

I took the briefcase, complete with cash and dynamite inside, and decided that it was stiff enough to make a splint out of. I still had the shroud line that attached the case to my rear and decided I would use it to tie the briefcase to my left leg. I first untied the front container bag from my right leg and put its contents inside the briefcase. Before tying on the briefcase, I threw my hand into the right side pocket of my pants and fell into despair; I forgot to take my tie from the airplane seat. A gift from Yvonne to me was now going to be in the hands of the FBI, and there was no way of getting it back. That tie was something of a comfort blanket to me in Vietnam, and the mother-of-pearl clip was a beacon of hope. Now, both comfort and hope were lost.

Like a lame horse, I was finished. The only thing left to do was wait for the barking police and FBI dogs to come for me. There I was, wrapped up in this big white shroud with a bum leg, but $200,000 richer. At least if I got home with the money, I could care for Richard at home for around fourteen years. I had some savings in the bank that could pay for Richard's care for a few months until I laundered the money or exchanged it somehow. The money would be wanted and identifiable for quite some time, rendering it completely useless and barely worth the paper it was printed on, so I had to keep it safe for the time being.

After some time passed, the pain was starting to come back, so I used another of the morphine syrettes and took a big gulp of soda from one of the cans. The silence was both eerie and peaceful in equal measure. To this day, I have no idea where I landed, but the trees were spaced quite far apart, and in the dawn light, I could see rows of thorn bushes forty to fifty yards away and a clearing that would take me through the woodlands. The trees weren't too close together, and the ground was slightly soft but not well-trodden.

There was a fallen tree trunk beside the tree I was resting against, and I was able to rest my ankle on it and elevate it higher to above heart level. I temporarily removed the attaché case splint and looked at the maps to see if there was some way to guess or pinpoint my location. All I saw on the map between Seattle and Portland was a large wooded area. I had survival training many years ago, and I remember very clearly being told not to remove the boot if a broken ankle is suspected and to keep the injury splinted. I wanted to take the shoe off but didn't and instead pulled it down slightly to see some bruising, and thankfully the fracture wasn't a compound fracture. I replaced the large splint, kept it elevated, and during that time I was trying to figure out how I could get some warmth. It was impossible to see a river or a water source on the way to the ground, and I didn't feel good enough quite yet to get up and walk. So, I decided to set up camp for the night and hope I wouldn't succumb to hypothermia, infection, or the authorities. All I could do was insulate myself in the parachute canopy.

A dense fog started to eclipse the area later in the morning when I woke up some hours later, and while they weren't directly overhead, I knew there were some helicopters and airplanes flying above the area. I had to try and get out quickly, but I was not going to be able to move swiftly. My first order of business was to get rid of the dynamite. Burying the dynamite there and then meant if I was caught on my way to freedom, I would have fewer charges on my rap sheet; with the dynamite in my possession, I could be charged with possession of explosives without a permit, possession of explosives with intent to endanger life, threats to kill, and maybe some more depending on how creative the prosecutors would be. If captured, I could lie and say the bomb was a ruse made from road flares that I had used to intimidate and later discarded, which would be a lesser charge than having an actual, illegal weapon in my possession.

I dug a hole with my hands in the soft earth and buried the dynamite, wires, and battery. They were all buried together, and while I attempted to bury them as deeply as I could, I knew that police sniffer dogs would always smell explosives, no matter how clever I tried to be in disposing of them. If dogs caught the scent, they were going to uncover it—as long as I wasn't uncovered, that was the main thing. This freed up space in the briefcase, and while still seated on the ground, I transferred the cash from the front parachute container into the briefcase but retained the empty container.

The fog would be the ideal cover, and there was a large branch or stick nearby that I used like a crutch to lift myself up. I had kept the backpack parachute harness on the entire time and took it off as I stood up. Lifting my left leg up to get the left leg loop off was horribly difficult.

I cut the canopy out of the parachute container, cutting along all the shroud lines so that I just had the nylon parachute. Then, taking a section of a parachute canopy, I wrapped it securely yet cautiously around my ankle and the attaché case. I made sure it was snug without cutting off circulation. Realizing I needed more support, I used another piece of the parachute canopy to fashion a sling. I placed this piece under my knee and brought both ends over my opposite shoulder, tying them to keep my foot elevated. I was conscious that this was just a temporary solution and only needed to get me out of the woods. It was slow and laborious trying to tie everything to myself again, and the cargo was heavy enough as it was without being significantly impeded by my ankle.

If someone saw me, the game was up. I hobbled along the woods, propped up with a large branch and my foot out at close to a right angle. I stopped now and again to quell my hunger and thirst with the limited drinks and snacks I had and to adjust the empty parachute container over my shoulder to stop it from slipping off and being found.

Knowing how much ground I was covering was impossible. The maps were completely useless, and the lack of any life anywhere made me start to question my sanity. As if hobbling through the woods alone wasn't bad enough, not knowing where I was going was making the hobbling so much worse and troublesome. I could see the sun and decided to keep moving south until I reached some form of civilization, worrying about how I would explain myself to anyone I came across if that time came. I rued not having some form of accomplice, but more often than not, an accomplice will always spill the beans about their partner in crime if they are captured. It would have been my luck to land somewhere safely on the ground, only to have my accomplice tell the authorities everything about me. I took regular rest breaks, and the morphine was a huge help. The instructions on the syrette prohibited more than one syrette within a twenty-four-hour period, but by perhaps eighteen hours, I had already had two, which made the trek a little easier.

***

The first signs of life other than the occasional bird came several hours later as I encountered my first public road separating two sections of the forest. I sat on the ground, staring through the clearing to see if any cars or motorcycles were approaching. I heard nothing and decided to make a break for it. As I got out onto the road, I lost my footing and fell. Just after I crashed to the ground, I could hear the rumble of a farm vehicle or truck nearby and scrambled up as quickly as I could, making sure I hadn't dropped anything. The throbbing pain in my ankle caused me to let out a shout, but I pressed forward and placed my back flat against a tree trunk after reaching the other side as the rust bucket truck drove past and out of sight.

I kept pressing forward, and throughout the day, I would guess that I covered seven or eight miles. I kept to the wooded areas for cover and had only seen a couple of dirt roads with no traffic whatsoever. As night fell, I came across an isolated house on the edge of the woods. I hid in the brush and staked out the house for around fifteen minutes. There were no signs of life, and it was a strange location for a house. It could only be accessed by a dirt road from the front of the property, which obviously led to the public road further down. There was a garage adjacent to the house and what looked like greenhouses in front of me as I approached the property from the rear. My clothes had dried considerably since landing, but they were still slightly wet, and the cold was starting to get to me since I had stopped moving. I was shivering more and more as my damp clothes sent unbearable chills through my bones. If I didn't enter this property, I knew that I was going to get hypothermia, and I needed a place where I could dry off and rest my ankle.

I hobbled to the back door and peeked through the glass panels to see a very well-maintained and tidy home inside. To my right, there was a little stone sculpture that looked out of place. I slowly bent down and slid it slightly to the left, and by the grace of God, there was a small key underneath. I sat down on the ground and removed my revolver from the briefcase after untying it from my ankle. If someone was here, they were going to allow me to take three changes of clothes of my choosing from their house and their car if it was in the garage.

At this stage, I was reckless and desperate. The occupiers of the property could have been asleep or out and could come back to find me at any moment. My policing brain kicked in when I unlocked the door and made my presence known with a "Hello," but nobody answered. It had become pitch-black outside, but I thought better than to turn any lights on. The only faint illumination came from the half-moon light coming through the glass panes of the front door, and there was a table sitting in the hall with envelopes on it. Even after establishing there was nobody home, I still moved as quietly as I could toward this table, where there were three envelopes with the home address on them: 18712 NE Erickson Rd, Brush Prairie, WA 98606, USA. I wrote the address down using the pen and paper resting by the telephone and kept the address. Just beside the telephone, there was another note with a paperclip over it that said something along the lines of, "A Thanksgiving gift from the little ones and us. Sorry we missed you before we left. Thank you for all your hard work this year, and we will see you when we return on Saturday." How lovely of them to give their nanny a tip and go away for Thanksgiving to give me cover that no criminal could ever plan for or organize. As soon as I deemed this a safe hideout, I immediately untied the money bag and removed the improvised parachute leg sling.

Downstairs was a living room with a large fireplace complete with logs and tinder, plus a door leading to the garage on my right at the bottom of the stairs. I entered the garage and saw what looked to be an old motorcycle under a tarp and tools lined up neatly along the wall, but what really caught my eye was a sharp pair of hedge clippers. I removed the hedge clippers and shuffled back to the living room, and over the next hour I chopped up the parachute, the green container bag, and the front reserve container. It took me so long because my fingers were frozen through and took some time to warm up. When I decided to light the fire, I placed all the notes I had gathered along with the matchbooks onto the grate, along with a bundle of twigs. There were long cook's matches resting beside a small coal bucket, and as soon as the fire was lit and the coals were smouldering, I started to feel much better. I decided to draw the curtains in the living room to prevent the flickering flames from being visible to anyone outside the home.

There were two piles of chopped-up material—a green pile from the butchered container bag and a white pile from the parachute canopy. Slowly but surely, the parachute and containers were disposed of in the fireplace. I lay on the floor with my bad ankle resting on the chair beside the fire and put the container and canopy into the fire a handful at a time. Now and again, I would put a log on top to keep the fire going. The parachute fumes gave off a horrible smell, and I became fearful that I was unleashing toxic fumes into the house, so I opened both the living room window and the kitchen window.

After drying off somewhat, I realized my suit was filthy, and while the last of the chopped scraps were burning, I went upstairs to see if the man of the house had clothes that would fit. Getting to the second level was not very dignified; I sat on the stairs and ascended them one at a time on my rear, propelling myself with my right leg while using my left hand on the handrail. The master bedroom with adjoining bathroom was right at the top of the stairs, and I pulled myself up to enter. In the wardrobe was a selection of shirts, sweaters, pants, belts, and shoes. I decided to take off the dirty and damp suit and change into something more comfortable before climbing into bed.

I had at my disposal an empty house for at least another twenty-four hours to rest, warm my bones, and eat, and hopefully the cops wouldn't come sniffing around. As the adrenaline was wearing off, the throbbing pain in my ankle was coming back, so I injected another one of the syrettes and slept for around six hours until the daylight rays awakened me. From the front-facing bedroom window, which was the master bedroom, there didn't seem to be another house nearby unless hidden by trees, and very little traffic drove by. There are only two things that allow criminals to get away with crime: luck and alignment. It doesn't matter how clever or well-planned any crime is; if a criminal is down on luck and certain things don't align, the game is over and the book of justice must be faced. I had the very basics of a plan, but I could never have planned for luck like this.

The therapeutic benefit of sleeping meant my ankle felt a little bit better, but it was still badly swollen. The fireplace had provided plenty of warmth, and there was plenty of hot water to freshen myself up in the adjoining bathroom. I decided to start scrubbing my face, and I even shampooed my hair a couple of times to get a head start on getting the dye out. I leaned over the bathroom sink, balancing on my good right foot, and cleaned myself off. I kept the washcloth, wanting to dispose of it somewhere. After three washes, the dye was fading slightly to the point of having a salt and pepper appearance. I had to take care to remove all the hairs and put everything back exactly as I found it.

The clothes I had gathered were slightly loose, and because the wardrobe was quite full, it was likely these items wouldn't be missed. I changed into a red knit sweater with a blue shirt underneath and brown slacks, and I kept the same shoes on, but having to take them on and off to dress was a pain. At the top of the wardrobe was a collection of hats, and I made sure to take one along with another raincoat. I went into another room to find another bag to transport the money because I thought the briefcase splint would be too suspicious in daylight and closer to civilization. I found a large army-type knapsack in what must have been their son's room on top of his closet and laid the case on the bed. However, I couldn't fit both the $200,000 and the suit into one bag, so I had to put the dirty but now dry black suit into the bag and retain some of the cash in the briefcase.

I decided to be bold and take another sweater, another pair of pants, and a pair of reading glasses that were in one of the bedside drawers. I thought they wouldn't be missed because the homeowners didn't take them on their travels. I crushed the other change of clothes into the knapsack, slung it over my shoulder, and carried it and the briefcase downstairs. Before I left, I had to take care to go around the entire house and remove all my fingerprints with a feather duster and wipe away any remnants of footprints that I had left. I cleared out the ashes from the fireplace into trash bags and just scattered them around their yard, allowing the wind to do its job. Outside, there was a storage box with fire logs inside, and I replaced the ones I used. In the garage was a single wooden World War II-era crutch that I hadn't noticed the night before, and I decided I needed to take it. The fireplace was spotless, the house was completely de-fingerprinted, and the house looked exactly as it did when I entered it. The final things I took were a bottle of water, a can of peaches, and a can of corned beef from the pantry.

Using the crutch was a great relief, and with another syrette of morphine, I limped out of the house and replaced the key under the little monument at the back door. My head felt woozy, and when the morphine kicked in, I was able to pick up a little bit of speed to make my way down toward the road. The main road was around a quarter mile off from the dirt road that led to the property. There were a few other farms nearby, and the last hope I had was to hobble down this road. Every few minutes, cars were coming past me, and I had no idea where I was going. Not a clue. The pain was starting to come back, and behind me I heard a car slowing down. I had the sinking feeling it was the cops, and it was.

"Are we lost, friend?" the voice said, and I didn't turn around to face him immediately, but after taking a deep breath, I did. He was from the Clark County Sheriff's Department, and he was probably wondering what this pathetic old man was doing hobbling down the side of the road.

"Ah…no, Monsieur!" I replied with a laboured French accent. "I wanted to surprise my daughter and her family for Thanksgiving, and it turns out that they aren't at home, but I was able to call someone to take me back into the town."

"I see, would your ride out of here not pick you up at the address you were at to save a cripple having to walk down this road here? By the way, where was the address you were at?" which was a fantastic reply that I respected very much. I got the piece of paper with the address out of my pocket and read it out to him.

"I keep address for le taxi driver, Monsieur; saying Brush Prairie in this accent makes it très difficile for the driver to understand," and then I let out a false, hearty laugh, in which the deputy joined in. I saw what looked like a bus approaching, and I raised my crutch at it, hoping it would stop. The small Volkswagen bus pulled in, and it was pale blue with the name of a community church printed along the side of it. The slide door opened beside me, and I greeted them while the deputy looked on. I asked for a ride into town, wherever that was. When they accepted, I bid the deputy adieu, and I smiled at him as he left. He didn't smile back.

All these elderly ladies were on board, and they were asking me where I was from, and I can't even remember what I said because the morphine hadn't worn off. The driver asked where I was going, and I told him I wanted to go to Portland but that anywhere in the city was fine. He said he was going to Grace Church or something like that. I said that I didn't know the area very well and asked if he could recommend a hotel to stay in for the night so that I could gauge how far I was from my own hotel. The hotel they recommended was the Heathman Hotel, explaining that it had an impressive collection of hundreds of author-signed books. I agreed and said I would try there, and then my plan was to get a cab to the Benson if it wasn't too far away. They asked if I could join their prayer meeting, but I politely declined and told them I was going to find somewhere to stay and go home in the morning.

The bus pulled in at the top of Southwest Broadway in Portland, and I bid everyone goodbye and declined any assistance because I would manage. The bus driver gave me a blast of the horn and waved goodbye to me. I limped over to a cabbie reading the paper and asked for directions to the Benson, and he told me to hop in as it was half a mile away. With the slow traffic of downtown Portland, I probably would have been quicker if I had just hobbled.

I was back at the Benson. I adjusted the eyeglasses I was wearing and pulled the hat down to cover my eyes a little bit. All I had to do was get to the room. When I shoved myself through the glass revolving door, I kept my head down and shuffled with my crutch over to the elevator. I didn't even look toward the reception desk on my right as I passed. When the elevator door closed and I felt it thrust upward, a sense of relief and shame collided to give me a unique feeling I can't even describe now. Pride isn't the correct feeling, nor is complete regret, but one of having completed something I felt I had to do.

I was trying to unlock the door so fast that my hands were shaking when holding the key, and I dropped it outside the door. I groaned to reach down for it, and when I fumbled the key into the lock and the door opened, I almost slammed it shut behind me. There was an alarm clock beside the bed, and after leaving at around 1 p.m. on November 24th to set out on my mission, I returned at 3:15 p.m. on the 26th. I flung the knapsack and briefcase on the bed and then flung myself into it. I had three days in which to manage my pain, remove the dye from my hair, and survive on the cans of food and remaining packs of nuts I had taken from the flight.

***

I spent the following morning washing the dye from my hair. It took a hell of a lot of washes, but eventually, it came out. Although my hair was a slightly darker grey, it wasn't too noticeable. On my floor, about twenty paces from my room, was an ice machine. I wrapped ice in a towel a few times per day to get the swelling down in my ankle because I needed to get into my Mountie boots in two days. I didn't feel the morphine was needed at this point, and the pain was somewhat manageable when the swelling went down. The stress of everything quelled my hunger, but I was able to source some water and snacks from the vending machine beside the elevator.

Leaving the room wasn't an option over the course of those three days, and when it came time to fly from Portland to Vancouver, the real test was here. I didn't see or care to look at any news coverage for the two days I was in the hotel room. I don't believe my hotel room had a television in it, but if it did, I never used it. I became fearful of them searching my bags at the airport, and having $200,000 in the bag was going to be an absolute disaster for me. So I took out my RCMP tunic and put it in the briefcase, with the front facing up, so my medals were visible in the event of it being searched. I emptied out all the money onto the hotel room bed, placed the knapsack at the bottom of the suitcase, layered the money on top of it, and put all the clothes on top of the money.

When I gathered everything to check out at 7 a.m. on the morning of the 29th, I was able to move with a well-concealed limp using the crutch, and I wore the spare clothes I had brought. When I got to the reception desk to check out, the receptionist was on the phone, and I just flashed my key, waved goodbye, and she waved back. I hailed a cab, and because I was an "old cripple" with grey hair and glasses, the cabbie loaded my stuff into the trunk and took me straight to Portland Airport. This taxi driver left me right at the door of the airport and not in the lower-level area where the shuttle bus was, probably because of the crutch. I expected to see posters of my face littered around, but there weren't any. It just looked the way it did when I was there a few days ago. I think there may have been one cop with one dog quite a distance from me, but they didn't approach.

The Hughes Airwest desk was just inside the second-level entrance doors beside the Delta desks, and I purchased a one-way ticket to Vancouver with my name as "Raymond Simard," and I again pretended as though I didn't speak much English. A security guard approached and requested to see inside my briefcase. When I opened it and he saw the tunic, he apologized to me in French and nodded to the ticketing agent to let me through. The ticketing agent took my suitcase, slapped a tag on it, and then it was out of my sight. I wouldn't be able to settle until I was given it back in Vancouver. They weren't looking for a grey-haired Canadian, so I was ruled out right away. My departure was upstairs this time. When I was sitting down, someone kindly asked if they could bring me a cup of coffee to save me waiting in line, and I agreed. I drank my coffee as the covered gangway was put on to take us to the aircraft, and I hobbled through the covered walkway and into the big yellow airplane.

I took my seat and sat at the window, waiting for the propellors to start turning so we could get in the air. What I did notice was a guy who sat in the row opposite me in plain clothes, and he gave me a nod. I nodded back to him, and he laughed. Most policemen would agree that we know our own, and he didn't need to flash his badge or gun for me to smell the air marshal in him. I chuckled back at him, and he put his finger up to his lip as if to tell me to keep quiet. I had no intention of saying another word to him or even breathing in his direction. When we took off and I was on my way back to Canadian soil, I still didn't feel like I was safe. I was still in the earliest days of looking over my shoulder for the rest of my life.

When we touched down in Vancouver, the air marshal helped me to my feet, and I shuffled down to the front exit door, where he helped me down the stairs. Vancouver airport didn't have covered walkways back then, and I was glad to finally have my feet touch the ground. I quickly hobbled into baggage reclaim, and bag after bag was going around the carousel. I was starting to become anxious when mine wasn't turning up; I wondered if they were searching bags, and I tried to remain calm as I watched a set of golf clubs and another few bags come around. When I saw my little black suitcase come off the carousel, I quickly grabbed it and rushed as quickly as I could to get to a bathroom. I took my tunic out of the briefcase and the rest of my uniform from the suitcase. I changed in the stall and wrestled and fought for my left boot to go on my left foot, which was incredibly painful.

Of course, nobody was going to check a policeman's bags, and when I presented the return plane ticket to the check-in desk, there was no issue, and the flight home passed without incident. In fact, because I was so hypervigilant, given what I had just done, I noticed how many people greeted me and said hello. Perhaps I was getting higher levels of sympathy because of my crutch, but I didn't mind one bit. Even leaving Montreal airport and conversing with the taxi driver on the way home, I still didn't feel the relief I thought I would feel. When I finally got back home, I didn't even have a triumphant laugh or cry. It was just an inexplicable hollow feeling.

Chapter 26
Montreal

Clifford Harding, April 5, 2002

Containing my emotions was incredibly challenging. There were few times in my life when I felt completely dumbfounded and unsure as to how to handle a situation. I had almost thirty-nine years of service and was always missing closure on the events of November 24, 1971. I decided to fly on April 4, 2002 and meet the man the following day, a day earlier than I had initially planned. I simply couldn't wait another day until that Saturday, so why should I care about a minor inconvenience to this guy if I'm early? I flew from SeaTac, the scene of the crime, directly to Montreal. This was less than a year after the terror attacks on 9/11, and security had been tightened considerably. It was a far cry from 1971, when there was so little security that an individual could purchase a plane ticket with a fake name, bring on a briefcase filled with explosives, and parachute from the aft stairs of an aircraft with a bag of cash.

I had never been to Montreal and was immediately captured by its beauty. I stared out the window of my cab to look at the hotel, and the city lights were simply stunning. I had arrived in the evening, and when I was researching places to stay before flying out, I stumbled across the Fairmont The Queen Elizabeth Hotel. This was an opportunity to somehow let go of the past and forge a way forward, despite being almost sixty-two years old.

This was a secret mission, but more of a personal one than an official one. I had to face the man himself. I always wondered how family members of murder victims could face the person who killed their loved one, but that morning of April 5, 2002, I understood it properly for the first time. I gave the cab driver the address I needed to go to, and it was only a short distance away. When we slowed down, I knew we were very close, and we pulled up outside the house, which was at the corner of the street. There was a large cherry blossom tree on the front lawn, and the house was an antiquated pale blue color and clearly hadn't had a drop of exterior paint in many years. It was a dull, overcast morning, and there was a darkness about this house. It seemed much older and as if the rest of the street had moved on with the times, and this was the only one that hadn't.

The cab driver drove off, and when I looked toward the living room window, the curtains were open. I paced up the path and restrained myself before knocking gently three times on the door. After around ten seconds, nobody answered the door. I knocked again and pressed my ear to the door, and just as I did, I heard shuffling movements on the other side. My heart skipped a beat when I heard the inside latch unlocking and the door slowly opening. There stood a slightly stooped-over man with a walking cane, and he looked me straight in the eye as he shook my hand firmly for a man his age. His eyes were definitely brown and seemingly cataract-free.

"Wonderful! Great to see you, Mr. Harding—you haven't changed a bit! Do come in and make yourself at home."

I walked past him and stood as close to him as I could, and because he was hunched over a little, it was hard to gauge his height, but I vaguely remembered that he was a little shorter than me, so he easily could have been five feet ten in 1971. He gestured for me to go to his sitting room, and I sat down on the couch, and he sat opposite me on a high armchair beside the fireplace. The tension was there from the second I stepped in the door and was building as I sat and looked at him from only two feet away. Above him was his portrait in his RCMP uniform holding his Stetson in his hand, and even though it was a black-and-white photograph, it bore a striking resemblance to the second composite sketch of Dan Cooper.

"Apologies; I know you were expecting me tomorrow, but I was in town and decided to come today. I hope that is okay," I said nervously.

"Oh? Sorry, Mr. Harding. When you reach my age, one day simply leads into another. If you hadn't mentioned anything, I would still believe today was Saturday. May I offer you some tea or coffee?"

"Coffee would be nice. Thank you."

The man hoisted himself to his feet and went slowly out to the kitchen. The kitchen was through a set of double doors in his living room, and he left the door ajar slightly. When I leaned forward to peek through the gap left in the doors, he seemed to move a little bit more freely when he thought I wasn't looking. When I heard the coffee pouring into the cup and him approaching the door to re-enter the living room, I sat back in the chair.

He handed me the mug and asked me, "So, how have things been with you?"

"Well, there've been ups and downs. I climbed the ladder in the Bureau; went through a divorce, but thankfully it wasn't too nasty; and I had a couple of grandchildren. How about you?"

He hesitated and looked at a family picture on the wall. It was of him in a nice suit with his late wife and his son.

"Well, since my wife passed, things have been pretty quiet around here. And then Richard…poor Richard…"

"Is that your son?"

"Yes, poor boy. In any case, the reason for your visit, as pleasant as it is, is something of a mystery to me. I always knew you were like a dog with a bone, Mr. Harding, and I imagine you have something you wish to achieve with this visit."

He sounded very friendly and amenable, and I couldn't, at this stage, imagine him not being Cooper. When the flight attendants said that he was nice and polite, not cruel or nasty, I could see why. This man was clearly quite likeable, and his tone of voice conveyed a gentleness but also a firmness.

"Well, Monsieur, I would like to ask where you were on November 24, 1971." I just had to come out and say it. I was no longer in the mood for small talk and had to get to it. My self-control had been depleted.

"Probably somewhere similar to where you were on January 16, 1961," and then he laughed sarcastically and shrugged his shoulders.

"What does that mean?" I inquired.

"That was, gosh, more than thirty years ago. Is there a particular reason why you are asking me this?" The man kept smiling, and he wasn't becoming defensive yet.

"You flew to Vancouver on November 22, 1971. I checked with some colleagues of mine. What were you doing there?"

"Oh yes, I can vaguely remember carrying out inspections of the Vancouver police stations. One of their inspectors had retired, and I volunteered to come down for support. That would be about right, I would think. So, I know this line of questioning, and I must ask you, what are you questioning me in connection with?" The smile was still there, and he wasn't breaking composure, which was making me feel slightly embarrassed and seriously doubting myself at this point. Then again, with this man's demeanor, I could see how he had evaded capture.

"Does the name Frank Martin mean anything to you?"

"No."

"Well, on that day, a man calling himself Frank Martin flew from Vancouver to Portland. I was able to track down and verify all the passengers on that flight from the old Hughes Airwest ledgers that they had kept. So, somebody flew from Vancouver to Portland under an alias." At this, the man gave a much broader smile when, in reality, he should have gulped.

"Oh, I see where this is going. That hijacking from Seattle, was it? Goodness me, that was almost thirty years ago. Was that 1971? I don't know why, but I had in my mind just now that it was 1973. Is that case still open after all this time? You sure don't know when to quit, do you?" Then this childish laugh came out, which was seemingly on brand with the childish Cooper the stewardesses described when he made them hold the money bag to see how heavy it was. Or maybe the old man was just off his rocker.

"You're quite right. What has led me here is the profile of the man who boarded Northwest Orient Flight 305, calling himself 'Dan Cooper.' To level with you, I went to dark places investigating this case. I lost my wife, I lost my home, I lost my good standing for many years in the FBI, and I have waited for some time for this moment. Sir, were you 'Dan Cooper'?" This was when the man's façade finally dropped somewhat, and the smile was wiped completely off his face.

"Who? Me? Oh gosh, no!" He started waving his arms emphatically, doing this whole "oh gosh gee willikers, I'd never do such a thing" act. It took everything in me to not jump across the room and strangle the man to fucking death.

It was probably the second hardest moment of my life, after Charlotte telling me she wanted a divorce.

"Well, Monsieur, there is evidence against you!" I snapped at him, and then he raised his hand.

"Now, Mr. Harding, I know you are here in a personal capacity because you have elected not to bring a firearm into the home of someone you feel is capable of extorting a lot of money from an airline. You have no handcuffs either, I presume. We are both evidence men, so please humor me by telling me what evidence you believe you have."

I took a deep breath to gather my thoughts before giving both barrels. "Well, the hijacker knew that the Boeing 727 airliner could take flight with its aft stairs deployed. You have that extensive knowledge from your time in Saigon, knowing what that aircraft was capable of, which was outside the knowledge of even the most experienced pilots of the day." When I said that, he nodded.

"I see. Go on."

"In that nice picture above your chair, you bear a striking resemblance to how the witnesses described the hijacker, and if I am not mistaken, the tie you are wearing in it looks very much like the tie left behind by the hijacker just before the jump." This rattled him. He was breaking, and he started giving me less eye contact. I definitely touched a nerve with the tie, and for what reason, I don't know. I didn't really notice the tie at first until I happened to see it as I was looking at the picture.

"Excuse me one moment; I am very keen to hear the rest of your story." He reached down to his side and brought an inhaler out of a little leather bag and took three long blasts of it. "Tell me, Mr. Harding, did this hijacker suffer from bronchitis and use inhalers too?" As he said this, he regained some of the smile I wiped off earlier.

"Well, the man was a smoker, which I assume you were

at that time."

"Yes, like every other man, never mind a policeman. Please, continue. I'm very keen to hear everything you have to say."

"Do you ever notice that we cops can sense one another?" At this, he let out the biggest grin yet and nodded. "Why did you ask for an unmarked vehicle to bring on the money and the parachutes? To anyone else in the world other than us, an unmarked car is simply a car, surely. Also, the fact that you took all the notes and as much evidence back as possible was another tell. You handled a hostage-taking situation like a hostage negotiation."

"I took? I handled? Don't you mean the hijacker?" Then he folded his arms and sunk back into his chair.

"Plus, asking for negotiable American currency? Not a very American thing to do, is it?"

"Well, clearly, this gentleman was giving you a reminder that in Canada, we have the dollar, as do Hong Kong, Australia, and various other places. Perhaps the hijacker should have been provided with Australian dollars. That would have been a right kick in the teeth—terrible exchange rate." He smirked back and was getting very comfortable in his chair. He was enjoying this conversation somewhat, and normally when people are on the receiving end of this line of questioning, it never gets as far as this without people asking for a lawyer. This man showed no sign of that.

"It also appears that a deputy from Clark County Sheriff's Department stopped a French tourist sporting a limp in the same leg you are limping on now—an old injury? It seems a remarkable coincidence that a Frenchman was in the area at that time and was easily overlooked all those years ago."

"Mr. Harding, I am eighty-one years old. I will not insult your intelligence by educating you on the fact that with age comes frailty. Have you got a grand finale lined up here somewhere?" Clearly, he was backed into a corner, and I knew I didn't have long until he either asked me to leave or threatened to call a lawyer.

"Another passenger on November 29, 1971 flew from Portland to Vancouver under the name 'Raymond Simard,' and the flight's arrival time was very close to your own return flight back to Montreal from Vancouver. Again, I haven't been able to track down or locate anyone living or dead by that name who flew to Vancouver that day. It seems remarkable that close to your connecting flights from and to Montreal were two unidentified passengers who I couldn't find identities for. The game is up. I have all of this against you, Monsieur; the evidence is certainly there."

He took a long pause, sitting back upright in his seat. He then leaned forward to me with his hawklike features and said, "Well, young man, out of all this evidence you have, does any of it involve money...or the parachute?" and that smirk just came straight back. In my eyes, it was like the sketches were looking directly at me as his bottom lip curled, waiting for my response.

"The circumstantial evidence indicates that, on the balance of probability, with all of these happenings and connections, you hijacked Northwest Orient Flight 305. My superiors do not know I am here; I am not wearing a wire. I just need to hear it from you. There is a warped opinion that this whole caper was a victimless crime. You threatened to detonate a bomb and showed the stewardesses a viable explosive device, probably traumatizing them. Those gentlemen flying the plane were likely terrified too. You may not have killed anyone, but those passengers were victims, whether they, you, or anyone else likes it or not."

"Mr. Harding, it does not matter if you are wearing a wire or not. If you must know, I was not the hijacker. I did not commit this crime, and not only are you missing money and a parachute, but what about the plane ticket? What about a picture of me at the airport? What about witnesses who can say beyond all reasonable doubt that they saw me in the airport and are willing to swear under oath that it was me they saw in the area? I regret to inform you that you are mistaken. There is no prosecutor in the United States or Canada that will successfully take anyone to court on these wishful deductions you have made. Although, if I may offer an opinion, I believe the actual hijacker of that aircraft did not survive that evening."

I knew I wouldn't get it out of him. I knew I wouldn't get him to say it. I knew it was him. He knew that I knew it was him, even though he didn't admit it to me. I did get that sense of closure when I was leaving, and when he shook my hand, he smiled at me. At least I got to tell him the effect his crime had on me, but I never got to find out why he did it. I know in my heart and soul that the man I sat in front of was "Dan Cooper," and that he was absolutely correct—no court in the land would have been able to successfully take him to court, never mind throw him in prison.

**

My retirement finally came on May 9, 2002. Nobody knew of my recent visit to Montreal, and up until recently, I hadn't spoken about it to anyone, not even my daughters. I always suppressed my innermost thoughts and feelings after being shut down so many times, and recalling all of this has been cathartic for me. After some time, I tried calling the man again, but anytime I called, he just hung up the phone, and he never said another word to me. I waited and hoped that knowing I had caught him would lead him to confess to the crime, but it never happened. Now and again, I checked on the internet for funeral notices in Montreal, and on January 19, 2009, I read that the man had passed away at the age of eighty-seven. Of course, like anyone fearing DNA analysis, he made sure that he was cremated upon his demise.

Hearing of his passing wasn't a relief for me, and I didn't even wish for the man to rot in hell. All I knew was that for thirty-seven years after his crime, he perhaps didn't sleep as easily as I thought he did, and for all that money he got, he lived in a modest home and died alone. I have my beautiful daughters, my granddaughters, and a career I am largely proud of. No amount of money would buy from me the simple joys I have in life, and I am sure he would have traded whatever cash he landed on the ground with on November 24, 1971 for what I had. This man was no hero. He was a common crook, no matter how honest of a man he tried to present himself as.

.

Chapter 27
Tena Bar

Dan Cooper, June 18, 1979

The day after I returned home, I made the necessary arrangements the following morning to have Richard's nurses put in place. I was told they would come to visit me to complete paperwork and that I would have to pay for three months up front for the contract to begin. I informed them I would see to it, and I went to the bank to withdraw thirty-nine hundred dollars from my savings. Back then, the Canadian dollar was almost at par value with the American dollar because Nixon stopped its convertibility with gold, meaning the $200,000 I had would have been worth much more twelve months earlier.

When two of the nurses came to visit me, they looked around the house and made me a list of things they would need for their work, particularly mobility items like a transfer sheet and a mechanically operated hoist to lift Richard out of bed if he needed it. They gave me a number to call and had these items delivered to my house, meaning another check of around five hundred dollars to deplete my savings. I had Richard's care and what he needed for three months, which was the time limit I had to somehow launder the money. I had no idea how I would ever be able to spend or change the money, given the media coverage the hijacking was getting on television and in the papers, even in Canada.

What I found strange was that the hijacker's name was being reported as "D.B. Cooper." This obviously wasn't the name I had provided for the ticket, and the incorrect name gave me some emotional distance from what I had done because I didn't have to keep being reminded of the name "Dan Cooper."

My ankle was still in considerable pain, and I couldn't risk seeking medical attention. I returned to the station, and to be honest, nobody seemed to notice I was gone. When cops become desk jockeys, they mostly fall off the radar inside the stations. If they did notice I was gone, nobody seemed to ask any questions. I had a noticeable limp, and this limp has remained with me up until this day. Other than the broken bones, there must have been accompanying nerve damage or some other muscular injury. Walking has caused me pain since, and after my injury, I could no longer mount a horse or climb stairs without struggling slightly.

***

After everything was in place at home, the nurses began their gradual transition to Richard being home full-time. For the first week, he was coming home during the day and returning to the Allan at night. By December 5th, two days from the discharge deadline, Richard was getting incredibly agitated, and I decided that he should just come home. The nursing staff at the Allan were sorry to see him go and were sincere in their goodbyes to him. Richard found it very difficult to settle at home. By December 1971, he had been in full-time care for almost a decade, and I had this image of Richard and me living happily ever after at home. It wasn't the case. Richard had become so used to his institutional home that his real home was an alien land to him.

Six weeks had passed, Richard was no closer to settling

down, and time was running out to get rid of the $200,000 I had. It was stuffed into the back of my closet, and now and again I took it out to run my thumb through the twenty-dollar bills and hold the bundles in my hand. I was very surprised that there were no communications to the station seeking information about the hijacking or any circulated memos from Depot. It was clear early on that the FBI didn't consider any suspects outside of the United States, which was good for me. Typically, we didn't receive lists of serial numbers for stolen or counterfeit money, but the banks certainly would have. I didn't want any of this money being circulated in Canada, never mind Montreal, because if an investigation started here, it could easily have ended with me.

***

Christmas was drawing near, and because Richard was taken care of during the day, I was able to spend more time in my office at the station. Framed citations adorned the walls, which were a testament to a decorated career in the Royal Canadian Mounted Police. But one particular frame was absent, which was that of being one of the most wanted men in the United States. My telephone rang one day, and I was immediately summoned to Le Port de Montréal. I limped to a patrol car and had the blue light on all the way, not because I was in any great rush to get to the scene but because driving had become painful for me due to my ankle. I was directed into a shipping container filled with narcotics with a street value in the millions and enough firearms to start a small war.

The drug and weapon seizure had been big news. It was a waterfront sting, resulting in the confiscation of not only the weapons and the narcotics but also stacks of cash. The cash totaled $1.8 million. The raid's success was credited to an anonymous tip, which was becoming the most effective method of intelligence for most police forces and governmental agencies. Due to the huge amount of cash and the significance of the find, I could use my position and authority to take control of itemizing and writing up all of the physical evidence.

We had testing facilities at our station, although they were limited. We had ways and means to test what substances were and if cash was counterfeit. I tasked our own technicians with testing the narcotics and told them that I would take responsibility for the cash to ascertain if it was real or counterfeit. However, I had been around long enough to know what cash was real and what was not. This cash was perfectly legitimate.

The confiscated Canadian money provided the perfect opportunity. What I needed to do was forge documentation that it was "counterfeit" to cover the money I had extorted from Northwest Orient. Banks in Canada had been issued with the serial numbers of the cash I had taken several weeks earlier, and I would never have been able to spend it.

Richard's nurses knew about this bust, and I told them I was working on it and would have to stay at the station through the night to catch up on paperwork on both the suspects and the evidence. This was late in the evening, and before I left, I grabbed the briefcase and knapsack containing the $200,000 in USD to bring with me. The cover was perfect, and they questioned nothing. Carrying a briefcase as someone in my position was not unusual, and I walked into the station without any worry. For all anyone knew, it was full of paperwork and statements. I took the evidence room key from my office, and I never had to sign the ledger for the key because I was responsible for it. If anyone else wanted the key, they had to go through their superior, who then came to me.

After unlocking and unbolting the evidence room door, it was just me and the vault. I opened up the steel door and took all the cash out of it. The stacks were all perfectly arranged into bundles containing five thousand dollars, consisting of 250 twenty-dollar bills. I counted 360 bundles, and gradually I replaced the cash from my briefcase with the good cash, but I ensured to disperse the cash evenly among the bundles. I spread thousands of my twenties within the Canadian notes, and it was taking hours because the bands on the cash were made of paper, and I had to take extreme care not to damage any of them.

Soon enough, I had a briefcase of good cash that had non-sequential serial numbers and was already in circulation. I had spent at least three hours switching the money when I heard a bang on the door close to midnight, which caused me to break out in a cold sweat. It was a junior officer offering me coffee, but I told him I already had a cup, and I shooed him away without giving him time to salute. It was a close call, and after this officer disappeared, I reopened the vault to place the money back into it and make the stacks look neat and tidy. I was quite spooked by this stage. I had three bundles of my American dollars left and decided I would stop and keep them.

I was wearing gloves throughout, like any good cop should do when handling evidence, and my work for the evening was done. I went home with a briefcase and knapsack full of legitimate Canadian dollars at around 2 a.m. That night, I had the soundest sleep I had had in years.

The following morning, I summoned two sergeants into the evidence room and opened the vault in their presence. I laid out all the cash and said that it was deemed counterfeit. I told them I had counted $1.8 million and that the 360 bundles all had 250 twenty-dollar bills each. I even offered them the chance to sit there all day and count it all if they wished. My agenda was for them to countersign the paperwork declaring that it was all fake money, which they did because they trusted that I had done my "due diligence" and had the cash checked. I locked the cash away and was never going to let anyone near it. Some news outlets called the station, requesting to photograph the money and the narcotics, but I declined.

A couple of days later, I was tasked with speaking to the media at a press conference alongside other senior policemen. Publicly, we announced that we'd be incinerating the "counterfeit" cash as a standard procedure to ensure it didn't re-enter circulation. While this was standard for counterfeit money, legitimate cash was typically returned to circulation. The process would usually be overseen by multiple personnel to ensure integrity and confirm that all counterfeit money was completely destroyed. My documentation was completely clean, indicating that the cash was counterfeit. I had the RCMP-headed paper, the documents were all stamped and countersigned, and the central banking authorities took my word for it.

The counterfeit cash destruction process is exhaustive and meant to ensure that not a single bill survives. Large batches are first soaked in a chemical solvent, reducing them to a pulpy mess. This pulp is then pressed and dried, resulting in brittle sheets that are then fed into an incinerator. After incineration, the ashes are combed for any traces of intact currency, which, if found, are reprocessed. The official team I had assembled, comprised of forensic experts and treasury representatives, would oversee the destruction of the seized Canadian money.

The day of the operation was nerve-wracking. The large incinerator roared to life, casting an eerie orange glow over the proceedings. One by one, we fed the brittle sheets into the flames, watching as the 1.8 million worth of "counterfeit" dollars turned to ash. The intensity and scale of the process ensured that, even if someone knew what I was up to, it would be virtually impossible to identify which bills were from the hijacking. This is why none of the cash from the hijacking of Northwest Orient Flight 305 re-entered circulation in the United States or Canada.

***

My routine became very peaceful, and Richard was managing well at home. He had gotten to know his care team and was quite used to having them there. When one of his nurses went to have a baby at the end of 1973, we thought he would take it badly, but he used to point at her baby bump and rock his arms from side to side as if he were holding an imaginary baby. He loved her, and although sad when she finally left, he got used to the new staff quickly. My home wasn't really my home anymore; it was almost like I was living in Richard's hospital, not Richard living in our home. As time went by, his needs increased, and he often awakened at night and needed support to use the bathroom. I couldn't help but feel that having Richard at home was starting to get worse for him, and it was a dilemma for me because home should surely be the best place for any individual. Perhaps that isn't the case for everyone.

At the start of 1974, I made the decision to retire. To be honest, I had considered early retirement before 1971 but had to force myself to stay on so as to not arouse suspicion if it ever came my way. The two and a half years of feeling trapped and wanting to escape into retired life were awful. What made matters worse was the need to look over my shoulder all the time. Sleeping properly at night became a challenge, and having to spin a web of lies as to how I could afford Richard's care was difficult. I told people that

Yvonne's life insurance had eventually paid out and that this was what allowed me to keep Richard at home. I was the freest prisoner ever to exist. The other prisoner in this story was Richard. Even though there were so many medically trained staff around him, he wasn't interacting with anyone else his own age like he could have done at the Allan. He enjoyed participating in things like art and music therapy, but there was none of that available to him at home. He just started fading away, and our connection seemed to be slipping away slowly.

At the end of June 1974, my colleagues arranged a banquet and retirement party for me. There was a short ceremony at the beginning, and I was presented with a keepsake Stetson and a retirement medal. I stood there, surrounded by the faces I had come to know over my thirty-five years of service with the RCMP. The weight of the Stetson in my hand was a tangible reminder of the journey, with each crease telling tales of cases and comrades. From the corner of my eye, I caught the glint of my retirement badge, freshly minted yet feeling like an old friend. Memories flowed freely as colleagues took turns sharing stories, some humorous, others heart-wrenching, each a snapshot of our shared past.

As a bagpiper began playing, the notes transported me back to countless ceremonies and moments of pride. Friends presented me with a plaque, its polished surface reflecting the years gone by. I felt a swell of emotions—a mix of gratitude, nostalgia, and the bittersweet realization that this chapter was coming to a close. Amid the merriment, there was also a sense of anticipation for the future and the knowledge that while my time in uniform might be ending, my connection to this storied institution and its people would remain unbroken. No matter how much time had passed, I missed Yvonne terribly, and I wondered how ashamed of me she was, looking down from heaven.

***

Loneliness was starting to get to me, even though my house was packed. Nurses had noticed that Richard was bleeding when urinating, and doctors were starting to come out. Like they were with Eric forty years earlier, he was dismissed as having urinary infections because he had no control of his bladder, and frequent accidents can cause frequent infections. For a year, Richard was eating as many antibiotics as his nurses could convince him to take, and doctors kept coming with more, saying that he was just having frequent urine infections.

It took three of us to get Richard to the hospital one afternoon in November 1975. The month of November and around Thanksgiving has always been a month of mixed emotions for me. The doctor I saw was quite sympathetic and admitted Richard for tests, permitting his nurses to stay with him throughout, which was a help. I went every day to visit, and his own nurses stayed with him night and day and slept on a chair next to his bed. The right side of his lower back was quite enlarged and swollen. Richard permitted his nurse to turn him in the bed so that I could see, and it must have been so painful for him.

Richard had tests run as much as possible over the next few days, although the medical team was always limited in what they could investigate with Richard's health, given how uncooperative he could be. Only one blood test could be completed, and the doctors said that the blood and urine tests indicated an advanced stage of kidney failure, which was what the nurses suspected. What got to me most was when the doctors told me that being at home with nurses wasn't the ideal environment for Richard, and his nurses looked at me with sad eyes to agree with them. The medical team did not wish to put Richard through surgery because he

wouldn't be able to comply with the aftercare requirements. I
knew there was no way Richard would understand the need
for medical staff to clean and dress his surgical wounds and
that he would need diet and fluid restrictions. Like so many
other children and young adults like Richard in that era, he
was simply written off and sent home to die.

***

By March 1976, Richard was completely bedridden and being
nursed in bed. He could no longer get out and into a chair,
and he was starting to find breathing challenging. He wouldn't
even allow an oxygen container to sit beside him, nor would
he put a mask over his face. At night, Richard would scream
with pain, and I could hear the nurses leave their room in
my house to go and administer morphine to him. Richard
allowed me to sit on a chair beside him, but he barely looked
at me. I always wanted to get inside his head, and I wondered
if he knew deep down what I had done and that my having
him at home was the root cause of his downturn in health. I
tried to reassure myself that my heart was in the right place,
which meant that Richard wasn't in the right place for him.

Soon enough, the same way Eric did, Richard started
to refuse food and water. There were times when I entered
the room and the nurses were praying with him and holding
his hand. Richard was full of morphine, so he didn't resist or
push any hands away. I wasn't there for Yvonne whenever she
departed, and I made sure to stay with Richard as much as I
possibly could. The nurses were giving us privacy, and in the
rare moments when Richard would open his eyes, he would
quickly fall asleep again or turn away whenever he looked at
me. The only word I heard him say on the morning of April
22, 1976 was "Mama." I hadn't heard his voice in weeks, and
just as I was feeling the elation of hearing his voice, Richard

closed his eyes and went into his mother's arms. I just stared at him, waiting for his chest to rise again, but it didn't. I was just too heartbroken to cry. He was twenty-nine and ten days short of his thirtieth birthday. When Richard's nurses came in, they hugged me and reassured me that he was in a better place now, and I couldn't disagree with them.

Over the coming days, former colleagues of mine, former care staff at the Allan, and others came to the funeral home to comfort me. Everyone told me that they respected my attempt to care for Richard at home, but I knew that some of it was insincere. I was asked if Richard was to be buried with Yvonne, and given that I had a secret that Richard's remains could potentially unlock one day, I chose for him to be cremated after his funeral service. Richard's funeral sermon was centered on innocence, and that is what Richard was. The world is a frightening place, and anytime he was aggressive or agitated in life, it was his way of communicating that the world was just too cruel for him.

A few days later, I collected Richard's ashes from the funeral home and kept them at the side of my bed. My house was quiet, and I had the peace I so desired, but nobody to share it with. At the time of Richard's passing, I had around half of the money from my heist left, which would support me on top of my RCMP pension. On top of nursing costs, I had clothes, bed sheets, specialized food Richard had to eat, and everything else, which burned through the money like the wind. It got to a stage where I couldn't even look at Richard's ashes anymore.

***

After Richard had been gone a few years, I decided to do some home improvements and get my home painted. I got a contractor who was going to replace the heating system, install a new bathroom and kitchen, as well as paint both the outside of the house and the inside. I agreed to pay for all the work in cash, and when the five thousand dollars worth of work was completed, I found a stark reminder of the past when I found the three bundles of American dollars from the hijacking. Once I got my hands on the Canadian dollars, I completely forgot about these three bundles. They were unimportant and of no value whatsoever. The only purpose they served was to be three skeletons in my closet and potential evidence if the buried dynamite was ever found. I needed to get rid of them while somehow keeping attention away from myself.

I don't know why I thought it was a good idea to return to the Pacific Northwest, but I wanted to. I went on the same journey on June 17, 1979 as I did on November 22, 1971. Montreal to Vancouver, and then Vancouver to Portland. By this stage, metal detectors were in place, and when they looked suspiciously at the little grey container I had, I explained that they were my son's ashes. I kept the bill bundles in my suitcase that I checked onto the flight with some clothes in them to conceal the money.

When I landed in Portland, I got a rental car, and of course I had to give my real name and identification. I shuddered when I looked around the terminal building, and this horrible feeling of dread came over me, so much so that I wanted to go to the bathroom to be sick, but I realized the last time I was in a bathroom in here was when I was preparing a bomb to bring on board Flight 305, so I kept composed.

There was a gas station near the airport that sold maps, and when I got a detailed local map, my first thought went to going toward Brush Prairie, but I didn't want to get too close to where I landed in 1971, as tempting as it was. I couldn't face it, so I wanted to find another open area on the map that may not have been searched before by the authorities back in 1971 or 1972. I drove along the 501 through Frenchman's Bar Regional Park, but there were a lot of people around. There were backpackers, hikers, and families on bicycles together, and it was all busy. It was nice to see families and people getting on with life, something I wish I was able to do.

Eventually, I stopped at the side of the road when I saw what looked to be a small beach out the window of the car to my left. I pulled the car in, collected the money bundles along with Richard's ashes, and walked down a little dirt road just off the 501. This beach was tiny, and I am not sure if it was a public beach, but it was situated on the banks of the Columbia River, and I could see right across to Sauvie Island. I removed my shoes and socks and rolled my pants up to my knees.

I held the three bundles of cash in my two hands, and Richard's ashes were sitting on top of them. I held them tightly and then slowly unscrewed the top of the urn. I walked into the Columbia River and stood just over an ankle deep in the water. I said, "Paradis avec Richard," and slowly extended my left arm forward for Richard's ashes to flow from the urn into the cold water. Then I threw the urn further forward and watched it sink below the surface into the river. I walked back toward the shore and looked at the three bundles of bills again. Although I wanted to be free of "Dan Cooper," I removed ten of the twenty-dollar bills and put them in my right pocket. I crouched down, which was somewhat painful given my ankle injury, and dug a small hole in the sand just at the edge of this small, isolated beach. I placed the bills inside the hole before replacing the sand with my fingers.

Staying in the area was too much for me, so I decided to return home to always look over my shoulder and die alone.

If anybody asks you who I am or where I am, tell them I am gone. Dead and gone.

My name is Gabriel Clement, and I was D.B. Cooper.

Acknowledgements and Final Thoughts

As always, no acknowledgements section would be complete without thanking my ever-patient and loving parents, Eimear and Tony and my big sister Emily for having to listen to a full year of D.B. Cooper info. Also to my son Ethan, who was nine and ten years old at the time of writing and who loved bonding with me over Cooper stuff. It brought us a little bit of closeness that was probably my highlight of the whole writing journey.

A huge and special thanks to Lucy Ceccarelli for all her hard work in the editing of both Canadian and American spelling, punctuation, and grammar. Thank you for dealing with all my Whatsapp voice notes, emails, and all else throughout the journey. I couldn't have done this without you.

The D.B. Cooper Mystery Group on Facebook has been without a doubt the best resource of learning about all things Cooper and to the whole group, thank you for all the kindness, time, and discussion granted to me when I needed it. Throughout tons of video calls, phone calls, text exchanges, and Facebook Live broadcasts I got a wealth of knowledge and inspiration. Special thanks to Eric Ulis, Nicholas Broughton, Ryan Burns, Pat Boland, Martin McNally, Tessa Lauren, Jon Higgins, Tim Wallace, Aaron Richardson, Chris Cunningham, Mark Meltzer, Joe Halliday, Paul Daniels, Dave Fudeman, Winston Strumbley,

Mary Johns, Tom Kaye, Larry Carr, Arlene Marie Gray, and literally hundreds more. Thank you for accepting me into the Cooper family/vortex.

As a historical fiction effort, I needed to lean on other books on the case written by Bruce A. Smith, Robert H. Edwards, Geoffrey Gray, Skipp Porteous, and Max Gunther. The books written by these incredible writers and researchers were of huge value to me, to the point where I read them all twice! I tend not to read books twice but there were so many gems in there that it was impossible to capture them all in one read through.

I travel plenty with my Autism/Neurodiversity advocacy and speaking, and I had the best company on the road and in the air with The Cooper Vortex podcast hosted by Darren Schaefer. Online resources are just too many to mention but www.norjak.org and www.citizensleuths.com were huge favourites and they kept me up late at night because I couldn't stop reading!

Special thanks to the RCMP historical archives online, and I was completely fascinated by the tradition and heritage of force and it's impact during war time Canada. A real institution and yet another rabbit hole I found myself perilously tumbling through late at night. I also want to take the opportunity to thank Tom Colbert for his efforts in getting the D.B. Cooper case files released into the public domain through Freedom of Information, and the monthly releases from the FBI Field Office in Seattle gave a great insight into the early investigation and the dynamics between the FBI agents and other offices during that period.

With the early research and conversations I had, I became convinced that Cooper wasn't an experienced parachutist and trying to get inside the mind of an inexperienced parachutist would be extremely hard if I only spoke to an experienced parachutist, so I found the best way to get inside the mind of an inexperienced parachutist was to become one. Thank you to all at Skydive Ireland and We Are Vertigo Indoor Skydiving; Nick, Levi, Aaron, Ailbhe, Rudy, Pete, Neal, Pamela, Mike, Simon, Graham, Oisin, Peter, and everyone else. Safe to say I have caught "the bug" and may one day become an experienced parachutist myself! The Irish weather and my work commitments were impeding my writing and publishing timeline so I made the trip out to Skydive Spain to jump during actual summer, not Irish summer. Thank you to Jezza, Lakshya, Roxens, Chris, Josh (Mr Buns), Danny, Saray, Enrique, Jared, and all the ground and air crews in Aerodromo de Juliana.

I managed to get my hands on some Vietnam War-era parachutes that I absolutely love and want to somehow display them in my house. Any pointers on that would be greatly appreciated! Some called all this extreme and unnecessary, but if method actors can become other people for films and television, why can't I do it for books?

The most important and heartfelt acknowledgement has to go to the passengers and crew of Northwest Orient Flight 305 who have told their stories and provided their insights in not only attempting to solve the case but in helping others learn about the hijacking and tell the story in various creative formats. It is very easy to forget that they were Cooper's victims and hostages, and I wanted to ensure that this was clearly pointed out several times in the narrative. I hope all found some form of peace, closure, and healing after being part of such an event.

***

Since it became known that I was writing about D.B. Cooper, so many people have asked me who I think the man was. Here it is...I have absolutely no idea who Cooper was.

When I started this in late 2022, I looked at some people but became frightened of being pulled deep into the Cooper vortex to the point where I would become institutionalised and never escape. I don't believe Cooper was an experienced military parachutist for the following reasons; he took the smaller canopy during the hijacking, he never insisted too much on his demands being met because the money didn't arrive in a knapsack, he got three parachutes instead of four, and the aircraft didn't take off with the stairs down nor did it go to Mexico. It seems that after Cooper got the money, he just folded. The money arrived in a big cotton Looney Tunes comedy bag, and he didn't once say, "Go into the terminal building and get me my knapsack! I have a bomb and you have ten minutes to get me the bag I asked for!".

When the flight crew didn't accommodate his destination request or to take off with the stairs down, there was no real argument either. It seems that Cooper became something of a meek and overwhelmed shadow of himself. It became somewhat close to the hijacker becoming the hostage. Instead of insisting on a functional fourth parachute, or a knapsack, he decided to tie the money to himself which took a lot of time. Refuelling also took a long time, so all of Cooper's daylight for the jump escape was gone. I admit that when I started the Cooper journey he was this cool bad-ass who was in complete control, but the more I read the witness statements and his behaviour, I found the man quite underwhelming.

As for the jump, did he survive the jump? Yes. Of course he did. A parachute jump is both of your feet leaving the exit door and falling down to Earth. Did he survive the landing? I honestly don't think so. He was described as being between 170lbs-180lbs and had around 60lbs worth of cargo including the cash and the briefcase. A minimum of 230lbs under a 24ft canopy would at the very least give a very serious injury at the bottom. In Spain during one of my jumps, I flared my 28 too early and it was a mighty crash at the bottom and having to do a Parachute Landing Fall (PLF) saved me from a very serious injury. A PLF is dependent on seeing the ground and horizon to orientate one's self. At night, Cooper probably had sight of neither. The idea that this man simply landed on the ground and walked away, is just extremely unlikely in my eyes. Just don't ask me about the money find on Tena Bar! Maybe he miraculously landed and stayed under the radar until his dying day. Although, none of the money turned up in circulation after the event. The only money of Cooper's was found buried on Tena Bar. Maybe it was aliens. I don't know. If in doubt…aliens.

I do think the best shot at cracking the case is getting DNA extracted from D.B. Cooper's tie. At the time of writing, there is an ongoing case championed by Eric Ulis to get the tie back from the FBI to have it examined with 2023 technology. There is so little physical evidence that I think this is the only way that a DNA profile of the hijacker can be obtained, perhaps matched with a descendent, and that could do it. I would love if we could know who Cooper was, for both personal interest, and for closure to those affected by the hijacking of Northwest Orient Flight 305.

As far as I see it, there are only three facts that everyone with an interest in the Cooper case can agree on; he was born male, he sat on seat 18E on Northwest Orient Flight 305 on the 24th of November, 1971, and that his name wasn't 'Dan Cooper'.

About the Author

Jude Morrow is an autistic best-selling author, entrepreneur, philanthropist and keynote speaker from Derry, Northern Ireland. Jude travels the world to showcase, through his talks, that autistic children can grow up to live happy and successful lives. Jude's first two books are published by Beyond Words, publisher of The Secret. Jude is the founder of Neurodiversity Training International, the world's premier autistic-led training and consultancy to nurture autistic people to thrive in business and embrace their creativity. Jude is also a two-time TEDx speaker, has been featured in Forbes, and nurtures parents, teachers and professionals to develop a kinder mindset toward autistic people, young and old. Follow and connect with Jude on Facebook, Instagram, Twitter, and Linkedin.

Other Works By Jude Morrow

Why Does Daddy Always Look So Sad (2020) – Beyond Words Publishing
Loving Your Place on The Spectrum : A Neurodiversity Blueprint (2022) – Beyond Words Publishing
The Ghosts of Riots Past (2022) Independently Published

Websites and Social Medias -
Follow, Share, Tag, Review! :) #DanCooper

https://www.judemorrow.com
https://www.neurodiversity-training.net/
Jude Morrow | Facebook
Jude Morrow | LinkedIn

Made in the USA
Columbia, SC
04 November 2023

25415980R00172